THE SECOND JOURNEY

JOEL BIGMAN

The Second Journey

By Joel Bigman

Trade Paper: 978-988-8843-70-1
Digital: 978-988-8904-03-7

© 2024 Joel Bigman

FICTION

EB222

All rights reserved. No part of this book may be reproduced in material form, by any means, whether graphic, electronic, mechanical or other, including photocopying or information storage, in whole or in part. May not be used to prepare other publications without written permission from the publisher except in the case of brief quotations embodied in critical articles or reviews. For information contact info@earnshawbooks.com

Published in Hong Kong by Earnshaw Books Ltd.

A Tang Jar

The water supply in the Xi'an Temple failed for unknown reasons in early spring. A week later, a freshwater spring sprang up behind the Small Wild Goose Pagoda. The tourists that day thought it was auspicious, since the water started flowing on the first day of the New Year.

The plumbers knew differently. This wasn't a natural spring. It was a leak in a modern pipe.

The main water valve was shut off, and two days later, a repair crew showed up with a backhoe, pipes, welding equipment, and, as is required during repair work at historical sites, an archeologist.

The archeologist, though young, was very careful, and the digging proceeded slowly. In the early afternoon he noticed a speck of white at the base of the widening pit. Upon closer inspection, it was found to be a sealed jar, typical of Tang dynasty (610-908 A.D.) ceramics. The jar was whole and unbroken, without any visible cracks or chips, though it had been stained over the centuries.

The jar was taken to the Xi'an Museum for further study, and the water line repairs continued.

Two years later there was a startling announcement: after extensive X-ray tomography work, researchers had concluded there was a manuscript inside the jar. The jar was finally opened

THE SECOND JOURNEY

a few months later. The cover had been sealed in place with beeswax, which had hardened and darkened over the centuries. The researchers slowly carefully scraped away at the wax with toothpicks, then placed the jar in a nitrogen-purged glovebox, to protect the manuscript from oxidation. When they removed the cover, they could see the yellowed edge of the rolled paper manuscript inside. Paper had been invented by Cai Lun in the 2nd Century, so that was not a surprise. The researchers debated how to remove the scroll; tweezers might rip the scroll, since the business end was so narrow. Food tongs were a possibility as well, but one evening, when the lab was empty, a graduate student simply turned the jar upside down, gave it a shake, and the scroll fell out.

The paper was dark yellow, but nobody knew for sure what the original color of the paper was, and how much was due to the eons that had passed. The paper did not crack when unrolled. It was a long document, over two meters long, written in the typical brushstrokes of the Kai Shu calligraphy style, popular in the Tang dynasty. The brush strokes were easy to recognize, but none of the researchers could read the text. It wasn't in Chinese! Carbon 14 analysis gave a date of between 653 and 663 C.E, which was the last decade of the celebrated Buddhist monk Xuanzang's life.

After a few false starts, the language was identified as being ancient Aramaic, and a translation was undertaken. The contents described an unknown Second Journey to the West undertaken by Xuanzang and his disciples, and it created a sensation in academic circles. The events described are not what one would expect in a Chinese tale of that era, and some scholars questioned whether this was in fact a Tang document, or perhaps a later forgery. Some even questioned the provenance of the document, and the veracity of the Carbon 14 dating.

JOEL BIGMAN

Professor Amsalem of the Hebrew University put these doubts to rest, when he realized that the stories in the scroll had parallels in the Babylonian Talmud. A team of Chinese and Jewish scholars worked together to reconstruct the original events, which are presented in this book, without further ado.

To quote the manuscript: "We do not yet know the details of that Second Journey: let's find out in the next chapter."

Kaifeng

We are sure you recall the Tang Monk, Xuanzang. He was famous for his great Journey to the West, a journey he embarked upon in order to collect Buddhist scriptures from India and bring them back to Tang China. He crossed mountains and rivers, forests and cities, and faced eighty-one obstacles on the way. Many demons wanted to eat him, for it was said that anyone who tasted of the flesh of this most perfected monk would gain immortality. The other obstacles, however, were more unusual, such as getting pregnant by drinking river water, or scaling a mountain covered with slimy, stinky, rotten persimmons.

Xuanzang could not have finished his Journey alone. The bodhisattva Guanyin, the divine embodiment of mercy and compassion, provided him with companions to aid him in his travels. Unlike Xuanzang, these companions were far from perfected; each was flawed and saw the Journey as an opportunity to redeem themselves.

The most famous, of course, was Sun Wukong, who we shall call "Monkey". He could be as playful as a child, a child with a dangerous weapon and a quick temper. He was born from a stone egg and learned seventy-two transformations from a Daoist Immortal which allowed him to change his shape into anything from a mosquito to a house. His weapon was the Compliant Rod, a steel battle rod that grew and shrank as needed. He challenged

Heaven itself and insisted he be referred to as The Great Sage Equal to Heaven.

Monkey rebelled against the heavens relentlessly, but even when he was finally captured, the gods found that they could not kill him. He was eventually subdued and buried under a mountain by the Buddha himself. Guanyin released him from his tomb under the condition that he help Xuanzang on his Journey. With his agreement, she placed a ring on his head, the magic headband that Xuanzang could tighten with a spell if Monkey got out of control.

Xuanzang was also joined by Zhu Bajie—literally Eight-Rules Pig—on his Journey. We shall call him Pigsy. He was a pig-demon, the personification of gluttony and lust, partly reformed during the original Journey. He had accepted the Eight Rules, namely right view, right thought, right speech, right behavior, right livelihood, right effort, right mindfulness and right concentration. Thus, his name. His weapon was the nine-pronged rake, refined from divine ice- iron, hammered by Lord Lao Tzu himself.

There were two other demons who joined our Tang Monk Xuanzang on his original Journey. Sha Monk, known as Sandy, and a dragon who was turned into a horse. They do not join Xuanzang on this Second Journey, so we will not discuss them further.

Our story starts with Xuanzang.

It had been five years since he had returned to Xi'an from his Journey, bringing with him 657 Buddhist Scriptures. The work in the Translation Bureau was progressing smoothly and didn't require much of his attention these days.

He was no longer a young man. Since his head was shaven, one could not see his graying hair, however, his white eyebrows, wrinkles and sun-beaten face all suggested he was considerably older than he had once been. His saffron robe hung loosely on his shoulders, and he used his cane more than he'd like to admit. His eyes, though, remained intelligent, clear and calm.

Our Tang Monk was not an adventurous man at heart. His Journey was motivated by a scholar's hunger for books, and his disciples always dealt with the demons, and fiends—he was far too timid for that. For all intents and purposes, he should have spent his remaining days in peaceful meditation, reciting sutras, and overseeing the translation project. Alas, Heaven decided otherwise.

Two days earlier, a wandering monk had shown up in hemp sandals, begging bowl in hand. In Kaifeng, he told a confused tale of unknown scriptures. Reports of this sort were common and rarely relevant; people expected and received a small reward for these new 'discoveries', which did not make for accurate reports. This particular wandering monk did not ask for a reward, however. He simply told his story and walked away, leaving only a scrap of palm leaf behind with a young temple monk. The monk saw some black markings on the leaf, and suspected that it was writing of some sort, so the following morning he handed it to his superior, who in turn gave it to Xuanzang, thinking that if anybody could read it, it would be him.

When Xuanzang first received the leaf, he was puzzled. He walked down the aisle past the rows of laboring monks and went out into the bright daylight. He peered at the bit of leaf again. There was no doubt. There was writing on it, in a script that he had never seen before. That in and of itself was quite remarkable, considering that he had traveled more than 50,000 *li* and visited more than a hundred kingdoms. Even more peculiar, the monk had insisted that he'd found the scrap in Kaifeng, just five hundred *li* away, and that the people who wrote it still lived there.

He had been pondering this script for two days, and a decision had to be made. Xuanzang arranged for a visit to Kaifeng.

It took three days for Xuanzang to free himself from the welcoming ceremonies and banquets. He was famous and admired for his Journey and for the scriptures he had brought from India, and as a result, it was impossible for him to travel quietly. With the conclusion of such formalities, he was finally able to start his investigation. His approach was straightforward — go to the marketplace and start asking people if they recognized the writing on the leaf. If the monk's story was in fact true, somebody would know where these people were. It took all morning, and, just as he had to overcome eighty-one obstacles on the Journey, he had to ask eighty-one people to get his answer. The writing had originated from a temple located on Earth Market Street, near the corner of Fire God Temple Lane.

The temple looked like any other temple, both pagan and Buddhist, but with one glaring difference: no gods. There wasn't a single statue, either inside or outside. There weren't even decorative carvings of tigers and dragons on the roof. There was an inscription on the entrance to the temple, Xuanzang scrutinized it but saw only regular characters rather than the odd script that he had seen.

The temple was nearly empty. There was a table surrounded by a dozen benches and several piles of books atop a platform in the middle of the room. Where the idol should have been were this any other temple, was a large ornate cabinet of unclear purpose. Xuanzang approached the platform and opened a book; it was filled with ordinary characters, though the content was unfamiliar to him.

"How can I help you?"

THE SECOND JOURNEY

A bearded man with a blue cap had approached while he was engrossed in the book. Our Tang Monk bowed to him and introduced himself.

"I am Xuanzang, a Buddhist scholar from Xi'an."

His host bowed in return.

"Welcome! Welcome! I am Jin, one of Sect Who Extract the Sinew. You are well known throughout the kingdom!"

Now, this temple belonged to the group called Djuhud, or Jews. These people were known for their strict dietary code, which included not eating certain tendons in their meat. Thus, the name 'Sect Who Extract the Sinew'.

Xuanzang couldn't deny his fame, so he remained silent.

"How may we assist our honored guest?"

"I am looking for scriptures written in these strange characters."

Xuanzang showed the scrap of leaf to his host, who nodded, and walked over to the cabinet. He opened the door and took out an ornate silver idol. Xuanzang had been wondering where they kept them; he watched the man carry the idol from the cabinet to the table where Xuanzang stood. Upon closer inspection, our Tang Monk saw that it wasn't an idol at all—just a case. His blue-capped host opened a clasp, and the case split open to reveal a large scroll written completely in that odd script.

"It's beautiful. Can you read it for me?" he whispered.

Jin's smile faded.

"I can read the sounds, but I don't fully understand the contents. We had an elder who knew more, but he died last year, taking with him much of the ancient knowledge."

"Where is this from?"

Jin smiled again. "From the West. You know about the West better than anyone else in Tang lands."

Xuanzang took pause. "But I don't know this. I've never seen such writing."

"There are lands west of India."

"I've heard of them. My goal was India, where I could find the source of Buddhism."

"Yes, that is clear, but there is more. We have some hope — a group of us are studying this text together and perhaps, we can unravel some mysteries."

"May auspicious stars accompany your studies."

Xuanzang bowed again, left the strange temple, and started walking down Earth Market Street towards the Buddhist temple where he was staying. The sights and sounds were familiar to him. The colorful small shrines at every corner, the shaven-head monks in their simple robes, carrying their begging bowls, the street vendors hawking steamed buns and fried vegetables. Everything looked, sounded, and smelled like home. A Buddhist should avoid such feelings of attachment, especially to mundane items, but after years of wandering in strange lands, it was good to be home.

Further west! He shook his head. As if his own Journey hadn't been far enough! Well, he'd found the source of the writing on that leaf, and though it was interesting, it wouldn't help him in his study of Buddhist scripture. He'd stay overnight in Kaifeng, then head back to the city of Perpetual Peace, Xi'an.

Xuanzang only slept a few hours each night as there was little time to sleep in a life full of chanting, meditation and study. His hosts at the large Buddhist temple near the western gate had laid out a mat in a small room for him. He undressed and lay down.

He had hardly fallen asleep when Guanyin Bodhisattva appeared before him. A Bodhisattva is one who has attained enlightenment but has delayed reaching Nirvana in order to help the others. Guanyin in particular epitomizes compassion and mercy. Xuanzang kowtowed to her nine times and waited to hear her message.

"Xuanzang, you are truly Tripitaka, the one with knowledge of all the Buddhist Scriptures!"

Xuanzang was not one to seek compliments or fame, though both had come to him; he could only bow his head in silence.

"There is wisdom in our writings, but not all wisdom is found in India, nor is all wisdom found in Buddhism. There is much to be learned from more distant lands."

Xuanzang had an idea where this was headed.

"More distant lands? Lands further west?"

"Yes, you have guessed correctly. There are wise teachings further west, and wise teachers as well."

"Someone could bring teachings. It can be done. But to find a teacher who will come to a distant land, and teach in a language he doesn't know? Who will do such a thing?"

"Someone like you. One who is dedicated to wisdom."

"I went to India to bring the true teachings back to my own land. Not to stay there and teach foreigners."

Guanyin knew it would be difficult, but aren't all such quests difficult?

"Yet such a sage must be found, a sage to teach the Sect Who Extract the Sinew, a Sage to bring new ideas into Tang lands."

"Perhaps someone could travel further west. Perhaps they can find such a sage. But who would go on such a mission?"

Guanyin was silent. Xuanzang knew how to wait, but so did Guanyin. When Xuanzang finally understood what Guanyin was really suggesting, he could not remain silent.

"Another trip? I can't do that, not again. I am too old, too tired. How could I hope to deal with the demons and fiends again?"

"You will have help."

"I had help last time and still barely survived. Besides, who would help me?"

"Monkey and Pigsy".

Xuanzang was silent. Guanyin waited.

"If they will come of their own free will, then I will go."

"They will. They're already here."

"Here?"

"Yes. You will see in the morning."

"Xuanzang, this is not merely a matter of helping the small Sect Who Extract the Sinew. There are very few of them, and who knows if they will exist tomorrow? Our Tang culture is so powerful that neighboring cultures absorb it, invaders adopt it. We are blind to the other cultures and learnings."

"What of my Journey to India? What of the teachings of the Buddha?"

"That is a rare example. We need to bring other ideas to our lands. Seeds that may grow into something new. The same is true of foreign lands. They can learn from the Tang, even if they are far away.

Guanyin returned to the Hall of Divine Mists, and Xuanzang returned to a troubled sleep filled with abrasive, vivid dreams. Confused images of caves inhabited by demons and monsters, of endless days riding through unknown lands, of Monkey and Pigsy quarreling with each other.

He woke in the morning just before sunrise, as was his habit, and had to clear his mind before he could start his daily meditation. He kept thinking of arguments he could have tried on Guanyin: he was too old, he'd already done his share of the work, and he didn't owe these strange idol-less people anything. He finally managed to push all that from his mind and settled in to his meditation.

There was some background noise, but it would take quite a lot to disturb an old Tang Monk in the middle of his morning

THE SECOND JOURNEY

meditation.

Xuanzang wasn't aware that a large black fly was buzzing around his head. He completely ignored the fly when it was in his ear. But when the fly flew up his left nostril, he couldn't help sneezing, and his concentration was disturbed. He opened his eyes and saw there was a large black fly dancing on his nose. Dancing?

He looked more carefully. The fly was kowtowing to him!

Xuanzang smiled.

"Welcome, Monkey! Welcome, Sun Wukong!"

The fly shook itself, and in a flash, Old Monkey stood before him, hairy-faced and with the beak of a thunder-god. Though his appearance would likely cause most to quake in fear, it only drew affection from Xuanzang. Monkey was dressed in a yellow robe and red boots, with two long phoenix feathers rising from his cap. His Compliant Rod had shrunk to the size of a needle and was hidden in his ear.

"Hello, Master! Hello, Hello! Are you ready? Shall we go?"

"How did you know there was another Journey?"

"Guanyin came to the Flower Fruit Mountain. She offered me a choice. She told me that you were going. She said I did not have to go with you, that I had fulfilled everything on the first Journey. I had to think long and hard. Life is good on Flower Fruit Mountain."

"How long did you think?"

"Long enough to say, 'Yes, yes!'"

Xuanzang laughed. "I did not want to go, but Guanyin said I'd have companions."

"I'm here! I'm here! And Pigsy is sleeping right outside the door, digesting last night's supper!"

"Ah, Pigsy. Guanyin said that Sandy and our dragon horse would not be joining us, so it appears that it is just the three of us at present. There should be a fourth, and maybe a beast for me to ride on."

"Master, disciples can be met on the way."

"True."

"When shall we start?"

"Now. Or as soon as we can wake up old Pigsy."

They went outside. Sure enough, Pigsy was snoring away as only a well-fed hog can.

Xuanzang gently tapped Pigsy on the shoulder. "Wake up! Time to go!"

Pigsy snored.

"Master, you know that approach won't work with Pigsy. Just let me…"

"No. We won't start this Journey with tricks or violence, even if meant in jest."

"Pigsy! My Disciple! Wake up!"

"Hmm."

"Food! Food time!"

Pigsy opened his eyes, pulled his heavy body up, and…

"Oh! Master! I'm here for the Journey! Where's the food?"

"I'm sure breakfast is waiting for us. Let's eat and part from our hosts before we go."

"Old Monkey thinks there's no food here. Idiot Pigsy ate it all up last night!"

"Quiet. Let's go."

They joined the monks at breakfast. Pigsy laid his nine-toothed rake in a corner and behaved himself, eating only five times as much as did the average monk. His brown robe hung loosely on him, which was a convenience if he ever found a feast waiting for him. If it weren't for his snout, one would merely think he was an overweight gardener.

After breakfast, they set on their way. Jin from the temple

THE SECOND JOURNEY

provided Xuanzang with a white horse, not as fine a steed as Bai Longma, the White Dragon horse of his first Journey, but a fine beast, nonetheless. Travel began easily, these were well-traversed lands that they had already visited, lands that were now free of demons and fiends.

They left Kaifeng and went to Liangxhou.

They left Liangzhou, and went to Qinghai.

They left Qinghai and traveled across the desert to Kumul.

They left Kumul, and followed the Tian Shan, the Heavenly Mountains, westward.

They went through Karasahr to Kucha, where they stayed a few days to visit the stupas and the other Buddhist holy sites.

They left Kucha, and traveled to Aksu, then crossed the Bezel Pass.

They visited Tokmak, home of the great Khagan of the Göktürks,

They passed Tashkent and finally reached the great city of Samarkand. This was as far west as they had traveled many decades ago. From this point on, the unknown awaited them.

From Samarkand the way west took them through Bukhara. The trail went along the fertile plains of the Zeravshan River; their travels thus far had been smooth and the inhabitants of these lands were generous towards foreign travelers. They awoke before daybreak each day, ate breakfast, and began traveling at sunrise, the old Tang Monk on his horse, his companions walking alongside. They would walk for the duration of the daylight hours and search for suitable accommodations in the late afternoon.

One evening, near Qiziltepa, at the end of an uneventful, yet tiring day, before our friends found lodging, they heard some deep grunting noises ahead. Xuanzang shuddered at the sound, but Monkey laughed.

"Master, don't worry! Don't worry! It's just one of Pigsy's cousins. Old Monkey will go first and take care of it."

The path followed a twisting canal. High reeds blocked their view in all directions. The grunting grew louder, now accompanied by loud thumps. Xuanzang shuddered despite Monkey's reassurances. The road opened up into a small clearing, where a giant man stood. He was dressed in a tiger skin draped over one shoulder, leather sandals bound on his feet, and he had a fierce black beard. He was entertaining himself by lifting huge rocks over his head and then throwing them half a *li* away. He paused when he saw the travelers.

"Hello to you!" he bellowed at them.

"Hello, hello, Mr Rock Lifter!"

"Allow me to introduce myself. I am Bear. Also known as the Second Samson."

"Samson?"

"Ah, you are from quite far away if you haven't heard of him, or of me. He was the strongest man on earth in his time, as I am in mine."

Monkey laughed.

"Strongest man? Maybe, maybe. But not as strong as Old Monkey."

"A challenge? From a furry contender?"

"A challenge! First strength, then a few friendly bouts."

"I am Bear, lifter of mountains, bender of steel!"

"And I am just a little old monkey!"

Bear picked up a huge rock and threw it a full *li* into the reeds. Monkey picked up a larger rock and threw it farther.

Bear piled five rocks in his arms and carried them across the clearing.

Monkey picked up six and danced daintily across.

Bear was enraged.

THE SECOND JOURNEY

"Come here, you skinny hairy nothing. I'll beat you to a pulp!"

Being from the West, Bear had never heard of old Monkey or his exploits. He had no clue that Monkey had challenged Heaven itself and had very nearly been victorious. He had never heard of Xuanzang and the Journey they had taken together. He knew not of how Monkey had saved Xuanzang from demons and monsters along the way. But lucky for him, Monkey was never one to be shy and was glad to educate this foreign Bear.

"Beat me to a pulp? You can try, but you don't know who you are dealing with!

> *My father was Heaven, my mother Earth:*
> *Born from a stone egg, I subdued dragons; I captured beasts.*
> *I was king of the monkeys at Flower Fruit Mountain*
> *I called myself the Great Sage, Equal to Heaven;*
> *The soldiers of the Jade Emperor himself could not subdue me,*
> *Laozi's brazier could not burn me*
> *I am Sun Wukong, the Handsome Monkey King!"*

The giant bear-man ran at Monkey, carrying a log the size of a ship's mast. He swung it at Monkey, who danced aside as the beam crashed into the ground. Again, and again the beam hit the ground, but Old Monkey was never under it.

"Tired, Old Bear? Let's see if you can dodge my Compliant Golden-Hooped Rod!"

Monkey pulled the needle-sized rod out of his ear, whispered a few words, gave it a shake and instantly, it was as thick as a rice bowl and weighed 17,500 *jin*!

"Take a blow from my little rod, Fat Bear!"

Xuanzang was struck with horror. He had believed Monkey

had redeemed himself on their Journey; even the Buddha had congratulated him on perfecting himself. He thought that the golden headband and its tightening spell was no longer needed. You will recall that Guanyin had placed a ring on Monkey's head, a simple crown that Xuanzang could tighten with a few magic words. The pain of this headband is what brought wild Monkey under control during the first Journey. Yet, Monkey was going to murder a stranger, for no reason at all! It was just a stupid contest. Had he forgotten everything in a few years on the Flower Fruit Mountain?

There was no time for Xuanzang to try the headband-tightening spell. The rod came down, and Bear, the Second Samson, did not budge. He planted his feet firmly on the ground and waited for the blow.

Our Tang Monk closed his eyes and screamed. But there was no blow, no splattering of blood and bone. He opened his eyes.

Monkey and Bear faced each other, their eyes glaring. Bear had caught the rod in his bare hands and had somehow wrestled it away from Monkey. Monkey was in shock. What human could even dream of moving his weapon, let alone grab it from his hands? Bear's eyes calmed and cooled. He lifted one knee and using it as the fulcrum, slowly bent Monkey's compliant rod into the shape of a horseshoe!

Silence. Even the insects stopped buzzing. The birds were quiet. The Heavens and the Earth held their breath. Our dear Monkey was shocked. Anger flared in his diamond eyes, but then died down. He backed away from The Bear, fell to his knees, and kowtowed four times.

"You are my Brother! Be my blood brother.

Bear did not know what to make of this.

"Brothers? How?"

"We'll take an oath. Like the Oath of the Peach Garden."

THE SECOND JOURNEY

"Peach Garden?"

Monkey faltered.

"Liu Bei, Guan Yu and Zhang Fei? You don't know of them?"

Strange as it seems to us, Bear had no way of knowing about events that had taken place centuries earlier in a faraway land. He didn't know of the Han Empire, nor did he know of its collapse into civil war.

Bear shook his head.

"These things are known in your land, but not here. Just as there are many things that are known here but will be new to you."

Xuanzang suddenly realized what had happened. Bear and Monkey complemented each other and Bear was their ideal guide in these Western lands.

He spoke, "Welcome! You are, in fact, Monkey's brother and our guide to these foreign parts! Will you join us?"

"Join you? Going where?"

"West, always west. To seek wisdom and scriptures."

"I have always wanted to go west, to where my people came from. I'll gladly join you!"

Monkey looked despondently at his crooked staff.

The Second Samson laughed and bent it back into shape as easily as you or I would cut a piece off a cake of Pu'er tea.

And thus Bear, the Second Samson, the Foreign Guide, joined our group of travelers.

We will leave our travelers for now, and visit a sage in a distant land.

Elisha

The weather was good, so Elisha, the son of Avuya, was teaching outside, under a tree. Twenty students, seated on rocks and the remains of a fallen tree, were gathered to hear his words. Blind Joseph sat in the front. He was their breathing, walking library. The ancient sages did not record their teachings, and had not done so for many generations. What was written was written, and what was oral, must remain oral.

Since the sages had been discussing the fine points of the Law for centuries, and much of the discussion centered around earlier precedents and opinions, the lack of a written record was problematic. This was solved by having scholars, who didn't necessarily have the sharpest minds, but with phenomenal memories, who would absorb the oral teachings for years. Often, though not always, these people could not see.

Elisha continued. "Let's consider the case of three oxen in the same courtyard. Let's assume that none of these oxen were known to be belligerent. We find that one of the oxen had been gored and injured, but nobody saw this happen, and there was no other indication of which ox did the deed. What points do you think are relevant to this case?"

The students were silent, looking down at the ground while they thought. One raised his head. Elisha nodded. "Yes, Saul."

"Who does the courtyard belong to?"

Elisha nodded. "That certainly can be relevant to the payment, but how can we decide who should pay? You see the problem. Yes, Joshua."

"I don't have an answer. I'm just thinking, if the injured party demands payment from one of the ox owners, the owner can always say, 'How do you know it was mine that caused this damage? And likewise the other. We can't even demand partial payment from any of them. So the injured party is out of luck."

"That makes sense," Elisha agreed. "But let's see if there are any parallel cases in other fields. Joseph, maybe you know of something relevant from, let's say, the laws of betrothal?"

"There's the case of a man who goes up to a group of women, and betroths one of them--but afterwards doesn't recall which one it was."

"An extreme case of forgetfulness, I would say. Not exactly gentlemanly, either. What's the ruling?"

"The consensus is that the man has to give all of the women involved a bill of divorce."

The students shifted uneasily.

"Saul," said Elisha.

"First of all, what is this case? It must be that none of the women remembers either. Or they all insist that they were the betrothed one. Perhaps the man was very wealthy. Wealthy and drunk."

Elisha smiled. "Very good, the case might not be very realistic. What was your second point?"

"The proposed solution has a cost. The women involved are now divorced women, so they won't be able to marry any priest."

"Also true. But, getting back to our case, I think it doesn't help us at all. Hard to draw a comparison between that case and our oxen."

The discussion continued in this way for a while, with Joseph being called upon to recall various ancient teachings that turned out to not be quite relevant to the case under discussion.

Elisha noticed that the sun was high in the sky. It was time to finish the discussion and send the students home to eat lunch. He recalled the story of his student Meir, who was teaching in the Synagogue Friday evening, and got carried away. One of the women in the congregation got home so late that the lamps had run out of oil and gone out, leaving her husband hungry and in the dark, waiting for her. It almost ended up in a divorce. It was important to keep track of time, even when one was enjoying the lesson.

Elisha rose, and the students rose out of respect, and waited till he had walked away from their outdoors study hall.

Elisha enjoyed teaching. Holding class outside, under a tree, always reminded him of Plato's Akademia near Athens. He understood the antagonism toward Rome, and by extension to Greek culture. But there was much they were missing by this wholesale rejection. What would his students think, if they knew that he had attended a performance of a Greek Play?

Without coincidence, there would be no story.

Most of his students had scattered to their mid-day meals. His best student, Saul, had stayed behind, and approached him.

"Sage Elisha. May I ask you a question?"

"Ask, Saul."

"Master, is it proper for a man to attend a Greek play?"

"Many would say not, Saul, as you well know."

"Sage Elisha, I am not asking many. I am asking just one."

"And are you asking about Greek plays in general? Or perhaps a specific one?"

"Master, for the sake of argument, let's say a performance of *Oedipus Rex* a week ago in Bet Shean."

Elisha smiled. "In that case, for the sake of argument, as you put it, what should one do if one observed one's teacher entering the theater?"

"That would depend if one was attending the performance oneself, or not."

"And if, again, for the sake of theoretical argument, one did attend the play, what would one think of it?"

"Most likely one would think that *Oedipus Rex* was a fable, a myth. It was impossible that such a thing ever happened. Yet perhaps the play had some truth in it, truth that is expressed better in fiction than in reality."

"If it had some truth, it would be an uncomfortable truth, of unavoidable fate. An idea that is different from the common perception of divine oversight, 'do the right thing and God will take care of you. Would that idea make you uncomfortable?' "

"Master, is being comfortable in your ideas the correct road to wisdom?"

Elisha sighed. "Saul, consider carefully how uncomfortable you want to be."

"Sage Elisha, some ideas that we now accept, did not originate with our people. We have already absorbed concepts from the Greeks and the Persian fire worshippers. The exchange of ideas is not merely historical. It will continue, even if we pretend that it doesn't."

"And yet we remain separate," Elisha noted.

"Blessed is our Lord, who makes a distinction between sacred and profane, between

light and darkness, between Israel and the nations, between the Seventh Day and the six work days."

Saul went on his way, but he left Elisha thinking. There was much to learn from the Greeks, and even the Romans. For example, the Greek writings were full of stories of distant lands and strange animals.

Elisha had seen some exotic animals. He occasionally saw war elephants, and once he saw a tiger in a gladiator show. The tiger was interesting, but the show was awful. He would not be going again. He'd never seen a monkey, and wished he would. They were almost human, but not quite. Or maybe humans were almost like them. The Greeks had fables about them. He'd read one about a prince who had trained dancing monkeys. They danced as well as any of his courtiers, and were dressed just as well. The monkeys performed regularly, until one courtier took out a handful of nuts and threw them on the stage. The monkeys immediately forgot their training, and reverted to their true monkey-selves, scrambling for the nuts as the audience laughed.

So the true nature of a monkey cannot be hidden forever. Likewise the true nature of a man. The sages knew that the world was large. How could they not, when the Romans were everywhere? Yet they limited themselves to the narrow confines of discussing the Law, thinking, yes, there are other peoples and things in this world, but none of them were important.

Let's leave Elisha to his ponderings, and return to our travelers. To find out what happened to them, read the next chapter.

Oven

We were telling you about the Tang Monk Xuanzang, who rode his white horse alongside his disciples: Monkey Sun Wukong, Eight-Rules Pigsy, who was often called just plain Idiot, and Bear, the Second Samson; the newest addition who had joined them near Bukhara, serving now as their Foreign Guide.

It was getting dark, and they needed a place to spend that night. There were no cities nearby, but there were scattered fishermen's huts. It was getting dark and they had to ask for shelter where they could. Xuanzang asked his disciples to wait among the reeds, while he and Bear went up to the nearest hut.

The hut was made of woven reeds and had a thatched roof. They entered through a small courtyard, where nets hung on poles, drying after a day's work. They walked between the nets and the traps, until they stood in front of the door. Xuanzang was going to knock, but as the door was also made of woven reeds, it wouldn't make much sound. Instead, Bear called out.

"Is anybody home?"

A short sun-wizened man came to the door and looked out.

"Guests! Here? An unusual pleasure!"

"Yes, we are travelers. I'm Bear, from a village not too far from here. My fellow travelers are from far away, from the Tang Empire in the East."

"I can see that he is from far away, from his face and his

clothing. But you are...Bear? The Bear? Weightlifter and general-purpose strong man?"

"Yes, that's me."

The fisherman scratched his head and peeked around Bear, searching, "You said fellow travelers..."

Xuanzang bowed.

"I will call for my two disciples to join us. They are a bit unusual-looking, but usually well behaved."

The fisherman smiled.

"Usually? Well, they are welcome. There isn't much room in my hut, but we can crowd in. Your horse can stay in the courtyard. I will roast a couple of extra fish for your dinner."

"Thank you, thank you. But my disciples and I are among those who have left the family. We don't eat any meat or fish. Only vegetables."

Their host wasn't familiar with the term "those who have left the family", though he had heard of itinerant holy men who had left their homes and lives to wander the earth. In any case, he thought it impolite to question our friends further on this point.

"I can prepare some rice and vegetables. Nothing fancy, but hungry you won't be."

Xuanzang called for Monkey and Pigsy to join them. They were there in a moment, thanking their host for his hospitality. He hid his surprise at their appearance and welcomed them into his hut. They sat in the courtyard for the meal of rice and vegetables.

After a time of polite conversation, their host could no longer restrain his curiosity.

"We know of the lands to the east. Traders come through with goods and stories, but they stick to the main roads and the cities. I don't think I've ever met somebody from there."

"We aren't traders. My disciples and I are on a quest to seek

THE SECOND JOURNEY

Western Scriptures."

"A worthy goal, though not one for a simple fisherman. I must ask, why don't you eat meat, or even fish?"

"We are Buddhist monks. Ones who have left the family."

"I don't know what a 'Buddhist' is. I can understand that you left the usual family life in order to search for a spiritual truth. But why not eat a chicken, or a fish? Surely these animals were created to serve as our food."

"One must have compassion for all living things. Animals are sentient; they have emotions. The fish tries to escape your net. The chicken fears the butcher's knife."

"Yet they are our food. How far does this 'compassion' go? What about an ant? Or a mosquito that is biting me? Plenty of those around here."

Xuanzang had an answer from the scriptures, "One must protect ants when sweeping the floor, and put shades on lamps for the safety of the moths."

Their host was impressed. "At least you're consistent."

Bear wasn't satisfied.

"Consistent? Maybe. But, also extreme. Eating animals is part of nature. It is simply the way things are. The lion kills and eats the deer. The spider catches and eats the fly. This is the way the world is, as the Creator intended."

Xuanzang had heard this argument many times before.

"Are you a lion, who has no choice, and no way to make a choice?"

Bear wasn't satisfied.

"Does our fisherman host have a choice? Does the shepherd have a choice? All of us have to make a living, whether he be the lion, the spider, or the butcher."

Pigsy couldn't resist talk of food.

"If you'd been on our first Journey, if you had been tied up and hung from the rafters, waiting to be some demon's next meal, you'd think differently about eating animals."

"Nothing for you to worry about here!" said Bear. "My people don't eat pork."

"I have heard that, why is that so?"

"It's our tradition. It's written in our law."

Xuanzang suddenly understood.

"The law. The book that I saw in your temple in Kaifeng."

"I don't know where Kaifeng is, or if our people live there."

"It's a famous city in Tang lands. And your people do live there. That is why I am traveling again, to help them." He handed the fisherman the leaf left behind by the monk.

He handed the leaf with the writing on it to Bear who glanced at it.

"Yes, that is our language and our writing. How did any of us get so far East?"

Xuanzang shrugged.

"There's a lot of travel on the East-West routes. Merchants from every land travel back and forth."

Pigsy was still focused on food.

"You don't eat pork, but you eat other animals!"

"It's our tradition."

Monkey couldn't restrain himself.

"I am only a monkey; my master is the wise one here. The other is Bear! How can you say such things? Here you sit, chatting and eating rice with your monkey blood brother and your pig-companion, and yet you talk about humans not having compassion for animals."

"You are not normal animals. And what about those ants and moths?"

"Ants are nothing? Let's see you make an ant!"

Bear scratched his head.

THE SECOND JOURNEY

"But the moth, it wants to fly into the flame. Why is that my concern? Maybe it loves fire, it's his religion, or philosophy, or art. Maybe he thinks that it is better to be happy for a moment, and be burned up with beauty, than to live a long time, and be bored all the while.*"

"You don't know me yet, Brother Bear. Someday you will see that a moth might actually be a monkey, just like a monkey can be The Great Sage Equal to Heaven."

Finally, they lay down on reed mats in the hut, and with the Tang Monk's horse safely tied in the courtyard with some hay, they drifted off to sleep for the night.

They woke at dawn. The hay was still in the courtyard, but the horse was gone.

Xuanzang was shocked.

"I have bad luck with horses. My first one was eaten by a dragon, my second one was a dragon, and this one has disappeared!"

"Do not worry master! I may be the Great Sage Equal to Heaven, but Old Monkey was also once in charge of the heavenly stables! We'll get that horse back!"

But try as they could, they couldn't find the horse. Somebody had untied it, opened the gate, and taken it off into the marshes while they slept. Monkey wanted to mount his magic cloud and search for the marsh outlaws who had run off with the Tang Steed, but Xuanzang forbade him.

"Monkey, it's just a horse. If I'm destined to walk, I'll walk. It will slow us down a bit, but we are not in a great hurry."

They started on their way; Monkey lead the way, followed by Bear and Xuanzang, and Pigsy taking up the rear.

"Bear, you are the 'Second Samson', but who was the first Samson?"

"It's a long story."

"We have a long way to travel..."
"Here is how it is told in our scriptures:

>'And there was a certain man of Zorah, of the family of the Danites, whose name was Manoah; and his wife was barren and bore not.
>
>And the angel of God appeared unto the woman, and said unto her: 'Behold now, thou art barren, and hast not borne; but thou shalt conceive, and bear a son.
>
>Now therefore beware, I pray thee, and drink no wine nor strong drink, and eat not any unclean thing...'"*

It was a fascinating story about events that took place many generations ago. It was long, as Bear had forewarned, and it helped Xuanzang and Bear pass the time as they walked. Monkey was scouting ahead of them, and missed the story, while Pigsy trailed behind, grumbling about food, and not paying much attention.

As the morning turned to afternoon, Xuanzang was getting quite tired, and though it was only spring, it was already getting quite hot.

In these far western lands, Spring was not as kind as it was in the Tang Empire. In the regions ruled by Emperor Taizhong, The Poem of Spring says:

>"The cycle of nature has made its turn.
>The great earth quickens, and all things seem new.
>Plums vie with peaches in their beauteous blooms;
>Swallows pile on carved beams their scented dust."*

Here, in the far lands west of India, the Poem of Spring says:
"The cycle of nature has made its turn.
The Eastern desert wind blows for weeks on end.
The great earth heats and all things seem old and dry.

THE SECOND JOURNEY

*Golden wheat ripens in the field,
and cattle churn the dust."*

The heat and dust distorted the view, so that even Monkey's diamond eyes could not pierce the haze.

But Xuanzang saw what looked like a great city on the horizon.

"Disciple Monkey, is that a city that I see, or is the heat and dust fooling me with a mirage?"

"Master, it's a city all right, but it's hard even for Old Monkey to see clearly. Let's get closer, and then we'll see what sort of city it is."

When they got closer, they saw a city with great stone walls and many gates. The gates were open, but the city looked deserted. Where was the traffic of merchants with money bags, or with fruit or live fowls tied with twine?

Pigsy was already concerned.

"Master, where will we beg for food here? These foreigners do not recognize those who have left the family."

Monkey gave him a gentle tap on the head with his compliant staff. Fortunately, it was only the size of a spindle at the time, so a loud 'ouch' was the only damage.

"Why did you hit me?"

"Because you are up to your old tricks, always trying to fill your belly. Can't you see that the city is empty?"

"Is it my fault that I was born with such an appetite?" asked Pigsy.

"Quiet, my disciples! Why does the city look abandoned? Is it a plague? Or has it been taken over by some demon king? Monkey, go see what is happening there, and don't cause any trouble!"

So, our Monkey went into town. Usually, people would stare at his strange appearance, gawk at this hairy body and his

"We have a long way to travel…"
"Here is how it is told in our scriptures:

>'And there was a certain man of Zorah, of the family of the Danites, whose name was Manoah; and his wife was barren and bore not.
>
>And the angel of God appeared unto the woman, and said unto her: 'Behold now, thou art barren, and hast not borne; but thou shalt conceive, and bear a son.
>
>Now therefore beware, I pray thee, and drink no wine nor strong drink, and eat not any unclean thing…'"*

It was a fascinating story about events that took place many generations ago. It was long, as Bear had forewarned, and it helped Xuanzang and Bear pass the time as they walked. Monkey was scouting ahead of them, and missed the story, while Pigsy trailed behind, grumbling about food, and not paying much attention.

As the morning turned to afternoon, Xuanzang was getting quite tired, and though it was only spring, it was already getting quite hot.

In these far western lands, Spring was not as kind as it was in the Tang Empire. In the regions ruled by Emperor Taizhong, The Poem of Spring says:

>"*The cycle of nature has made its turn.*
>*The great earth quickens, and all things seem new.*
>*Plums vie with peaches in their beauteous blooms;*
>*Swallows pile on carved beams their scented dust.*"*

Here, in the far lands west of India, the Poem of Spring says:
"*The cycle of nature has made its turn.*
The Eastern desert wind blows for weeks on end.
The great earth heats and all things seem old and dry.

THE SECOND JOURNEY

*Golden wheat ripens in the field,
and cattle churn the dust."*

The heat and dust distorted the view, so that even Monkey's diamond eyes could not pierce the haze.

But Xuanzang saw what looked like a great city on the horizon.

"Disciple Monkey, is that a city that I see, or is the heat and dust fooling me with a mirage?"

"Master, it's a city all right, but it's hard even for Old Monkey to see clearly. Let's get closer, and then we'll see what sort of city it is."

When they got closer, they saw a city with great stone walls and many gates. The gates were open, but the city looked deserted. Where was the traffic of merchants with money bags, or with fruit or live fowls tied with twine?

Pigsy was already concerned.

"Master, where will we beg for food here? These foreigners do not recognize those who have left the family."

Monkey gave him a gentle tap on the head with his compliant staff. Fortunately, it was only the size of a spindle at the time, so a loud 'ouch' was the only damage.

"Why did you hit me?"

"Because you are up to your old tricks, always trying to fill your belly. Can't you see that the city is empty?"

"Is it my fault that I was born with such an appetite?" asked Pigsy.

"Quiet, my disciples! Why does the city look abandoned? Is it a plague? Or has it been taken over by some demon king? Monkey, go see what is happening there, and don't cause any trouble!"

So, our Monkey went into town. Usually, people would stare at his strange appearance, gawk at this hairy body and his thunder-god beak. The ruder ones would often make unfriendly comments. He had steeled himself to ignore such comments despite his willingness and desire to pick a fight with some ignorant locals. He knew that it would upset Master Xuanzang, resulting at best in a lecture on seeking merit, and at worst a tighten-the-headband spell. But today, in this far-western dusty land, Monkey was ignored. He looked around. The busy city gate wasn't completely deserted. There were guards, who looked healthy enough but hardly glanced at him. He strode in along the main street, a market street lined with shops selling bright Tang silk, purple Roman robes, dark northern furs, sturdy African sandals.

And food!

Baskets of golden wheat, piles of red pomegranates, round cakes of dried figs and fresh yellow dates.

The stores were open, but there were no shopkeepers, and no clients. The streets were empty. He could hear a roar in the distance, towards the center of town, so he decided to follow the sound, and see where everybody had gone.

The roar was a crowd. Thousands had gathered around a large building near the center of the city. There was a sign on the building, but our Monkey had difficulty in reading it. As Xuanzang had noted in his previous journey:

> *The alphabet of their language is brief and simple, having only twenty-odd rudimentary letters, with which a vast vocabulary is formed by a methodical spelling system.**

How these people managed to have a complete civilization with so few characters was a mystery to him. "Old Monkey will never learn to read these chicken-scratches!" he said to himself.

He couldn't get close enough to see what was happening.

THE SECOND JOURNEY

He reached for the compliant gold-banded rod, now the size of a spindle, tucked behind his ear. A few blows with the staff should clear the way. It would also leave a trail of dead bodies and steaming human meat patties, so he thought better of it, and with a magic sign, a few words and a shake of his body, turned himself into a fat bumblebee with a vicious stinger.

He flew over the crowd, through an open window and into the building. What could be so entertaining to so many people?

There were twenty foreign sages in the building, having a heated argument about an oven! Old Monkey listened carefully and while it was hard to follow, the question seemed to be whether this specific oven was ritually pure or impure, or maybe whether it could become impure or not. The tone was getting heated, and the sages were shouting and yelling. The most elderly among them were the most excited.

Our travelers were not used to such behavior. Sages could certainly debate the fine points of scriptures and traditions, but always in a proper dignified manner. Here the venerable sages behaved like vegetable vendors in the market.

Monkey looked closely. One of the sages had drawn a picture of a peculiar oven, one that could be disassembled into pieces. Was this considered a proper oven, in which case it could become ritually impure, or was just a collection of oven parts, and thus not susceptible to impurity like a complete oven would be? The Great Sage focused his bumblebee diamond eyes on the drawing and saw there was a snake demon wrapped around the oven. He knew how to deal with demons!

Impetuous Monkey! He shook himself, returning to his regular size and shape. He pulled the Compliant Rod from his ear, gave it a shake, and it became as thick as a rice bowl. He sprang into his Horse Stance, and only then realized that he was about to attack a drawing. The snake he saw was an embodiment of the twisted arguments coiling around the oven. What would Master say?

Lucky Monkey! Nobody had noticed him, so he slipped into the courtyard, hid in the branches of a tree, shrank his rod back to needle size, and listened to the argument.

It was a fierce battle. One tall scholar defended himself against all the others. He was gray-bearded, wore a rust-colored scarf tied around his head, a white cloth wrapped over one shoulder and around his body, and simple leather sandals. He punctuated his arguments by beating his worn staff on the ground. His words were like a pair of swinging swords, his arguments the quick deadly pecks of a crane, his shouts could raise the souls from Yama's domain of the dead. The other scholars surrounded him with arguments, warding off his attacks with flicks of their logic.

"Eliezer! You have to accept the majority opinion!"

"The majority is wrong! How can I accept? The oven is pure!"

"It's impure, Eliezer. Impure! Accept our ruling."

In his heart, Monkey knew Eliezer. He must have hatched from a sister foreign stone egg and been toughened in a local kiln. Did he ever rule in a western Flower Fruit Mountain, or live in a Foreign Water Curtain Cave? He could stand against them all, even without knowing the Transformations. And, being a westerner, he could not call on Guanyin for assistance, or petition the Jade Emperor to help him in his battle.

"You are all wrong." Eliezer repeated. "Watch! If I am right, the carob tree will prove it."

All the scholars looked at the tree in which our Monkey was hiding. What were they waiting for? A proof? The tree was supposed to do something, to give a sign that Foreign Brother was right.

Dear Monkey! He pulled out a handful of his hair, chewed

it into small pieces, and whispered "Change!" The hairs turned into hundreds of moles, which scrabbled and dug in the rocky earth, and pulled the tree and its roots to one side to a distance of 100 cubits.

The crowd roared when they saw the tree move. But not the sages. They laughed at Eliezer.

"A carob tree isn't an argument. You ran out of proper proofs and are resorting to cheap magic tricks."

"You are all wrong. Watch. If I am right, the aqueduct will prove it."

All eyes turned to the aqueduct running along the edge of the courtyard. They waited for another sign. The water flowed gently down the slope of the water channel. What were these sages waiting for?

If he could make the water run uphill, his brother might win. Monkey thought for a moment, made a magic sign with his fingers, then again whispered, "Change!"

The moles all jumped into the water and turned into fish.

The fish stuck their snouts in the muddy bottom of the channel and waved their silver tails as if they were swimming downstream. Their motion pushed the water back upstream. The water was flowing uphill. Our Monkey knew that they couldn't keep it up for long. More water would flow from further uphill, and soon the aqueduct would overflow. Fortunately, a few seconds sufficed. The crowd roared again. The sages saw the water running uphill, and their shouts once again filled the dusty air.

"An aqueduct isn't an argument. You ran out of proper proofs and are resorting to cheap magic tricks."

Eliezer pounded his staff three times on the ground. The sound reverberated throughout the study hall and the courtyard. "You are all wrong! Watch. If I am right, the very walls of this study hall will prove it."

Monkey gave himself a shake, and all the fishes jumped out of the water, and turned back into hairs on his body. He sat in the now stationary tree and scratched his head. What kind of sign would they expect now? What could walls do? They could fall down! But if they fell down on these old sages, he would lose merit. Not to mention that Master Xuanzang would be very angry.

"See, you can't even get the walls to do anything! You've run out of stupid signs."

Dear Monkey. He couldn't bear to hear Brother Eliezer insulted like that. He plucked the compliant rod from his ear, shook it, and it again became as wide as a rice bowl. It weighed thirteen thousand five hundred *jin*, and when leaned against the side of the study hall, the walls started leaning in. Soon the assembly of scholars would be crushed.

Master Yehoshua, who was leading the argument with Eliezer, scolded the walls:

"If scholars are contending with each other in matters of The Way, why are you getting involved in the discussion?"

The walls did not fall out of respect to Master Yehoshua, but they did not straighten out of respect to Master Eliezer.

Master Eliezer cried out, "A voice from heaven will prove me right!"

Old Monkey did not know how to help now. "Old Monkey can't talk like these foreign scholars. They'll know right away that I'm a fraud. Maybe Guanyin can help me."

You may recall that on the first Journey, Monkey constantly ran into obstacles he could not deal with, despite his powers. His usual recourse was to get the Bodhisattva Guanyin to help.

He flew back to Xuanzang and the other travelers as a bee, then returned to his usual self, so he could speak to them.

THE SECOND JOURNEY

"Master, I need some assistance with an argument here. I'm going to get some heavenly help. I'll be back soon!"

Without waiting for a response, he mounted his magic cloud, and headed to the gate of heaven.

In less than half an hour, the Potalaka Mountain, home of the Bodhisattva, came into sight. He lowered his cloud halfway up the mountain and walked up to the summit. The Twenty-four devas, the Great Mountain-Guardian, the disciple Mokṣa, Child Sudhana, and the Pearl-Bearing Dragon Girl all came forward to greet him. "Why did the Great Sage come here?" they asked, and Monkey said, "I must see the Bodhisattva."

Guanyin had already known of old Monkey's arrival, and appeared before him. "Your journey has hardly started, but you've already come, Monkey."

"Yes. I am traveling with the Master in the land of the Western Peoples. I found a brother sage there, and I helped him in his battle with the other sages. A battle of words and signs, not a battle of weapons."

"Words are sometimes the right weapons. What help do you need?"

"I need a voice from Heaven to declare that Sage Eliezer is right."

"In the past, you have received help in battling demons, either from myself, or from other celestial beings. But in this case, even the Jade Emperor cannot help you. These lands are too far away from our realm. You must ask for help from the emperor in a different heaven, in the Far Western Heaven."

"Who is he? Where can I find him?" asked Monkey.

"He is Olam-Tzu, World-Master. The westerners call him Ribbono Shel Olam. You'll have to find your own way to his heaven. If your brother sage is one of his favorites, I expect it will not be too difficult for the Great Sage Equal to Heaven to find him."

He kowtowed to Guanyin, left, and stood outside the gate. How was he to find this World-Master? Would he help a Tang Monkey King, Great Sage Equal to Heaven?

He closed his diamond eyes, spun around eight times, and mounted a magic cloud in an unknown direction, trusting to luck and the World-Master to help him find his way.

The wind made a great sound, like a giant wild goose calling. After many thousands of *li*, the wind and sound stopped. Only a still quiet was left. Adventuresome Monkey! He opened his eyes and found himself in the Western Heaven. Though he'd spent plenty of time in the normal Heaven in the East, much of it busy wreaking havoc, he didn't know what to expect in the Western Heaven.

The first thing he saw was four marvelous creatures.

They had the likeness of a man.

Each one had four faces.
Each one had four wings.
They had the hands of a man under their wings on their
four sides
As for their faces, they had
the face of a man
the face of a lion
the face of an ox
and the face of an eagle*

This World-Master kept some strange creatures. He walked on.

There was lightning everywhere.
Singing, but no singers,
No gates,

THE SECOND JOURNEY

No guards,
No palace,
No silks,
No tapestries.

The Western Heaven was a bare place compared to the Eastern celestial realm.

This heaven was quite empty. Besides the odd multi-faced creatures, he didn't see any humans at all. He chose a random direction and walked quickly, treading lightly on the clouds, and looking for a landmark of some sort. One could easily go in circles in this place, and never even know it. He noticed a blue sheen in the distance and headed towards it. As he approached, he found an elderly sage wearing a white robe and a blue hat, sitting upon a glowing sapphire block. Monkey thought to himself: "old Monkey must find this Foreign Jade Emperor, the World-Master Olam-Tzu. I can ask this old sage or try my chances with the four-faced creature. Let's try the old sage."

"Oh, venerable one! I am a traveler, one who has left the family. I am on a quest with my master, the Tang Monk Xuanzang, along with two other disciples. I am looking for..."

"You are Monkey, Sun Wukong, the Great Sage Equal to Heaven, and you are looking for the World-Master, Olam-Tzu," said the sage.

Since the old sage seemed to know everything about him, Monkey thought it best to be silent and wait.

"You want to help your soul brother, Sage Eliezer."

Monkey could only nod his head.

"Come."

He led Monkey to a well. A sign above the well said, 'Sapphire Speaking Well,' in normal characters that our Monkey King could read. His confusion was noted.

"The sign adjusts itself to its audience," the sage explained,

"Look in the well."

———∽∽———

Meanwhile, Xuanzang, Pigsy and Bear were waiting at the edges of the crowd outside the study hall. They heard shouts of excitement. Bear, their Foreign Guide, could explain some of what they heard.

"Something about a tree moving, and water flowing uphill. I can't make out the details."

Pigsy was concerned.

"It's been a long time since Monkey went in there. This is far away from normal civilized lands. Maybe something has happened to him. Should we go look for him? Or better yet, let's just leave and look for some food."

His master, Xuanzang, wasn't happy.

"Pigsy, we are not going to abandon Monkey. Certainly not in favor of finding food. But I am nervous. When he disappears, there is generally a demon around who wants to make a snack out of me, hoping to gain immortality."

Pigsy chuckled.

"Well at least no one is going to make a snack out of me here. These wise foreigners don't eat pork."

Bear settled the issue.

"Let's go closer. I want to see what's happening in there."

Using his elbows and a few guttural words, he cleared a path for them through the crowd. Xuanzang thought they might be honoring him as a venerable foreigner, or perhaps drawing back because of Pigsy's looks, or maybe Bear's imposing size had its desired effect. In any case, they soon reached the center of the crowd, at the edge of the courtyard.

The argumentative sages were still at it.

Master Eliezer repeated, "A voice from heaven will prove me

THE SECOND JOURNEY

right!"

"Fool, you've said that a hundred times this morning! Where's your heavenly voice?"

The crowd snickered. Shouts started.

"Maybe your heavenly voice has gone for a walk?"

"Mr Voice of Heaven is asleep! Bang a drum to wake him!"

Xuanzang turned to Bear, clearly concerned.

"Don't worry. It's just a legalistic argument between sages. They won't get violent. They never come to blows over things like this."

"Never?"

"Well, hardly ever."

Xuanzang always had his goal in mind. He needed to help the people in Kaifeng with their scriptures. He could try to gain the knowledge needed to help them himself, but it would be better to find a local sage or teacher who would come back to the Tang lands with him and become their teacher. At least that is what he thought when he started this Journey; seeing the behavior of these sages was leading him to reconsider that idea.

Maybe he yet would find calmer sages on this Journey. Time would tell.

Meanwhile, in the Far Western Heaven, Monkey looked in the Sapphire Speaking Well. He could see the study hall and the courtyard with his diamond eyes. He could even see the sages out in the courtyard, pointing at the displaced tree and the miracle aqueduct. He saw Xuanzang, Idiot Pigsy and the Foreign Guide Bear as well. They were unharmed, not bound and waiting to be cleaned and steamed, as often would happen in the past when he went off to find help.

The elderly sage motioned to Monkey to step aside, walked up to the well, and whispered a few words. He turned and winked at Monkey.

"That should do it. Let's see them deal with a voice from heaven."

In the Far Western Region on Earth, in the courtyard, a loud whisper from heaven was heard.

"Why are you differing with Master Eliezer? The Way is in accordance with his opinion every time."

The crowd was silent. The sages were silent. Eliezer stood in front of them all, smiling and quietly tapping the ground with his staff.

"What do you say about the oven now?"

Xuanzang turned to Bear.

"Hmm, a very strange discussion. All the sages disagreed with Master Eliezer, so he brought some miracles as proof. The proofs were rejected. Trees and aqueducts are not logical proofs. But then Eliezer got a voice from heaven to support him. The voice said that not only was Eliezer right in this argument, but that he's right in all of them! The Law and the Way are mandated by Heaven, as brought to the people by the ancient Master Moses, thus, if a voice comes out of heaven, the argument is settled. I think everybody will go home now; or go drink some beer and talk about it."

Xuanzang was concerned. "Can't these arguments get out of control?"

"There have been cases where Sages have been temporarily excommunicated." Bear paused, noticing the confusion on Xuanzang's face. "Oh, I should explain. That means that nobody talks to them and they can't participate in some religious rituals."

"Difficult for someone who enjoys these arguments to be isolated that way," Xuanzang noted.

"Very difficult."

"Has anything worse happened?"

Bear paused and scratched his head.

THE SECOND JOURNEY

"I...Well...Let's say it's an uncomfortable topic. It's like... when you have something embarrassing in your family, and so you prefer not to talk about it with strangers."

"I understand, though I am not a stranger."

"You are an honored foreign visitor, but that is not the same as family."

Xuanzang knew not to press further. His porcine disciple had a different angle on the recent events.

"Great!" said Pigsy. "If the show is over, maybe we can finally find some vegetarian food."

Being a scholar himself, Xuanzang knew that defeat was not easily conceded, even when faced with the will of a god.

"Wait, Pigsy. Wait."

The crowd was silent. Many looked at Master Yehoshua, who sat on a stone wall with his head between his knees. Thinking, or perhaps simply beaten. Some of those at the edges of the crowd slipped away to their food stalls. A hungry crowd would be dispersing soon, and the first to man their stalls would sell the most food.

Finally, Yehoshua raised his head, stood on the ground and quietly said, "It is written: it is not in heaven." (*Deuteronomy* 30:12).

Silence. Then a roar from the crowd.

Bear signaled to Xuanzang that he'd explain later, once they'd gotten away from the noise.

———∞———

At the Sapphire Speaking Well, Monkey and the elderly sage saw and heard as well. The sage was unperturbed, until Yehoshua stood and said, "It is not in heaven." Then a slow benevolent smile spread across his face.

"My sons have defeated me. My sons have defeated me."

He turned to our dear Monkey.

"I gave the Law and the Way to my people many generations ago, as written scriptures. When the sages heard the voice from Heaven, they thought the argument was over. But Yehoshua remembered that in the original scriptures, it is written that "the Law is not in Heaven." He has defeated Heaven with Heaven's own word!"

Only now did Monkey understand that this sage was the World-Master, Olam-Tzu himself. Yehoshua was his real brother, for he was in fact the Great Sage Equal to Heaven.

Yet there was something Monkey did not understand.

"Olam Tzu, why are you alone in your heaven? In the heaven of the Tang lands, there are many gods."

Olam Tzu sighed "It's a long story. There are other gods, but not here. I'd rather not talk about it."

Monkey understood the West was a strange place, lacking in harmony even among the gods. To find out what happened to our travelers next, let's read the next chapter.

Angels

Our friends continued on their way. Our dear Monkey led the way, followed by Eight-Rules Pigsy, carrying his nine-toothed rake, and finally the Tang Monk, Xuanzang, now with a cane in hand, walking next to Bear, their Foreign Guide.

The going was slower now that Xuanzang was walking. He missed the horse, but would not complain, as it was his destiny to walk. When they reached a large tree, he requested to stop and rest, even though it was only mid-morning. They sat on some rocks scattered under the tree, ate some dried fruit, and drank from their water bottles.

Bear and the disciples sat wordlessly, but there was a silent conversation going on, grimaces and shrugs, all indicating that having old Xuanzang travel on foot was not a viable arrangement. It seemed that they all agreed that despite his insistence on traveling by foot, something needed to be done.

Yet, what could be done? By late afternoon, Xuanzang was exhausted. He wouldn't say a word, after all, no one knows how to handle suffering better than a Buddhist monk; but Monkey was keeping an eye on his old master.

"Master, let's stop here for the night. This is a good place to camp. We'll get a fresh start in the morning."

"But the sun is still high. We can go a bit further."

"Yes, you and I are both used to long journeys. So is Pigsy. But

Bear, strong as he is, isn't used to this kind of travel."

Monkey looked at Bear, the question lingering in his diamond eyes.

"I am strong, but I admit that my feet are starting to hurt. Thank you, Monkey, I didn't want to say anything, but let's rest here."

Pigsy put down their luggage while Bear built a small fire. After they'd eaten, they spread out their sleeping mats around the coals, and stretched out. The sky slowly darkened, and they looked up at the stars, each thinking of his distant home. The same stars filled the sky in the East and in the West, but the constellations that men made of them were different, as were their dreams.

Our friends woke up the next morning at sunrise. Pigsy and Bear packed up the luggage, while our Monkey climbed a tree to have a look around. Xuanzang was rubbing his feet, getting ready for the day's travel.

Everybody was subdued, lost in thoughts of home. Disciple Monkey was worried, how Xuanzang would continue on the Journey without a horse?

His sharp eyes saw the animal just as Pigsy's nose smelled it. A donkey was approaching them. It came from the same direction they had. Maybe it had been following them.

Pigsy glanced at Monkey and Bear, each offering a short nod in turn. With that, Monkey climbed down the tree, shrugged with his palms up, and pointed at Bear. Bear understood.

"Xuanzang, look who has joined us." Bear said.

"Oh. I see. A donkey. Another disciple?"

"I think not. But maybe a means of transportation..." Bear hinted.

Xuanzang understood, but declined. "The donkey must belong to somebody. I can't ride a stolen or lost beast. I'll continue on foot."

"You're right, Master Xuanzang. A lost beast should be returned to its owner. We should go back to town and try to find the owner. But there's one problem," said Bear.

"What's the problem?"

Bear explained. "We should go back and display this donkey in the marketplace. Then his owner can identify the donkey and take him home. The owner is supposed to describe the donkey, some mark on his head, a ribbon, a saddle...something to show that the animal we have belongs to him. But look at this donkey!"

The donkey had four legs and a tail, and a donkey head, but there were no markings, no saddle, and no saddlebags. Nothing at all. Not even rub-marks from a harness. Just a completely smooth gray donkey. Nobody could claim him.

Xuanzang slowly realized what Bear meant.

"So, I could ride this donkey."

"Yes."

"Wonderful! Maybe Bodhisattva Guanyin sent him here."

"Possibly, though I don't think she normally comes this far west."

They had no saddle, but Bear wove some thin willow branches into a frame, and along with an old blanket, managed to jury-rig one.

Xuanzang mounted the donkey and they continued on their way.

Soon they could see a city in the distance.

"Monkey, what do you make of that city in the distance?"

"It's just a small town, Master, but it has a shimmering aura."

Xuanzang shook with fear, and nearly fell off his donkey. "Demons? Here? Some god's escaped spirit animal? A cave full of fiends?"

"Don't worry! Don't worry! It's a good aura!"

"They have Buddhists there?"

Bear laughed. "No demons here, nor any Buddhists. Just scholars. You are seeing the 'aura' of their arguments."

"Old Monkey sees an aura of wisdom."

Xuanzang thought for a moment.

"Maybe argument and wisdom are the same this far west."

They continued on their way, Xuanzang lost in thought. When they arrived, the Tang Monk turned to the Foreign Guide, "Bear, would it be proper to join their discussions? As an observer, to learn."

"Why not? You've learned their language, at least a bit. How many languages do you understand?"

"I don't exactly know, maybe fifty or so. But many of those languages are similar or are dialects of the same language. Like the languages of India, or the Turkic and Persian languages. So, it's difficult to count them. My concern is that I won't understand the discussion, even if I understand the words."

Bear reassured him. "Don't worry. The study hall is open to all, just sit in the back and listen until you feel comfortable enough to contribute yourself."

"Very good. Monkey, Pigsy, please go find some vegetarian food for us to eat. Keep an eye on one another and stay out of trouble!"

Xuanzang, our wise Buddhist monk, knew how Monkey liked to pull tricks on Pigsy, and how jealous Pigsy was of his other disciple. Their first Journey would have gone much more smoothly were it not for their rivalry.

Bear went off to find them a place to sleep that night, while Xuanzang went into the study hall.

There were hundreds of scholars and students in the hall. The youngest ones sat in the back rows, listening to their elders teach and argue. Xuanzang wanted to join them but felt doubly uncomfortable. He was a foreigner and an outsider in this place, and he was two or three times the age of these young students. Then he noticed an old man sitting at the end of the eighth row, with empty spaces on the bench on either side of him. Most of the scholars were dressed in the local Roman fashion, but he wore a simple robe of rough fabric, and carried a shepherd's staff. His face was framed by his bright white hair and white beard, so much so that he seemed to be glowing. Xuanzang made his way over to him, and in his accented formal Hebrew, asked if he could sit next to him.

"Venerable sage, may I join you on this bench?"

The old man looked up at him wearily and nodded towards the bench.

Xuanzang sat down.

"Master Sage, have you attended these sessions many times?" Xuanzang asked.

"This...this is my first, and likely my only time. And, and though I once thought of myself as a sage, today I find that I am ignorant."

The sage stuttered a little but spoke slowly enough that Xuanzang could understand him. Had Xuanzang been aware of the Hebrew Scriptures, he may have recognized Moses, who was 'slow of speech and heavy of tongue'. But our monk was unaware of that verse, so he continued, politely ignoring the speech problem.

"With age one learns the limits of knowledge," Xuanzang said. "That is a type of wisdom. How many years have you lived?"

"I am now eighty years old. Though in a way, m...more than a thousand years old. And you? You are a foreign guest, and though not a child, you are not as old as I am."

"I come from the East, looking for wisdom. I have lived

foolishly for fifty-five years."

The foreign sage sighed.

"I don't understand anything at all, but I should understand everything."

"You don't know the language well enough?"

"No, it's..." The elderly sage trailed off. He looked around and realized that nobody was paying attention to them. "Where are you from?" he asked finally.

"The Tang Empire, a year's travel east of here. I am a Buddhist monk, a scholar."

"I don't know what a 'Buddhist' is, but I know of...scholars. Do you have scriptures in your land?"

"Yes, of course." Xuanzang said. "I've devoted my life to the study of our ancient scriptures."

"What are the origins of these scriptures?"

"These are the teachings of the Buddha. At first, they were passed down from generation to generation orally; they have since been recorded in writing."

"How long ago did the Budd...Buddha teach?"

"About one thousand years ago." Xuanzang told him.

The old sage sighed. Xuanzang waited.

"Imagine that your Budd...Buddha came to your temple today and found that he didn't understand any of the teachings."

"How could that be? Generations of monks have preserved the scriptures!"

"Yes, that's what he thought too. And yet, when he attended the lessons...he, he didn't understand anything at all. The scholars had preserved his words, but they had also interpreted and reinterpreted them, so much so that the lessons didn't m... make sense to the Buddha himself."

Xuanzang thought for a moment. "It could happen. After all, there are several schools of Buddhist teachings, and they are not identical."

The old sage sighed again. "It did happen."

Xuanzang looked at the old man again. His clothing, the staff, his odd accent.

"Reincarnation?"

"No."

"But you are..."

"Moses, known as M...Master Moses, who brought the Word of the Lord to the people, and who cannot understand what the youngest student here understands with ease. It is hard to believe, I know. I'll explain. I have a special relationship with our G...God. A personal relationship. We speak face to face, like a man speaks to his friend."

"Like my relationship with the Bodhisattva Guanyin," Xuanzang suggested.

"Perhaps. I am not familiar with this person. This morning our G...God invited me to Heaven, as he was preparing his scriptures for his people. I noticed that he was decorating the letters in the scroll. I asked him, 'Why are you putting little crowns on the letters?' He told me that 'after many generations, there will be a man named Akiva, the son of Joseph, who will derive hills upon hills of laws from each thorn of these crowns.' "

The man called Moses paused for a moment.

"'Let me see him,' I implored. God told me to turn around, and so, I, Sage Moses, turned around and found myself in the back of this hall. I sat down, and have been listening to this Akiva's teachings, but I don't understand anything at all."

Xuanzang knew when to speak, and when to be quiet. They sat as the lesson went on.

Finally, one of the students asked Sage Akiva, "Master, from where do we derive this law?"

The answer was quick to come.

"This law was handed down to Sage Moses on Mount Sinai."

Moses sat up straight. "Well, that at least is correct. They haven't forgotten me."

Xuanzang was pleased for his new friend.

"You will return to Heaven now?"

Moses smiled.

"Yes, when I turn around, I will walk right back to where I was. Come with me, fellow student. May I ask your honorable name, scholar from the East?"

"Xuanzang."

Moses didn't even try. "It's d...difficult to pronounce."

"As are your names for me. I was called River Float as a child, since I was sent floating down a river as an infant, and rescued by a monk from the Gold Mountain monastery."

"Oddly enough, I had a similar experience when I was a few months old, in Egypt."

Moses and Xuanzang rose from the bench, turned around, and walked right back into the Western Heaven, where Moses' god, the World-Master, met them. It was curious how similar the two looked, Moses and his god.

The World-Master greeted them.

"So, what did you think of Akiva, the son of Joseph?"

"Impressive. Why didn't you give the scriptures through him, instead of through st...stuttering me?"

Fire flared briefly in his god's eyes, "So I have decided."

"What will be S...Sage Akiva's reward?"

"Watch."

They followed the World-Master to a copper basin supported by many-faced beasts. It was filled with a still pool of water. They peered in and saw Akiva being slowly tortured to death by the western version of Lingchi, the death by a thousand cuts.

Moses could not control himself.

"World-Master!" he exclaimed. "This is the reward for your teachings?"

"So I have decided."

Xuanzang saw that this was a final word, and that there was nothing more to say. They followed the god of Moses as he retreated from the scene unfolding in the basin; as he sat on his sapphire block, he continued adding the little crowns to the letters.

Xuanzang was beginning to wonder how he would get back to Earth and his companions, when a delegation of messenger spirits arrived, the Angels. To Xuanzang they looked more like marsh bandits than divine beings. They were not happy that their god was giving the Scriptures to Moses.

"Master of the Universe, what is this mortal, born of a woman, doing here in Heaven among us?"

"He came to receive the Torah, the Scriptures."

"These Scriptures are a treasure you hid for nine hundred and seventy-four generations before the creation of the world! Now you want to give it to humans made of flesh and blood? It should be given to us, the pure and holy angels!"

"Moses, you answer them."

"B...But they will burn me with their flaming breath!"

"Hold onto my throne, and you will be protected."

Moses put a hand on the sapphire block and turned to Xuanzang.

"Are you good at arguments? I'm a p...poor speaker, and these celestial beings will run circles around me."

"I've been successful in debates, but I know nothing of your teachings. As Sun Tzu said, 'Know yourself, know your enemy, never know defeat.' My ignorance can cost you dearly."

"Nonetheless, please help me."

Xuanzang had no choice but to use his ignorance as a weapon.

"World-Master, this Scripture that you are giving Moses, what is written in it?"

"I am the Lord, your God, Who brought you out of Egypt from the house of bondage."

Xuanzang turned to the angels

"Angels, were you in Egypt? Were you in bondage?"

The angels looked at each other, but had no response.

"World-Master, what else is written in it?"

"You shall have no other gods before Me."

This seemed very strange to Xuanzang. He knew full well there were many gods, and Moses' god must know this as well. He glanced at the World-Master, a question in his eyes. The World-Master gave Xuanzang that cold hard stare that gods produce when they are being obstinate. Our Tang Monk knew better than to pursue the matter further and turned back to the angels.

"Angels, are there temples to many gods in the Western Heaven? You are angels, automatically serving the World-Master. Why do you need that 'No Other Gods Before Me' law?"

Again, the angels had no response.

Xuanzang, being ignorant of these teachings, had to ask the World-Master for help again.

"What else is written in it?"

"Remember the Sabbath rest-day and sanctify it."

"Angels? When do you ever work that you need a rest day?"

The angels at this point looked uncomfortable. A few of the lesser ones had slunk off. The Angel Mob was losing momentum. Moses, in the meantime, had gained confidence, and took over the argument. Following Xuanzang's lead, he first turned to his god.

"What else is written in it?"

"Do not take the name of the Lord, your God, in vain, do not

THE SECOND JOURNEY

swear falsely in court."

Moses turned to the angels. "Do you conduct business with one another that takes you into court, and into making false oaths?"

There was some muttering among the angels, but not one of them had a response.

"World-Master, what else is written in it?"

"Honor your father and your mother."

At this point, Moses just looked at the few angel leaders who still remained. Words were not necessary.

"World-Master, is there more written in it?"

"You shall not murder, you shall not commit adultery, and you shall not steal."

Moses turned triumphantly to the angels, victory in sight.

"Are you angels inclined to do evil? Do you need these laws?"

The remaining angels finally agreed that the right decision had been made, and the Teachings, the Torah scriptures, should be given to the humans, not to the angels.

———∽∽———

In the meantime, Bear had returned to the study hall, but saw no sign of the Tang Monk or his friends. Soon Monkey and Pigsy arrived, having happily managed to fill Pigsy's stomach. Monkey quickly realized that something was wrong.

"Where's Master Xuanzang?" Monkey asked.

Bear didn't have any information. "I don't know. I only arrived here a few minutes ago and have seen no sign of him."

"Old Monkey will get some help," Pigsy said. "Don't worry, nobody wants to steam and eat a Tang Monk around here. We'll find him."

With that, our dear Monkey flipped up to his magic cloud, and flew to the Western Heaven, to ask World-Master to help find Xuanzang.

When he arrived, he immediately kowtowed nine times to the World-Master, who once again appeared amused by this.

"Ah, my simian friend, Great Sage Equal to Heaven!"

"Equal to the Eastern Heaven, not the Western One!"

"I am here for your help. I'm looking for..." Monkey caught sight of his beloved sage, "Master, you're here!"

"As are you. You are acquainted with World-Master?"

"Yes, yes. We have met before. When I helped Sage Eliezer in his argument."

"So, you have friends in high places everywhere."

"Everybody likes Old Monkey. Except for demons, fiends, and occasionally the fat one with the nine-toothed rake," Monkey said.

Xuanzang smiled. "You two are brothers. Sometimes brothers quarrel, but they remain brothers.

"It's time to return to Earth, Master Xuanzang."

So Xuanzang took his leave of the World-Master and joined Monkey on the magic cloud back to their companions.

What else will our heroes discover on their Journey? Let's find out in the next chapter.

Orchard

We had left Xuanzang and Monkey on the magic cloud, traveling back from the Western Heaven to Earth. They landed just outside the study hall, and looked for their friends, Pigsy and Bear, who had stayed on Earth, but before they could find them, two of the older sages exited the study hall. One was Sage Akiva. Xuanzang had seen the second one in the study session, when he was sitting next to Moses, but did not know his name.

"Elisha, let's wait here for Ben Zoma and Ben Azzai to join us," Akiva said. Then we'll meditate together, and the power of the Chariot will take us to the Orchard of mystical knowledge."

Xuanzang heard 'knowledge', but our dear Monkey heard 'Orchard'.

"Master, we should go with them to the Orchard!"

"Monkey, Sage Akiva is taking only a few of his close colleagues with him. How could we go?"

"Don't worry Master, don't worry."

Xuanzang immediately began to worry, as Monkey scampered into the study hall. The study hall was nearly empty. There were only two venerable sages left there. They must be Ben Zoma and the Azzai! Monkey made a magic sign and recited a spell, saying to the sages, "Stay! Stay! Stay!" This was the magic of immobilization, with the effect that the two sages sat wide-eyed and transfixed in the study hall.

Monkey transformed himself into a fly, and landed on Xuanzang's ear.

"Don't worry Master. We will go to this Orchard."

The fly rubbed its wings together, buzzed a magic spell, and Xuanzang took on the form of Ben Zoma, while Monkey was transformed into Ben Azzai.

Sage Akiva noticed them. "Ah, you are here. Let's go."

They followed Akiva and Elisha down the Cardo, the main street of the town, exited the gate, and walked out to an olive grove. Akiva led them to the edge of an old quarry. They sat down on some fallen pillars. Akiva and Elisha started chanting something in their foreign language. Xuanzang and Monkey did not know what they were chanting, so they started quietly reciting sutras. Xuanzang chose the Mahaprajnaparamita Sutra, one that he had brought back from India and translated into Chinese. He recited it in the original. Monkey was not the studious type, so he recited the Heart Sutra.

Xuanzang was used to meditating, and expected to fall into his usual quiet state, but he found himself drifting into a different kind of trance. His eyes were closed, but he saw bright flashes of blue light, rotating wheels, and strange animals. He thought of the Hukou waterfall as a rushing sound filled his ears, then of thunderstorms on the Tian Shan Mountains as a crackling noise joined the rushing. Then he heard a voice. It was Sage Akiva.

"You can open your eyes now."

And behold, there appeared a chariot of fire, and horses of fire*

Akiva stepped into the chariot, oblivious to the fact that it was made of flames. Xuanzang, despite, or perhaps because of his adventures, was reluctant to take such a risk. Monkey reassured him.

"Master, don't worry, don't worry! I know these horses. I was in charge of them, when I had my first job in heaven."

THE SECOND JOURNEY

Xuanzang looked on as Elisha climbed into the chariot. Both he and Akiva looked unharmed, both bearded sages beckoning Xuanzang and Monkey to join them. Xuanzang stroked his chin, and his own beard reminded him the he was now a foreign sage, Ben Zoma, and that he should behave as Ben Zoma, and not as the Buddhist Monk that he remained inside.

He climbed into the chariot, followed by Monkey, who made a show of being the elderly Ben Azzai, and climbed slowly into the chariot. The chariot was a war chariot without no seats, so they held onto the frame of the fiery vehicle, and waited for it to move. They were surrounded by flames, so they could not see where they were being taken. There was no sensation of motion, so Xuanzang was not even sure that they moved at all.

Finally, the flames died down. They had stopped in front of a golden gate, guarded by divine creatures armed with spears and swords. Xuanzang shuddered, but Monkey reassured him. "It's just the divine heroes: Pang, Liu, Kou, Bi, Deng, Xin, Zhang, and Tao. I've met them before. They'll let us in."

Akiva led them off the chariot, and onto the path through the gate. The divine heroes paid no attention to them, though one did bare his fangs at Ben Azzai, perhaps smelling the simian behind the human. After going through the gate, Akiva signaled them to wait a moment, he had something to say to them.

"When you come to the place of pure marble stones, do not say, 'Water! Water'!"

Monkey and Xuanzang nodded their agreement, as did Elisha. Unlike Elisha, they had no idea what it meant.

Monkey whispered into Xuanzang's ear. "Master, did you understand that?"

"Monkey-Ben Azzai, Akiva made a very deep mystical-philosophical statement there. One we should take to heart. But no, I have no idea what he's referring to."

After this exchange, Monkey was unusually quiet.

They passed the place of pure marble stones. It was a large plaza, paved in white marble with dark green veins. He didn't see any water, or any reason to say, 'Water, water', but he did notice the thirty-three palaces that surrounded the plaza. Wasn't that the Scattered Cloud? And next to it, the tall one looked remarkably like the Vaiśrvaṇa, Monkey stroked his beard, or rather the beard of Ben Azzai, and wondered.

Akiva led them through the plaza onto a wide street lined with fine buildings. Monkey first recognized the Morning Assembly, then the Transcendent Void. These were the heavenly treasure halls, it was hard to be mistaken. Sure enough, they passed the Precious Light, the Heavenly King, the Divine Minister and many others on the street.

They continued on their way, passing the Tower of Homage to the Sage, an oven for refining herbs...

"Master, don't you see?"

"See what, Disciple Monkey?"

"The palaces, the treasure halls."

"I only see a few stone buildings."

"Master, someone has cast a spell on your eyes. We are in the Tang heaven. Soon we will see the Treasure Hall of Divine Mists."

Xuanzang looked off in the distance. "I only see a farmer's thatched hut."

Monkey scratched his head, stroked his foreign beard, and realized what the secret was.

"Master, they cast a spell on your eyes. It didn't affect me, because of my diamond eyes."

Xuanzang was doubtful. "If so, how do I break the spell?"

"Master, say, 'Water, water'."

"We were told not to."

"That's why! That's why! It will break the spell."

THE SECOND JOURNEY

Xuanzang shrugged, and mumbled, "Water, water."

"Oh. The Treasure Hall of Divine Mists. Not a farmer's hut."

They followed Akiva and Elisha into the hall, and into the Imperial Presence. Xuanzang was going to kowtow, but Monkey signed him not to. It was safer to pretend the spell was still working.

Akiva and Elisha had a long discussion with the Jade Emperor/Farmer. Xuanzang could see that Sage Akiva had a lot of respect for a simple farmer, as he thought the Jade Emperor to be. This did not surprise Xuanzang, as some of the most powerful Daoist Immortals lived simple lives, as did famous poets and Buddhist monks. He himself had been raised by a monk in a Buddhist temple, and wondered whether Sage Akiva had started life as a simple farmer.

Xuanzang was thoughtful as they left the Treasure Hall of Divine Mists. Where were the promised mysteries of the Orchard that Sage Akiva had invited them to? How could Akiva and Elisha remain oblivious to what they were really seeing? He caught himself—this was a stupid thing to think, considering that Xuanzang himself had been in the same situation a few minutes earlier.

Monkey didn't like the situation either. He prided himself on his sharp vision, and seeing the others effectively blind rubbed him the wrong way. He thought of a plan to cure the foreign sages of their curse. He could see that they were headed towards Lao Tzu's palace. He knew the way well, having spent some time in the master's alchemical furnace. In fact, they'd be passing the furnace area soon.

Monkey pulled out a hair, made a magic sign, and it turned into a gourd. He filled it with water from a fountain along the avenue, and waited until they were near the furnaces. As he expected, Lao Tzu came out to greet them. "Welcome, welcome."

Soon Akiva and Lao Tzu were deep in a mystical conversation. Sage Akiva probably thought he was speaking with farmer or a shepherd. Elisha was listening intently. Monkey was hiding behind Xuanzang. Five hundred years earlier, Monkey had stolen Lao Tzu's magic elixir. Lao Tzu tried to destroy Monkey by locking him in his alchemical furnace, but failed. There was bad blood between them, and it was best not to stir up old troubles.

The conversation went on.

Lao Tzu pointed out, "The name that can be named is not the enduring and unchanging name."

Akiva nodded his approval, and added, "Silence is a fence to wisdom."

Lao Tzu gave his own version of the same thought. "Therefore, the sage manages affairs without doing anything, and conveys his instructions without the use of speech."

Monkey tried to get Elisha's attention, without being noticed by Lao Tzu. They'd been standing by the hot furnace for some time, and Elisha was bound to get thirsty.

"Master Xuanzang, please move closer to Elisha."

Xuanzang didn't understand what Monkey was after, but it was a simple request, so he moved closer.

Monkey slipped out from behind Xuanzang, and offered the gourd to Elisha. Elisha reached for it, Monkey pulled back behind Xuanzang, but not fast enough. Lao Tzu glared at him, but chose not to interrupt the 'I am just a simple shepherd' game, and pretended not to notice who Ben Azzai really was. Sage Elisha was thirsty. He hadn't thought about it before, being too engrossed in the conversation, but the offer of the gourd made him thirsty.

"Ben Azzai, why are you hiding that gourd?"

"Elisha, son of Avuya, what do you want?"

"Water, water — I'm thirsty. This..."

Elisha's eyebrows went up.

"This baking oven, which is not for baking bread, has made me thirsty."

Sage Elisha looked around. He was surrounded by divine palaces. Celestial beings wandered around. Nothing was what it had seemed to him a moment ago. Ben Azzai had tricked him into saying, 'Water, water', and only now could he see reality. Akiva was in a different reality, thinking he was gaining mystical insights from simple folk in the Orchard. As it is written, 'they have eyes, but do not see.' Elisha needed to rethink everything, starting with Ben Azzai.

"Ben Azzai, you had me say those words. Why?"

"So you could see, so you could learn." Monkey answered.

"Is this the Ben Azzai I have known for twenty years?"

Xuanzang, now Ben Zoma, interrupted. "Does it make a difference? Who is wise? He who learns from every man."

Monkey Ben Azzai added, "Do not despise any man, and do not discriminate against anything, for there is no man that has not his hour, and there is no thing that has not its place."

Elisha was further confused. "You look like Ben Zoma and Ben Azzai. You two speak with their voices, but you are not the people I know. And this is not the Orchard of mystical knowledge that Akiva took us to."

Elisha stroked his beard, and added, "Silence is proper for the wise."

The visit continued, with Lao Tzu glaring at the ersatz Ben Azzai, Xuanzang and Monkey trying to hide their identities as best they could. Elisha was confused, and only Akiva calmly continued in his esoteric discussions. He listened intently as Lao Tzu suggested, "May not the space between heaven and earth be compared to a bellows?

'Tis emptied, yet it loses not its power;
'Tis moved again, and sends forth air the more.
Much speech to swift exhaustion leads, we see;
Your inner being guard, and keep it free."*

Soon the fiery chariot appeared, and though Sage Akiva would have liked to stay longer, they had no choice but to find their places on the chariot, and return to their own time and space. Lao Tzu aimed a parting fireball at our Monkey, but the chariot pulled away, and it flew harmlessly into the distance.

When they arrived at the study hall, Monkey and Xuanzang stepped into an alley. Monkey made a sign, and they returned to their original forms. He made another sign, and the real Ben Zoma and Ben Azzai were freed from the immobilization spell.

What further adventures will our friends have in these far Western Lands? Let's find out in the next chapter.

Leviathan

Our four friends continued on their journey. Pigsy led the way, carrying his nine-toothed rake, followed by our Monkey, with his Compliant Rod shrunk to the size of a needle and tucked in his ear. Their master, the Tang Monk Xuanzang followed on his donkey, while the Foreign Guide Bear walked next to him.

As they walked, they noticed a town on the side of a hill. Bear explained where they were.

"This is the 'House of Gates'. There are some famous sages in this town, both dead and alive," Bear said.

Xuanzang was surprised at this.

"What do you mean?"

"Sages have lived here for generations, so the burial caves are famous for their occupants. And Sages still live here, so it is famous for their teachings as well," Bear said.

Xuanzang was pleased. "We're here to search for wisdom, let us visit this place. Perhaps we'll find a teacher as well."

Pigsy had a request. "Master, though I am an idiot, I'd like to sit in the foreign study hall. Maybe some of this foreign wisdom will seep into my thick skull."

Monkey couldn't resist. "Idiot you are, and Idiot you'll remain. You won't be able to sit for ten minutes without getting hungry."

Xuanzang wasn't pleased. "Monkey, there is no need for

that. If Pigsy wants to try and gain some wisdom, we should encourage him, not insult him."

"Thank you, Master. I will eat a big meal before I join the sages, so I won't be hungry for a while. But I am worried...You see..."

Our Tang Monk knew what the problem was.

"Bear, we need your guidance here. Since Pigsy..."

Bear understood.

"...looks like a pig...It'll be okay. He'll get some looks at first, but no one will say anything. It's very bad to insult somebody. And pigs who walk on two feet aren't proper pigs. But we'd better feed him before he tries this."

They walked through the open-air market just outside the town. Xuanzang took some of the silver he'd been given for the trip and bought bushels of bread and melons for Pigsy. Dear Pigsy. He devoured it all and followed his meal with a couple bunches of fresh garlic as seasoning. His friends brought him to the entrance of the study hall. Bear had a few words with a student who stood at the entrance, and our Pigsy was in among the sages.

Pigsy knew he looked different, and so he was shy. He found a seat in the back of the hall, and tried to look inconspicuous, which, as is often the case, made him look even more conspicuous. As Bear had predicted, he got a few looks at first, but they stopped after a few minutes. Following the discussion, our Pigsy was feeling more and more deserving of his nickname, Idiot. After the other students' initial shock at his presence, he was ignored for a while. As the lesson proceeded, however, more and more of the students and sages glanced back at him. He did not understand why, until the Master Sage stopped the lesson.

"Who's been eating garlic here? You know I can't stand the smell!"

THE SECOND JOURNEY

Pigsy hid his snout inside his robe, and hoped nobody would notice him, but then he heard the sound of someone walking out of the study hall. Then another and another until an eerie silence filed the room. He risked a look; the study hall was empty. Only the Master stood in the front, teaching no one.

Pigsy hurriedly got to his feet and went outside. The students very carefully avoided looking at Pigsy, but he overheard them talking about the garlic incident. When one of the sages had heard the Master's angry comment about the garlic-eater, he immediately rose and left the hall, so the guilty party wouldn't be embarrassed. The other students understood what he had done, as he was known to not eat garlic, so they all got up and left too, so that no one would be embarrassed.

In the end, the only 'student' left in the hall was the guilty party, Pigsy. He didn't see any of his friends outside the study hall, so he sat quietly and listened to the conversations around him. After a while, the topic of garlic and embarrassment had run its course, and the conversation wandered off into other topics.

He overheard Sage Yonatan talking about a monster fish.

"In the future, the Celestial Being Gabriel will hunt Leviathan. Is it not written, 'Can you draw out Leviathan with a fishhook?' Gabriel will only be able to do this with the help of the Holy One, World-Master."

Pigsy had met many monsters in his time, but never this giant fish.

Yonatan continued, "I've heard that when Leviathan is hungry, his breath boils all the waters of the sea."

Just then, Monkey arrived, followed shortly thereafter by Xuanzang and Bear. They had tied the donkey by the entrance to the courtyard; considering it unlikely that any sage would steal it. Pigsy beckoned Monkey to be quiet and join him. Monkey was annoyed but did as he had been asked. Then he heard the sage's discussion.

"It's good that his head rests in the Garden of Eden, otherwise, no one would be able to stand his stench!"

"When he drinks, it takes seventy years for the sea to rise back to its normal level!"

"What is it?" Monkey asked Pigsy.

"It's a monster fish called Leviathan! A Celestial Being named Gabriel will hunt him one day."

Our Monkey could hardly contain himself.

"A monster! A monster! It isn't so boring out here after all! Let's listen carefully. Maybe we can go monster-hunting."

"On that day, the World-Master will make a feast for the sages from the Leviathan's flesh."

"Fish meat patties! Old Monkey knows how to prepare them!"

The students wandered back into the study hall. Pigsy had had enough of his search for wisdom and didn't join them. Besides which, he still looked like a hog and smelled of garlic.

Our Monkey wasn't able to control himself.

"Master, Master! Let us go subdue this monster!"

Xuanzang thought for a moment.

"If it's a demon or a fiend, it's okay to destroy it. And you do need the challenge. The two of you should do this together. No arguing or tricks! But how are you going to find this fish?"

Monkey scratched his furry head. "They said his head was in the Garden of Eden. But I don't know where that is. Maybe we can get some Heavenly help."

"No need. You forgot something, the stench of his breath. An old pig can smell that stench from ten thousand li away!"

The two of them mounted Monkey's magic cloud and sped off, spiraling their way into the sky.

Bear piped up, "Master Monk, how long will this take them?"

"It's difficult to know, Guide Bear. A journey is easy to start

THE SECOND JOURNEY

and difficult to finish. But Monkey's cloud moves fast. His cloud can go 108,000 *li* in one jump!"

Meanwhile, Monkey and Pigsy were having a difficult time finding this Garden of Eden. At first, they flitted back and forth, thinking Pigsy would pick up the scent, but he didn't catch half a whiff of a giant stinky fish. Finally, Monkey realized that they should be more systematic, so they rode the cloud in a spiral pattern, gradually covering more and more territory. But still, nothing.

"Pigsy, is your snout working?"

"It works. You see that marketplace, fifty thousand *li* away? One of the stalls is selling guava fruit. I sense it from here. I can smell everything except that giant, rotten fish."

"Let's think. Pigsy, where would one typically find a garden?"

"Near a palace or a temple?"

"Yes, but this garden has a smelly giant fish in it. Or at least his head lies there. It doesn't sound like a palace or temple site."

Pigsy thought for a moment. "We've been looking on Earth. Maybe it's in Heaven."

"Which Heaven? And what god would tolerate such a fish? What would be a good place for a garden? What do gardens need?"

Pigsy knew about gardening. He waved his rake as he spoke. "Water. They need water."

"So, let's find water!"

Monkey took the magic cloud higher and higher, until the world was spread out like a carpet below them.

"Monkey, there are rivers and lakes everywhere!"

"Yes, but this garden must be special."

Our Monkey searched with his diamond eyes. There were

many seas, but they were all salty and not suitable for gardens. There were rivers everywhere, but no sign of a special place. Then he saw it. A dark green area with four rivers flowing out of it! In a few moments the magic cloud brought them closer.

Monkey peered through the clouds. No sign of a fish. He looked up at Eight-Rules. Pigsy had hidden his snout in his robe.

"Horrible! Horrible smell!"

Our Monkey smiled, baring his fangs, and in no more than a moment, they had landed in the Garden.

The Garden was huge. Green grass covered the ground, and trees of every kind were scattered about, all dripping with heavy, ripened fruit.

Monkey was delighted.

"It's like the Immortal Peach Garden! But with all kinds of fruit. It's the Flower Fruit Mountain and the Immortal Peach Garden together! A happy union!"

The brothers walked through the Garden together. Pigsy held a hand over his snout, grumbling and snorting as they walked along.

"Pigsy, which direction?"

"I don't know! The stench is so powerful I can't tell."

Pairs of animals wandered past them. Antelopes, deer, tigers, pheasants. They showed no signs of fear. Pigsy was surprised.

"Elder Brother, they must realize that we're vegetarian Buddhists!"

"Maybe, Pigsy. What's that tree?"

"It's a fig tree. A giant ancient fig tree. But there's something on it—a vine of some sort."

"That's no vine, Idiot Pig, it's a snake! I bet this snake is a demon. They mostly are."

"This snake is huge, so he's old. Ancient. He's probably been here for thousands of years! Monkey, if we can make him talk, he'll tell us where that fish is!"

Pigsy wanted to finish this fish hunt as fast as possible. He grabbed his nine-toothed rake in the middle of the handle with both hands, smacked the snake's head with the handle, and swung the rake around to give him a taste of the nine prongs.

The snake reared up. Its head swelled, two horns sprung from its head, and it roared like a demon, fire spewing from its mouth.

His eyes flashed forth the stars of dawn; His nose belched out the morning fog. His teeth, like dense rows of steel swords; His claws curved like golden hooks.*

Too late, Pigsy realized that this snake had arms, and was lunging at him with a three-pronged pitchfork. He parried with his rake, but the pitchfork scratched his head, and blood flowed over his face.

Old Monkey grabbed the snake's tail and pulled, while Pigsy attacked with his rake. The fiendish snake roared and twisted, but Monkey slowly pulled him off the tree. Pigsy ran around the tree as the snake was unwound, smacking its head as he went.

Stretched out along the ground, the snake was a full *li*, five hundred meters in length. Monkey held its tail, and Pigsy had its horns locked in the teeth of his rake. The snake spoke:

"Mr Pig, would you like to eat a special fruit? The fruit of knowledge!"

Now, Pigsy and Monkey, having come from the Tang Kingdom, didn't know who this snake was. He was the ancient snake of temptation from the beginning of time. When Man and Woman were first created, they lived in this Garden, and the World-Master told them that they could eat fruit from all the trees, except for one tree, the Tree of Knowledge.

This first Man and Woman were like small children, or like the apes in the Flower Fruit Mountain, so of course they were tempted by that one forbidden tree. Still, they managed to resist the temptation until this serpent convinced them 'just to taste' the fruit, with dire consequences: the World-Master threw them out of the Garden, and they had to work for a living, rather than just eat fruit off of the trees.

Despite his insatiable hunger, our dear Pigsy was not tempted by the serpent's sales pitch.

"I'd love to eat that fruit! But first I want to skin you, stuff your skin with that fruit and broil the whole thing. Then I'll suck up the entire *li*-long snake sausage. It will be a small snack for me!"

"I'm ancient. I have powers!" hissed the snake.

"None that will help you now. You've run into the two warriors of the East, and you're done for! There's only one power than can save you."

"Which power might that be?"

"Your tongue, not the forked-tongue lies you sell. But a fact. Tell us!" Pigsy said.

"Tell you what?" The snake licked its face with its forked tongue.

"The fish! Where's the fish?" demanded Pigsy.

"Fish?"

"Leviathan! I can smell it!"

The snake hissed.

"Oh. He's here, but you can't disturb him!"

"Why not?"

"If you disturb him, the entire earth will shake. And he will destroy you."

Monkey laughed.

"Destroy? Don't you know that Old Monkey was born with a head of bronze and a crown of steel   Unbreakable by the mallet or the ax"*

THE SECOND JOURNEY

Monkey took his compliant rod from his ear and leaped forward to the snake's head.

"Here, see if you can swallow this little stick!"

The snake fiend couldn't resist a challenge, especially such a simple one. His tongue flipped out, and our Old Monkey's rod was gone!

Dear Monkey! He giggled and whispered a few words.

The snake's eyes bulged out, "what was that?"

"Just a small rod, Mr Snake."

A few more whispered words, and the snake was visibly inflated, and incapable of speaking.

"I'll shrink it again, and you'll tell us where the fish is hidden."

The snake could only roll its eyes in response.

Monkey shrank the rod and waited. The snake had no choice but to answer.

"The fish is here, right under the tree. Over the ages, dust has built up on him, so it looks like a hill. But he's here, asleep. That's why it smells so bad here."

Monkey was pleased. "Asleep? We'll wake him up. We're in the monster-exterminating business."

"Don't wake him!" the snake pleaded. "There will be trouble. Only Gabriel can handle him, and nobody's seen him for eons."

Pigsy took a good look at their captive. "You look like a monster yourself. Have you been making trouble here in the Garden?"

"Who, me?" the snake hissed, doing his best to sound innocent, and failing miserably.

"I don't sense any other candidates here. Except that buried fish."

"I don't make trouble, I only make...friendly suggestions. Besides which, you look like a monster yourself. Half man, half pig."

Pigsy was losing patience. "I'm one who follows the eight rules, a monk who has left the family. You will regret calling me a monster."

"Your rake doesn't frighten me."

Monkey broke into the conversation, "You've already forgotten your pain of a few minutes ago. I can see you're a demon, and we only needed you for one thing. That fish. You shouldn't insult my brother, that's something only I'm allowed do. Right, Idiot?"

"Exactly, Elder Brother, Great Sage Equal to Heaven!"

The snake laughed, then suddenly grew quiet. He made a small squeak, and his eyes started bulging out again.

Our Old Monkey didn't have time for games. "I'd like my rod back now. I could shrink it and you could spit it out, or I could grow it, and explode it out. I wonder what kind of trouble you've caused…One less demon will do the world some good."

A few whispered words, a small explosion, and the full-sized rod lay on the ground. Pigsy and Monkey were covered with snake meat. They ran downhill to a nearby stream and rinsed off the blood and flesh. Monkey shrank the rod and cleaned it well. When they emerged from the water, they saw vultures circling above.

Monkey waxed philosophical. "Such is the cycle of nature."

Pigsy and Monkey looked up at the hill. The tree was on the top of the hill and was now covered with snakeskin and flesh. Vultures were already pecking at the flesh. If the fish was sleeping below them, how could they wake it?

They went partway up the hill. Monkey shook a few drops of water off the rod, said 'grow', and it was back to full size, standing upright in his hands. He lifted it, and let it drop.

The earth shook from the weight of the rod. But no reaction from the fish underneath.

THE SECOND JOURNEY

"Maybe that snake demon lied to us."

"We'll find out soon, Monkey."

Monkey plucked hairs from his body, chewed them into little pieces, spat them out and cried "change"! Now there were a thousand monkeys. He shook his rod, and now there were a thousand rods as well.

"Pigsy! Lead the orchestra!"

Pigsy held his rake in both hands, lifted it, and stamped it into the ground. He lifted it again, shouted "Now"! And all the monkeys drove their rods into the ground. Each rod weighed 54,000 *jin*, 27,000 kilograms so the entire hill shook; figs and bits of dead serpent fell off the tree, and a cloud of vultures swooped up into the air.

They beat the ground thirty-six times, but the fish did not awaken. They beat the ground another seventy-two times, and again, the fish did not stir. They had beaten the ground a total of one hundred and eight times. Nothing.

Monkey was concerned.

"The one hundred and eight blows match the one hundred and eight stars of destiny. They should have done the trick. Maybe I destroyed that snake demon too quickly. He lied to us. We'll have to find another informer."

Just then the hill exploded. Rocks, trees, dust, water, Pigsy and Monkey were all thrown into the air. Monkey quickly mounted his magic cloud, chittering and laughing. He grabbed Pigsy out of the storm, and the two floated above the eruption, waiting for it to settle.

"So that snake was honest after all. Nothing lost by his death."

When the dust finally cleared enough to allow them to see the fish, they could only make out its head; the body and tail were lost beyond the horizon.

"Monkey, maybe it wasn't such a smart idea to wake this

demon."

"Let's give him a taste of my rod, and we shall see!"

Monkey gave the fish a few smacks on its snout, but the fish hardly noticed.

Monkey was surprised. "Hmm. I thought that would turn him into a fish patty. He's much bigger than I thought."

Just then, he remembered that there were another thousand monkeys somewhere; they had scattered when the hill exploded. Monkey whistled and they all came flying towards him, tumbling onto his magic cloud.

"We can't do anything from this cloud. The footing isn't good. Let's go!"

A thousand monkeys and one pig jumped onto the fish's slippery snout. Monkey led them in the attack.

"One, two, three!"

A thousand and one giant rods and one nine-toothed rake smashed into the beast's head at once. The beast shuddered and roared, and a thousand and one monkeys flew off into space, followed by one pig desperately holding onto his rake.

They landed by the gates of the Western Heaven. Monkey whistled, and the thousand monkeys turned back into hairs on his body.

"Come, Pigsy. The Western Jade Emperor can help us. He calls himself World-Master, Olam-Tzu. If he really is the Master, he'll help us defeat that fish."

They entered the Western Heaven, ignored the four-faced beasts, and went directly to Olam-Tzu.

The World-Master was sitting on his sapphire block and rose to greet them.

"Ah, my simian friend! And his porcine companion! How are you?"

"Fine, fine! We're just having a small problem with a Western monster. One of yours."

"I'm not usually in the monster destruction business. Which monster is this?"

"A giant stinking fish, hiding under a hill in a special garden." Monkey explained.

"Ah, Leviathan. I could help you with this, but I'd rather not. You see, I made him. As a plaything."

"You made a monster fish as a toy?"

"More as a pet. I knew the day would come when he'd have to be destroyed, but I can't bear to do the job myself." He turned towards Pigsy, "Mr Pig, may I ask your name?"

Pigsy was still dazed from the explosion, but quickly gained his composure and introduced himself, "I am Eight-Rules Pig, also known as Pigsy, and sometimes as Idiot."

He kowtowed nine times, to Olam-Tzu's amusement.

"Only eight rules?" asked Olam Tzu. "You are a lucky pig. It is a great honor to meet one who can call himself Idiot. It is a sign of great wisdom. Mr Pigsy, would you be so kind as to strike the gong? I should like to call my assistant. He can help you."

"I would be glad to! But where is it?"

Olam-Tzu reached into the folds of his robe, and brought out a tiny bronze gong, one that could easily fit into a bowl of tea. He then pulled out the matching mallet, no larger than a chopstick.

Pigsy gently raised the gong, holding it by its frame, and tapped it with the tiny mallet.

All of heaven shook with the reverberations. Pigsy and Monkey fell to the ground, covering their ears. Below them thunderbolts struck the earth.

When the vibrations finally ceased, Pigsy and Monkey pulled themselves gingerly off the ground.

"Yes, I know. Sorry about that. I'm also always surprised at the racket it makes. It's just that my assistant, Gabriel, isn't so young, and his hearing isn't what it was a few millennia ago. Please don't mention that to him, pretend you don't notice, and speak loudly."

Soon Gabriel slowly floated down.

"He's not hard of hearing," Monkey thought to himself, "His ears are simply too high!"

Gabriel was huge. His feet touched the same clouds that they were treading on, yet when they looked up, all they could see were his ankles, far above them. He was a giant, though a roughly made one. He looked like a child had clumsily formed him out of mud, without much attention to detail.

Pigsy snuffled. "He smells of earth."

The World-Master agreed.

"Yes, that's what he's made of. One of my first. Rather clumsy, but effective. Eons later, when I fashioned Men from clay, I did a much better job. I'll explain the task to him. Things have to be spelled out slowly and clearly for Gabriel."

The World-Master called out, "Gabriel! The Fish! It's time!"

Slowly the words came out.

"Leviathan."

"Yes. We knew the day would come. Now is the time."

"Yes."

"These two foreign sages will help you."

"Yes."

"Go, then," Olam Tsu commanded.

Gabriel slowly bent his clay knees, and with a surprisingly swift leap, flew into the air. Monkey and Pigsy followed as best as they could. They drifted down towards the Garden, and Leviathan flew up to meet them. Monkey and Pigsy charged right towards the monster, and landed on his head. Monkey again jabbed the beast in the eye with his rod and Pigsy attacked his gills. The monster, enraged, shook itself violently, throwing them off. Gabriel seized his tail, and swung him round and round, finally flinging him far away over the horizon.

"Finally, I can breathe without that horrible stink attacking my snout."

Monkey wasn't convinced.

"Monsters don't give up so easily. Wait."

A few moments later, the fish came flying back at them, clouds fleeing as he streamed past them. His gray skin sparkled and beams of angry blue light projected from his eyes. Monkey changed into the largest form he could but he knew it still would not be enough.

Gabriel was weaponless and single-minded. His philosophy was simple: "what doesn't work with force, will work with more force." He grabbed Leviathan by the tail and started whipping him around again.

Pigsy was disturbed, asking, "Monkey, why does he think it will work this time?"

"Pigsy, I'm not sure thinking has much to do with it. The World-Master was sure this would work. Speaking from experience, monsters are not easy to destroy, even monsters that attack Heaven itself," said Monkey.

"Yes, Monkey, I know you attacked Heaven, but in the end even you were subdued." Pigsy reminded him.

"It took considerable effort," Monkey retorted.

While they were talking, Gabriel kept spinning around faster and faster, until both he and Leviathan were just a spinning blur.

"When he lets go, the monster will fly far away, but sooner or later he'll come back."

But Gabriel didn't let go. He just kept spinning around.

"Monkey! Watch out!"

Pigsy and Monkey crouched down as two clear balls, each the size of a large palace, flew overhead, glowing blue as they disappeared in the distance.

"What was that?"

Monkey scratched his head. "Eyes. Gabriel is spinning so fast the beast's eyes have flown out."

Gabriel gradually slowed down. When he finally stopped, he was holding the tail of a very large and very dead fish. Pigsy was impressed but saw a problem. "What will he do with it now? If he lets it drop back to the Garden, the entire planet will shake."

"He could fling it off, like he did before. It won't come back. But it might hit some other world or heaven out there." Monkey paused a moment, "I have an idea. Do you have a sword or a knife?"

"Just the rake."

"Maybe old Gabriel here has one."

"Gabriel! Do you have a sword?"

Gabriel's head was so far away that he didn't even notice that Monkey was speaking to him. Monkey shook himself and turned into a vulture.

> Wide wings.
> Sharp beak.
> Nature's blessed cleaner.

He spread his wings and drifted on the updraft to Gabriel's roughly shaped head.

"Gabriel! Do you have a sword?"

Gabriel answered with a slow massive nod, and slowly reached to his left thigh. There was no sword there, but as his hand approached his thigh, the image of a long-handled broadsword appeared, and gradually became a clay three-dimensional sword. Gabriel plucked it off his leg, leaving a sword-shaped depression that slowly healed. He handed the sword to Monkey, who grasped it with his talons, and flew down to the cloud where Pigsy was waiting.

THE SECOND JOURNEY

Pigsy was confused. "A clay sword? What good will that do?"

Vulture put the sword down, shook himself, and turned back into his Monkey form. He picked up the sword and considered this.

"You're right, Pigsy. Even an Idiot is right sometimes. A clay sword is useless. A little Daoist alchemy will take care of this."

Monkey grew himself as large as he could, tilted his head straight up, and slid the sword down his throat. Pigsy watched as Monkey got warm, then hot, till he was finally glowing a dark red color. Pigsy knew better than to disturb him. Monkey slowly cooled down and pulled the sword from his mouth.

The clay sword was no more, and Monkey brandished a shiny steel sword, the handle encrusted with rubies. Monkey gave the sword a few trial swings.

"If the Dragon King of the East Sea had such a weapon, I would never have taken the rod! It's a shame to use it for such a task, but it needs to be done, and my rod won't do it."

The two travelers carefully skinned the monster and laid the skin out in the sun to dry. Then they chopped up the fish into small vulture-sized pieces. They saved a few lumps of fish flesh, for they planned a feast for the foreign Sages back at the House of Gates. By the time they had finished, they were both covered head to toe and tail with fish gore and guts. Vultures and seagulls were already circling overhead.

"Down to the river, Pigsy!"

They both flew down to the garden and cleaned themselves in one of the four rivers in the garden. Monkey took extra care in cleaning the blade. They flew back up to Heaven. Monkey returned the sword to Gabriel, who stuck the steel blade through his clay belt, and let it hang there. Then they went see The World-Master, who was sitting on his sapphire block, weeping. "It is done?" he asked.

"Yes."

"I knew this would be necessary someday. He was a mistake in the first place. Gods have regrets, too, you know."

Monkey and Pigsy waited quietly. One does not interrupt a deity's mourning.

Olam Tsu sighed. "Well, it was not the first mistake I made. At least this time I didn't have to deal with it myself. You wanted to ask me about the skin. Take it. It's yours."

The two travelers bowed and left.

Monkey grew his compliant rod to an enormous size. With himself at one end, and Pigsy at the other, they rolled the monster skin onto the rod. Monkey whispered a few words, and the rod, skin and all, then shrank to the size of a spindle. Pigsy carried the fish steaks, Monkey the rod and skin, and the magic cloud took them back down to the House of Gates.

Xuanzang and Bear awaited them. Bear was curious. "Were you successful?"

Pigsy waved the sack of fish meat in front of Bear in response. "We prepared a Leviathan steak dinner for the sages. Though Monkey and I can't join, we only eat vegetables."

Xuanzang had a different question. "Did you seek help from Guanyin again?"

"No, no! She doesn't intervene much here. The World-Master sent us someone to help. Gabriel."

Bear was impressed. "Gabriel the angel?"

"I'm not sure what an 'angel' is, but there was a giant terracotta soldier, like an Emperor might bury in his tomb, but alive..." Pigsy trailed off, his mind quickly switching to more pressing matters. "Where should we set up the feast?"

"Best outside," said Bear. "I doubt the sages will want it in their study hall. I'll take care of roasting the fish. You vegetarians would probably prefer to stay away from that."

THE SECOND JOURNEY

Monkey disagreed. "After having butchered the monster, I don't think roasting him would bother us much. But go ahead. Pigsy and I will set up the monster-skin tent."

Bear wasn't convinced. "After all that talk about watching out for the ant and the moth, and 'let's see you make an ant,' you've gone and killed a wonder of nature. Killed it and cut it up into steaks. You may as well roast it and eat it too."

"Not a 'wonder of nature'! Not a wonder at all. A monster! Monsters exist for destroying! They are the enemies of all that is harmonious in nature. Creatures who've outgrown their proper place in the world, and threaten the rest. A snake should be a snake, a fish should remain a fish. Neither should become a monster or demon. They are also Old Monkey's entertainment!"

Bear was skeptical. "I'm not one of you Buddhists. I'll sweep up the ant, step on the spider, and let the moth burn himself in the lamp. I'll never be a vegetarian, but I won't eat that giant dead fish! I'll settle for rice and lentils today."

An hour later, the foreign sages were feasting, and many thanks and compliments were given to our travelers. Monkey, Pigsy and Bear sat at a table on the side, and ate fruit and nuts. Xuanzang sat with them, but did not eat. This monster hunt may have been entertaining for Monkey and Pigsy, but did not bring them closer to their goal.

We don't know where our friends will travel next; let's find out in the next chapter.

Circle

"At the hour of the Dragon, the clouds will gather," said the Master "and thunder will be heard at the hour of the Serpent. Rain will come at the hour of the Horse and reach its limit at the hour of the Sheep. There will be altogether three feet, three inches, and forty-eight drops of rain."*

We were following the Tang Monk Xuanzang and his disciples as they explored the Far West in search of a foreign sage to bring back to Tang lands, a learned man who would teach scriptures from the far West. As you know by now, the group included the Tang Monk Xuanzang, Monkey Sun Wukong, Pigsy, and Bear, their Foreign Guide. And the Donkey.

Our travelers continued on their way at sunrise. Vultures flew overhead as the path wound its way down a mountain. They saw a freshwater lake in the distance. As they got nearer, they saw huge mudflats surrounding the lake. The lake had shrunken, and there were even small trees growing in the mud.

Pigsy was wrinkling his snout in disgust, when Monkey finally noticed the smell.

"What's that? It's awful!" said Monkey.

Pigsy knew. "The tribe of hogs has a great sense of smell. The better to find food. That was food before, but now it's rotting fish, it's no longer food and it stinks. Not as bad as Leviathan, but it stinks. Not even Pigsy can eat that!"

THE SECOND JOURNEY

"Have you forgotten your vows again, Pigsy?" admonished Xuanzang.

"No Master. I'm a hearty eater but remain strictly vegetarian. Simple food for me, and lots of it!"

"Vegetarian, but a killer," mumbled Bear, but it wasn't the time or place for another argument

They heard sad chanting coming from a small building. It was built of plain stone and sat at the end of a paved entrance way lined with stone columns.

"What is this building? What's that sad music?" Xuanzang asked.

Pigsy volunteered to help. "I'll go find out for you, Master."

"You know these foreigners don't like the way you look, Pigsy."

"I keep forgetting. That's why I'm called Idiot."

Bear had a better idea. "Xuanzang, this sounds like a religious matter. It's best that you go yourself. I shall accompany you and explain as best as I can."

"Yes, that seems most reasonable, Bear. Monkey, Pigsy, just wait out here. Keep an eye on each other so you don't get into trouble."

With that the Master and the Foreign Guide entered the building, leaving the disciples standing alone in the courtyard.

There were about twenty men inside, all wearing striped prayer shawls and small black boxes on their heads and arms. The shawls were the size of small blankets and had blue and white strings tied at each corner. The boxes were tied on with black leather straps. Most of the men sat along a stone bench which spanned the walls of the room; all but two men, one who stood in front of a table and appeared to be reading off of a scroll and another who kept interrupting him.

Xuanzang was excited.

"Scriptures!" he whispered to Bear.

"Yes. This is the first time you've seen them?"

"I've seen them, but never heard them read," answered Xuanzang. "He's reading it to all of them. Like a teahouse storyteller."

"Be quiet, and maybe we can get close enough to see."

The Scripture was written in black ink on parchment. You could see the dark and light patches on the parchment that reflected the pattern of the animal's skin. The writing was in that weird foreign alphabet script. Some of the letters had little crowns on them.

The storyteller read a short section, then the second man chanted for a few moments, then again, the storyteller. Back and forth they chanted, like a ball being passed back and forth in a children's game.

"Why the second storyteller?" Xuanzang asked.

"Translation. The text is in ancient Hebrew, which few today understand. So, a verse is read and then translated into common Aramaic."

Xuanzang smiled.

"Like Sanskrit scriptures that need to be translated into Mandarin but done in real time. Why do they read the original if nobody understands it?"

Bear explained. "It's sacred."

Xuanzang understood. "Like Sutras."

Bear listened carefully. "They're having special rain prayers. There's been little rain so far and the rainy season is almost over. I think they're fasting, no food or drink. It's part of the prayer ritual."

"That's why the lake is half empty."

"Yes. It might be best not to tell your disciple Monkey what is happening here. He'll be off to find the right Dragon King to help, but this is out of the realm of Dragon Kings."

Xuanzang sighed. "Oh, he knows that, he just doesn't always remember it."

———∞———

Meanwhile, our disciples were outside waiting as patiently as they were able; in other words, after five minutes they were both bored, and one of them was getting very hungry.

"Monkey, when Master and Bear finally come out, they'll be hungry. I should take the bowl and go beg for a vegetarian meal."

Monkey understood the situation better. "Don't."

"Why not?"

"Don't you see what's happening here, Pigsy? There's a drought. The lake is drying up. They're doing some rain-making magic in there right now. They don't have any food to give us."

"So, we will just sit here and wait?"

"No! I can go and...Pigsy, it's no use. I can't enlist the help of a Dragon King here. We're too far away from the Middle Kingdom. We'll just wait."

Pigsy quieted his rumbling stomach and managed to wait until the Tang Monk and Bear emerged, a bearded young foreigner in tow.

Xuanzang greeted them. "Good. You're both here. I expected you to be off fighting demons somewhere."

"That's always fun for Old Monkey. My compliant rod has gotten some exercise recently with Leviathan, and it's still itching to turn some fiends into meat patties. But there aren't the right sorts of fiends and demons around here. What did you learn in the prayer house? Will they manage to make it rain?"

Xuanzang was surprised. "How did you know about the rain? I guess you did pick up some wisdom over the years. They've been praying for rain for a few weeks already, but with no success. The Western Jade Emperor, The World-Master are not listening to their pleas for some reason. They will instead go to the Circle Maker, to see if he can help."

Monkey was confused. "Circle Maker?"

Bear explained, "He's from a family of rainmakers. They have some special power. A better connection to Heaven than the rest of the people."

Xuanzang understood.

"Like Lu Shao-Chun, the Daoist wise man."

"Maybe. I've never met a Daoist teacher," Bear said.

He added some important information.

"All of us have been invited to join this young Master Reuven on his way to the Circle Maker. It's a day's travel."

Pigsy liked the idea. After all, who wants to stay near a stinking lake?

"If we can find some food to fuel this trip, then let's go!"

All Master Reuven could round up for their trip was a cake of dried figs and a small bag of dates. He apologized. "This will have to do. Times are difficult, as you know. It isn't a long trip, though it's uphill. If we start at dawn tomorrow, we should get to the Circle Maker by early afternoon. You can stay with me tonight."

He led them up the street to a wooden gate, which opened to a courtyard. There were a few chickens and a goat in the courtyard, a small house, and the opening to a water cistern.

"There's still a little water in the cistern, a bit muddy, but potable if you let it settle for a bit. I can't offer you proper guest accommodations—you can see how I live," Master Reuven said. "We'll all sleep on the roof tonight, it's the coolest place in the house at night. We'll leave just before dawn. I can't afford to light my lamps during the week. I only light candles on Friday night, in honor of the Sabbath, so we'll have to finish our day soon."

THE SECOND JOURNEY

Bear explained.

"Our laws don't allow for lighting fires on the Sabbath day. It's prohibited in our scriptures:

> *Six days shall work be done, but on the seventh day there shall be to you a holy day, a Sabbath of solemn rest to HaShem; whosoever doeth any work therein shall be put to death. Ye shall kindle no fire throughout your habitations upon the Sabbath day*
> *Exodus 35*

"So, we need to light candles on Friday afternoon, so we'll have light on the Holy Sabbath."

The sun was setting, so they settled down on straw mattresses, and got some rest.

When Reuven woke them, it was still dark. By the time Xuanzang mounted his donkey and they started walking, there was barely enough light to see the path. An hour later the sun rose, and along with the sunlight came the heat.

Pigsy couldn't help complaining. "Just some dried fruits and muddy water to fuel us through this furnace? Remember the vegetarian feasts we had in our first journey?"

Our Tang Monk Xuanzang wouldn't let that go by.

"True, Pigsy, but do you remember the demons on that journey? Or how many times we were nearly the food at a banquet ourselves?"

Reuven calmed them down, "Don't worry. It's a hard climb, but it will get cooler as we go up the mountain."

Sure enough, it did get cooler. When the sun was high in the sky, they stopped to rest under an ancient carob tree. Pigsy tried eating a few of the crescent shaped fruits still hanging from the tree, but they tasted like slightly sweetened wood, so he spat them out, and managed with a few figs and dates, just like everyone else.

They reached their goal in the late afternoon. A bearded man, dressed in plain gray robes, meditated under a fig tree at the mountain's summit. Though the others couldn't see it with their mortal eyes, our dear Monkey could sense a golden aura about him, as if he was a bodhisattva, or perhaps a Daoist Divine Teacher.

Xuanzang saw him as a master sage, calm and contemplative. Maybe this was a candidate to return to the East with them?

Master Reuven signaled them to wait patiently.

The man opened his eyes but did not move beyond that. Master Reuven approached him. "Honi, I've been sent to ask you to pray, so rain will fall."

Honi closed his eyes and prayed for a half hour, but no rain fell. Maybe he wasn't a Divine Teacher after all.

Honi arose, and drew a circle on the ground with his staff, and challenged the World-Master:

"World-Master, your children have turned towards me. They know that I am like a member of Your household. Therefore, I take an oath by Your great name that I will not move out of this circle until you have mercy upon Your children and answer their prayers for rain."

A light drizzle started. Xuanzang waited for the rain to get stronger, but nothing happened. The few drops left small dark spots in the dry dust, but that was all. Xuanzang was patient, but Monkey couldn't help but whisper in his ear. "Old Monkey hasn't seen such a poor showing of rain-making in a long time."

His master signaled him to be quiet. Reuven spoke to the rainmaker. "Master, we have seen that you can perform great wonders, but this light rain is not enough. If we don't get more rain, many will die. It seems that a small amount of rain is falling

THE SECOND JOURNEY

just to fulfil your oath, so you may leave your circle, but it is not nearly enough to save us."

Honi close his eyes and shouted to Heaven. "I did not ask for this light drizzle, but for proper rain that will fill the cisterns, ditches, and caves."

Rain began to fall furiously, until each and every drop was as big as the mouth of a barrel. Our dear Monkey led Xuanzang to safety under a ledge of rock, afraid that a couple of barrel-sized drops would send his aged master on his final journey too soon.

You will recall a similar rain from the Slow Cart Kingdom, in the First Journey:

Marvelous rain! Truly.

> *Pouring and showering, it's like waves churning in a sea upturned.*
> *At first the raindrops seem the size of a fist;*
> *In a while they fall by the buckets and pans.**

Small craters began to appear wherever a drop landed, and Reuven had taken shelter under a large tree. He shouted to the rainmaker over the noise of the rain.

"Master, we have seen that you can call on God to perform miracles, but now it appears to us that this rain is falling only to destroy the world."

Honi opened his eyes and saw what kind of rain his prayers had brought. He remained in his circle and shouted once more, "I did not ask for this harmful rain either, but for rain of benevolence, blessing, and generosity!"

Finally, the downpour dissipated and the rain began to fall in the usual manner. Night approached and the rain continued. The ground turned to mud, water fell in front of their ledge, and Monkey thought it would turn into another Water Curtain Cave.

You will recall that Monkey started his remarkable career as the Monkey King, in the simian dream-world hidden in a cave behind a waterfall. His subjects were thousands of monkeys who adored their leader.

As the rain continued to fall, a few other people joined them under the ledge, seeking refuge from the downpour.

Xuanzang was impressed. "This miracle worker really does have great influence over the Western Heaven. This rain will save the crops and prevent the famine that surely would have struck. He has saved many lives!"

Though he was pleased with this sage's success in rainmaking, Xuanzang's heart fell. This Honi was a miracle worker, not a teacher.

Monkey was starting to wonder. "True! True! Yet I must ask, when will it stop?"

"It will rain forever, and all we have to eat is a few dried figs!" Came the desperate cry from Pigsy.

Bear just stared out into the darkness, mumbling some foreign sutra.

There was no visible sunrise and as day broke, they saw only the curtain of water in front of their ledge, the rain pouring the same as the day before. There were many more people on the mountaintop. They were all huddling under various roofs, rocks and trees, cold and miserable. Honi had left his circle and stood in an open space, oblivious to the rain. Occasionally someone brave would run out to him. There would be a brief conversation with a lot of hand motions before they inevitably gave up and returned to the crude shelter they had.

Now Xuanzang was concerned, "What's happening?"

Reuven and Bear went out into the storm to find out. First, they spoke to a wet, bedraggled family, complete with a few goats, under a tree. Then they ran out to Honi, who stood steadfast in the rain, and spoke with him. Our travelers saw some excited hand motions but could not hear a thing over the drumming of the rain. Finally, they ran back and ducked through the waterfall into their little cave.

Bear explained. "All of those people? They've fled their houses—they've been flooded out. This mountain is the highest spot around. It's the safest spot for them. But they're miserable."

"Old Monkey doesn't understand. There's been enough rain. The circle rainmaker can ask for it to stop. I think the 'three feet, three inches, and forty-eight drops of rain' have already fallen."

"Everybody here asked him already. Master Reuven even asked, in the name of all the sages. But he always has the same answer: "our tradition over many generations is that one does not pray for an excess of good to stop."

We do not know of their condition when the rain did finally cease; let's find out in the next chapter.

Samson

We left our friends huddling under a rock ledge, while Honi's downpour drenched the mountains. It was very cramped, with Reuven, Xuanzang, Monkey, Pigsy and Bear all crowded together. There wasn't enough space to lie down, let alone sleep.

Monkey wasn't tired, but he was antsy, and he could not sit still. He spent some time throwing stones at a nearby tree, but that form of entertainment lost its novelty quickly, especially when you never missed. Some other distraction would have to be found.

Monkey called out, above the sound of the rain. "Brother Bear! You are called The Second Samson. But who was the first Samson?"

"Well, the story goes like this:

"And there was a certain man of Zorah, of the family of the Danites, whose name was Manoah; and his wife was barren and bore not. And the angel of God appeared unto the woman..."
Judges 13

Xuanzang interrupted him. "Guide Bear. You told me this story a few weeks ago, when we lost my horse. Allow me to tell the story. I believe I can tell it in a way that my disciples will understand."

All people like a good story, even if the people are monkeys or pigs. They both listened carefully as Xuanzang raised his voice above the sound of the downpour.

"Many years ago, there lived a barren woman of the tribe of Dan. One day, when she was out in the field, a celestial being visited her, and told her this prophecy:

"You will become pregnant, and you must not drink any wine, for your son will be a holy monk from the day he is born. He shall never drink wine or cut his hair, for he will be a hero, and fight the enemy Philistines.'

This was a good prophecy, and so the woman ran off and shared it with her husband. He trusted her, more or less, but being a man, wanted to hear the prophecy himself. So, he prayed, and sure enough, the celestial being came around again, and shared with him the same prophecy, and he became satisfied that it was real.

A year later, in accordance with the prophecy, a son was born to this couple. They named him Samson.

Now, this Samson was a special child. He had three souls. A Monkey Soul, a Pig Soul, and a Bear soul."

At this point, Monkey and Pigsy were hooked on the story. Bear was amused at this alternate approach to the classic tale.

"Pig Samson fell in love with a Philistine woman, the daughter of their enemies. He had to have her. His parents wanted him to take a local girl, but Pig Samson lusted for the Philistine one."

"We hogs always want what we shouldn't have!"

"Pig Samson went with his parents down to Timnah, the village where this girl lived, to seal a wedding contract with her parents. On the way, a lion suddenly jumped out! This was not a job for Pig Samson, but Bear Samson ripped that lion in half with his bare hands.

A month later, Samson went back to Timnah for the wedding feast with his parents. He walked ahead of his parents to make sure that the path was safe. Soon he walked past the carcass of the lion, and found that there was there was a beehive inside, full of golden honey. He scooped up some of the honey, ate, saved some for his parents, and waited for them. When they caught up with him, he gave some of the honey to his parents, but he didn't tell them from where he had gotten it.

Monkey chuckled. "That doesn't sound like a Pig. Even Old Monkey has a hard time keeping secrets. That must be Bear Samson still or maybe he even has a little Monk Samson soul too!"

Xuanzang continued. "Now, there were thirty young Philistine men at the wedding feast—to be his companions and drink with him. And Monkey Samson thought he'd pull a trick on them with a riddle. 'I'll tell a riddle. If you can guess the answer, I'll buy each of you a suit of clothes. But if you can't guess it, you each have to buy me a suit of clothes!"

Our Monkey was excited. "Let's hear the riddle! Let's hear the riddle!"

"The riddle was: Out of the eater came forth food, and out of the strong came forth sweetness."

Old Monkey liked that. "A tough one. Clever Monkey Samson!"

"For three days the men thought about it, but they could not guess the answer. Monkey Samson was pleased."

"Of course! Of course!" cried Monkey, taking great delight in the tale.

"But like many a monkey's plans, it didn't work out as expected."

"That's right! Always surprises for Old Monkey!"

Xuanzang continued. "The thirty companions refused to

give up. They called the bride aside and threatened her: 'Get the answer from him! If you don't, we'll burn down your father's house and all of his fields!'

"So, she got to work on Samson. She wept, and cried, and begged, "If you truly loved me, you would tell me' — every trick in the female book. Monkey Samson knew what she was up to. He hadn't told anybody where that honey had come from, not even his parents. But she kept it up, and let's just say it wasn't much of a honeymoon anymore. Soon Samson was upset, and he was no longer clever Monkey Samson, but rather lustful Idiot Pig Samson. He finally broke down and told her.

"Sure enough, the next day they told him the answer to the riddle: 'out of the eater came forth food, and out of the strong came forth sweetness. What is sweeter than honey? And what is stronger than a lion?

Pigsy shook his head, "I know I'm only Idiot Pigsy, but I should have figured that out. It's food, after all."

Xuanzang continued. "Samson was not pleased, to say the least. He reprimanded the man, "If you hadn't messed with my wife, you wouldn't have figured it out!"

"Now, Monkey Samson went berserk! He owed them thirty sets of clothes, not an insignificant debt to pay! So, he went down to the nearby Philistine city, killed thirty young men, and stripped the clothes from their bodies."

Pigsy chuckled, "That's you, Old Monkey!"

Monkey nodded, "It was once me, but I've achieved the Right Fruit, I am not like that anymore. Unless we're talking about fiends and demons!"

The story went on. "Monkey Samson was fed up with the Philistines and stomped off. But a month later, Pig Samson grew stronger than Monkey Samson, and he again lusted for his wife."

"A true hog never forgets his old lusts!"

"So, he returned to Timnah only to find that his father-in-law had given his wife to another man! Unhappy Pig Samson quickly turned into a vengeful Monkey Samson; and Monkey Samson would get his revenge!

"He caught three hundred foxes, and tied them tail to tail, with a torch between each pair of tails. He lit the torches and set the foxes loose in the Philistines' fields. He watched the panicked foxes run, each pair pulling this way and that! He delighted in such chaos. Watch the ripe grain go up in flames! You can imagine that the Philistine harvests were rather poor that year. You can also imagine how angry they were. In retaliation, they went and burnt down his father-in-law's house, with his wife and father-in-law still inside.

"Monkey Samson wasn't going to take this lying down. He started a fight with the local Philistines and killed many of them."

Pigsy was concerned. "He should be careful! Maybe somebody will try a tighten-the-headband spell on him!"

"The Philistines decided to lay siege to The House of Two Gates, one of the towns of Dan, to force them to give up Samson. The townspeople went to Samson and told him that they had no choice but to give him up. So, he let them tie him up and hand him over to his enemies. But, as soon as he was in the Philistines' hands, Monkey Samson broke free of his ropes, grabbed an old ass's jawbone, and smacked them around, killing a thousand of them.

Pigsy knew where this was going.

"Monkey Samson is losing merit. He hasn't yet learned, and he never will. But neither did Pig Samson!"

"Pig Samson went down to Gaza, another of the enemy's towns. This time, he went to visit a whore he knew. He went to his whore, but the Philistine men found out that he was coming, and waited by the city gate, so they could catch him when he left.

THE SECOND JOURNEY

At midnight, Samson woke and realized what was happening — he then became Bear Samson. He broke down the city gate, and carried the gate, complete with doorposts and locking beam, up the mountain to Hebron. No one dared follow him.

"'Pig Samson's carnal appetite had no limits. Soon, he fell in love with a monster spirit in the form of a beautiful woman. This monster spirit was called Delilah and it had a monstrous appetite for silver. The Philistine leaders offered her a huge amount of silver, if she could find out the secret to Samson's strength. Thus, every night she would stroke his hair and ask him, 'Tell me, what's the secret of your strength? What can overpower you?'

Monkey Samson knew that she was up to no good, so, he told her lies.

"'If you bind me with seven fresh bowstrings, I will lose my strength, and be like other men." So, she tied him and had some of the Philistines wait in the back room. Then she woke him with a cry, "Philistines are attacking, Samson!"'

Bear Samson jumped up and tore the bowstrings off as though they were thin silk threads.

Monkey didn't understand.

"If Samson knew that Delilah was up to no good, why did he play this game with her? He knew it could be his doom."

Pigsy answered. "Elder Brother, you were born from a stone egg, and now you are awakened to nothingness. You expect Samson to think with what is sitting on his head, while he is actually thinking with what is between his legs. Listen carefully to the story. She's stroking his hair..."

Xuanzang went back to the story.

"'If you bind me with new ropes which have never been used, I will lose my strength, and be like other men." So, she tied him and had some of the Philistines wait in the back room. She woke him again, "Philistines are attacking, Samson!"

Bear Samson jumped up and tore the ropes off as if they were thin silk threads.

"'If you weave my hair in the loom, I will lose my strength, and be like other men,'" he lied again, so, she wove his hair into the cloth and had the Philistines wait in the back room. "Philistines are attacking, Samson!"

Bear Samson jumped up and shattered the entire loom into splinters.

"Old Monkey doesn't like this story! Everybody makes mistakes, but he keeps making the same mistake over and over again. He's not Bear Samson, or even Pig Samson, He's Idiot Samson, no matter how strong he is!"

Xuanzang went on. "This is both the strength and danger of passions. And why we, my disciples, have abandoned such passions.

"She said unto him: 'how can you say I love you, when your heart is not with me? You have mocked me three times and haven't told me where your strength lies.' She continued to drive him crazy, day after day, until he did a stupid thing."

Monkey just shook his head in despair. Pigsy understood Samson better.

"Sounds like Old Hog again. Hard to think straight when a lady is around."

Xuanzang was pleased at his disciple's burst of understanding. "Right! Exactly. Pig Samson said, 'If you cut off my hair, I will lose my strength, and be like other men.' She knew for certain he was telling the truth, so she met with the Philistines and told them: "this time it's for real, I'm certain. Bring the silver with you."

Pig Samson fell asleep on her knees and she cut off his hair. She woke him once more with a shriek, "Philistines are attacking, Samson!"

THE SECOND JOURNEY

"Pig Samson jumped up, but his strength was gone. The Philistines grabbed him, struck out his eyes, and bound him with brass fetters. Pig Samson thus found himself blind, confined to perform heavy work in their prison. But his captors failed to notice something."

Our dear Monkey was also a Great Sage, so he guessed it. "His hair! If you cut off hair, it grows back again!"

"Exactly. The Philistines had a festival for their harvest god Dagon and they brought Samson into their temple for entertainment. This was a broken Pig Samson. Remember Pigsy, how we felt when we were bound and hung up from rafters, waiting to be steamed?"

Pigsy only nodded. When he got into trouble, Monkey usually saved him. Though that same Monkey also got him into trouble plenty of times. But who would save Samson?

"They jeered at him and thanked their god for helping them to defeat him. Samson asked to stand between two pillars that held up the roof. There were three thousand people standing on the roof, besides the thousands inside the temple.

He wrapped his arms around the pillars and prayed to World-Master to give him his strength one more time, so he could take his revenge on the Philistines. He became Bear Samson one final time, pushed against the pillars with all of his strength, and the temple collapsed, killing Samson and everybody in and on the temple. Thus, Bear Samson killed more of his enemies in death than he did in life."

Xuanzang fell silent, and our friends were left with their thoughts and dreams as the rain continued.

We will leave Xuanzang and his companions in the rain, and we turn to the adventure of our miracle worker, Honi, the Circle Maker; let's find out in the next chapter.

Slow Cart

We will leave Xuanzang and his companions as they continue on their damp travels, and we now tell you of the adventure of our miracle worker, Honi, the Circle Maker.

Rainmaking is a tiring business. Once the rain died down, Honi sloshed his way through the mud and the puddles back to his home. He lived in a small, simple house, with a carefully maintained thatched roof, a raised floor, and drainage ditches dug around his yard. One couldn't be too careful in his business.

His wife met him at the door. She was wearing a plain, undyed woolen dress, her head covered with a faded red scarf.

"Oh. Looks like it's been a tough week at work. I haven't seen you this worn out in years! Come inside. It's been raining, as I'm sure you know, but the roof has held up."

She helped him pull off his muddy sandals, washed his feet, and led him inside. She sat him down on a stool and brought him some hot leek soup in a stone bowl. After he ate, he dragged himself to bed, lay down on his back, and collapsed into a deep sleep.

He woke to the sound of rushing air. When he opened his eyes his saw clouds flying by, and the moon perched high in the sky. He expected to see the rafters of his home, and the inside of his thatched roof, yet the sight of the night sky didn't surprise him. He rolled over and looked over the edge of his bed. Just as

THE SECOND JOURNEY

he suspected, he was flying through the air, the Earth far below him. Another glance told him how this had happened. Four cherubs, like those of the Temple, were holding the four legs of the bed, their wings slowly beating against the cold air.

What are cherubs, you ask? Cherubs are celestial bulls. They're golden beasts with the bodies, legs and heads of bulls, and the wings of eagles.

They rose higher and higher, until they were above the clouds. As Honi watched, the Cherubs morphed into four dragons. Poor Honi! Having been born and lived in the Far Western Regions, he had never seen a dragon before!

"Who or what are you?"

The dragons introduced themselves:

"Aoguang, Dragon King of the Eastern Ocean."

"Aoqin, Dragon King of the Southern Ocean."

"Aorun, Dragon King of the Western Ocean."

"Aoshun, Dragon King of the Northern Ocean."

"Where are you taking me?"

Auguang acted as their elder brother and spokesman, or spokes-dragon.

"To a rainmaking contest, of course!"

Soon they landed in the courtyard of an ornate palace. The dragons disappeared, but a group of thirty or forty elders entered the courtyard and continued through a yellow gate into the palace. Honi followed them.

The Custodian of the Yellow Gate announced them.

"Your majesty, the village elders wish to speak."

The King's throne was high and wide and decorated with pearls. It was called the Lion Seat, and was covered with fine cotton cloth, and required the use of a jeweled footstool in order to mount. The king was only middle-aged, but time had not been kind to him. His hair had turned white, and he was thin and weak.

"What is it?"

The elders all kowtowed.

"There has been no rain for the entire spring, and we fear a famine. We request that the Holy Daoist Fathers pray for rain to save the entire population."

The king answered, "Let the village elders withdraw. There will be prayers, and there will be rain."

The king turned to the Daoist priests, but before he could ask them to start the rain making ceremony, he heard a voice: "I will make it rain."

"And who are you?"

"Honi, I am known as the Circle Maker."

"Strange name. Strange clothes. Where are you from?"

"From a distant land to the West."

"Another one of those Buddhist charlatans?"

Honi answered, "I do not know of these Buddhists. I do know about rain."

"Our Daoist priests have been providing rain here for many years. Would you like to challenge them to a contest?"

Honi spoke genuinely, "if it will help the people of the village".

"There will be a contest. If you lose, circle maker, you will be taken to the block and beheaded immediately. The Daoist will be first."

They all went out to the courtyard where the altar stood, the king walking slowly with a cane. The Daoist priest approached the altar. The king and his attendants ascended the Five Phoenix Tower to watch the proceedings. Honi stood next to the altar, anxious to see what the Daoist would do.

"What is your name, Daoist rainmaker?"

"I am the Great Immortal Tiger Strength. I will bring rain.

THE SECOND JOURNEY

Rain will come down from the sky and your head will come down off your neck."

"We shall see."

His hands folded before him, the Tiger-Strength Immortal bowed to the king, and turned to the altar to start his ceremony.

Honi spoke to the Daoist rainmaker, "Tiger Strength Immortal, I am a foreigner. Please explain how you will make it rain."

"Your head will leave your shoulders soon. What difference does it make to you?"

"Indulge a dying man."

> "All right. When I ascend the altar, I shall use my ritual tablet as a sign. When I bang it loudly on the table once, wind will come; the second time, clouds will gather; the third time, there will be lightning and thunder; the fourth time, rain will come; and finally, the fifth time, rain will stop, and clouds will disperse."*

Honi nodded. "I wish you luck, though it means my doom."

The altar was a platform about thirty feet tall. Banners flew on all sides with the names of the Twenty-Eight Constellations written on them. There was a table on top of the altar, and on the table was an urn filled with burning incense. On both sides of the urn were two candle stands with huge, brightly lit candles. Leaning against the urn was a tablet made of gold, carved with the names of the thunder deities. Beneath the table were five huge cisterns full of clear water and floating willow branches.

A glimmering black and blue sunbird perched on Honi's shoulder, opened its long, curved beak, and chirped loudly. Honi was about to shoo the bird away, when it chirped again. This time he heard it clearly. It was Monkey, transformed into a little bird.

"Don't worry! Don't worry! I've settled it with the right people! He won't succeed!"

Honi had no idea what he was talking about. "Which people?"

"The Old Woman of the Wind and the Second Boy of the Wind.

"The Cloud-Pushing Boy and the Fog-Spreading Lad.

"The Squire of Thunder and the Mother of Lightning.

"The Four Dragon Kings: Aoguang, Aoshun, Aoqin, and Aorun

"They will not respond to this Tiger Strength Immortal. But when your turn comes, they will bring the rain!"

"How will I know what to do?" asked Honi.

"You are the Circle Maker, Honi. Just do what you know how to do." Monkey replied.

The Daoist rainmaker struck his tablet once, but there was no wind. He struck it twice, but there were no clouds. He struck it a third time, but there was no thunder or lightning. He struck it a fourth time, but there was no rain.

In sheer desperation, the Daoist added more incense, burned more charms, recited more spells, and struck his tablet again and again, more loudly than ever.

The sunbird on Honi's shoulder chirped.

"He failed! He failed! Old Monkey has too many tricks for a fake Daoist!"

"Monkey?"

"Sometimes Monkey is a bird, sometimes a fly, but he always has a trick or two up his sleeve!"

The king was watching the proceedings from the Five Phoenix Tower. He turned to his queen. "We have seen this procedure many times. It has always succeeded. Why is it failing now?"

The queen shrugged. "I don't know. But we have no choice but to let this strange foreigner try."

THE SECOND JOURNEY

The king raised his hand, and the Daoist stopped his desperate ceremony.

"Let the foreigner try his hand at making rain. Remember, you must succeed if you want to keep your head!"

The sunbird chirped, "Are you ready?"

"Yes, as ready as I will ever be."

"Good," said Monkey "I will wait for your signal."

"Signal?"

But it was too late. The bird had flown off.

Honi had no use for pagan altars, so he climbed down, leaving the Daoist with his charms and tablets on top. He found a piece of chalk in his robes, drew a large circle on the paving stones, and stepped inside. He heard a loud chirp, then:

"Old Woman of the Wind! Second Boy of the Wind! Wind time! Wind time!"

The roar of the wind could be heard instantly, as tiles and bricks flew up all over the city and stones and dust hurtled through the air. Just look at it! It was a truly marvelous wind, not at all similar to any ordinary breeze.

Honi drew a second, smaller circle, inside the first one, and stepped inside.

"Chirp, Chirp! Cloud-Pushing Boy! The Fog-Spreading Lad! Now! Now!"

Honi drew a third, smaller circle, inside the second one, and stepped inside.

"Chirp, Chirp! Squire of Thunder! Mother of Lightning! Now! Now!"

A bolt of lightning struck the altar, which burst into flames. The charms, the tablets and the priests were all consumed in a moment.

Honi drew a fourth, smaller circle, inside the third one, and stepped inside.

"Chirp, Chirp! Aoguang, Aoqin, Aorun, Aoshun! Now! Now!"

> *The dragons gave order, and rain filled the world,*
> *So great was the downpour that all the streets and gulley's*
> *of the Cart Slow Kingdom were completely flooded.**

The king, cowering under his awning, shouted to Honi over the roar of the torrential rain.

"Stop! Stop! Anymore and the crops will be ruined."

Honi never asked for rain to stop, but he was in a foreign land, and he wanted to keep his head on his shoulders.

He rubbed out the smallest circle with his foot, and the rain subsided.

He rubbed out the next circle, and the lightning and thunder stopped.

He rubbed out the next circle, and the fog lifted, the clouds dispersed.

He rubbed out the outer circle, stepped outside, and the sun appeared.

The king's daughter tossed him a red embroidered ball. Honi caught it, knowing that this would make him the king's son-in-law.

He heard a sweet voice in his ear.

"Honi, Honi! You've slept for a day and a half! Come eat."

Honi shook his head, trying to clear the other voices from his head. It took a few minutes, but they were all gone.

The dragons.

The sunbird.

The pagan priest.

The king.

All were gone. All was a dream. He was alone. Except for his wife.

"Honi, Honi, wake up!

"Why is there a blue feather on your shoulder?"

We don't know what happened to our travelers as they continued on their damp way; let's find out in the next chapter.

CAVE

After a day, a night, and another half day, the rain finally stopped. The clouds dispersed and bright light illuminated The endless mud and dripping trees, The endless mud stretching from hill to valley, Sticking to boots, weighing them down. The dripping trees splash on hats and coats, Drenching travelers, though the sun shines bright in the sky.

Master Reuven and Bear had a lengthy discussion in their tongue, punctuated by many hand motions. When they were done, Bear explained the situation to our travelers, "Master Reuven was explaining that travel is impossible today…"

Monkey cut him off and continued the explanation, "It's too muddy today for travel. But the mountain soil is rocky, and not very deep, so he expects that we'll be able to travel tomorrow. We should be fine so long as we are careful when crossing the ravines, as the water may still be rushing."

Bear was confused. "How…have you learned our language?"

"Your language isn't for civilized old monkeys, though I did pick up a bit. But even a deaf man could see your hand motions and what you are pointing at. Besides, what else would you be talking about?"

"Ha! Before long you will speak our language, even if you are an old monkey." Bear surveyed the area, saying, "We should build a fire and dry out. Your master is not a young man and we need to warm him up. It will get cold at night, and a chill is not good for any of us, certainly not an elderly sage. But the wood on the ground is too wet. We'll never be able to light a fire with that."

"Old Monkey can help!"

Dear Monkey! He jumped from tree to tree and collected dead branches for firewood. They were wet on the outside, but dry on the inside, so it was still possible to burn them. The wood that was lying on the ground was soaked through and through.

Starting a fire with flint and steel would be hard with the damp wood. Fortunately, one of the villagers had brought fire in a firepot when he fled his home and had managed to keep it dry and alive during the storm. Bear took a small knife, peeled the wet bark off a branch and partly peeled off shavings, until the stick looked like a pine tree. This was used as kindling, and soon they had a nice fire going, with a pile of wood drying next to it. Burning brands were taken from it, and by dusk there were small fires scattered across the mountaintop.

They changed into dry clothing and spread their wet clothing out to dry.

Our Tang Monk sighed, "I can't count the times when water has caused me trouble. I lost my water in the desert on the way to the Wild Horse Spring and barely survived. Pigsy, do you remember that cursed river water we drank from?"

"The belly-ache water that made us pregnant? It hurts just to remember it!"

"And the scriptures that we lost on the way back from India? Water is like…"

"Like women! You need them, but they cause too much trouble!" Pigsy shouted.

"Disciple Pig, I thought you had left your lust behind!"

"It's never behind, Master, just carefully ignored."

They slept soundly through the night and woke to the sound of the other storm refugees getting ready to go home. There was barely enough light to see, but people were already loading up their donkeys and eating breakfast. Several of these refugees stopped by our friends to share their bread with them before setting on their way.

Pigsy was pleased. "We don't even need the begging bowl here!"

Xuanzang understood the situation better.

"They're being very generous. I doubt that they have much themselves, yet they're sharing with us."

"Without our even asking!"

Xuanzang noticed that Bear was feeding the donkey but hadn't eaten anything yet himself. "Why aren't you eating?"

"I have to feed the donkey first."

"Why?" asked Xuanzang.

"It's part of our Way. It's how we interpret our Scriptures:

> *That I will give the rain of your land in its season, the former rain and the latter rain, that thou mayest gather in thy corn, and thy wine, and thine oil.*
> *And I will give grass in thy fields for thy cattle, and thou shalt eat and be satisfied.*
> *Deuteronomy 11*

"Just as our God first gives grass for the cattle, then food for us humans, so must we feed our animals first, and only then are we permitted to eat."

"You do have compassion for animals, Bear, even though you are not a vegetarian."

"Xuanzang, it's more than compassion, it's compassion combined with responsibility."

"What do you mean?"

"It's not enough to feel compassion. One is required to act. Like the people who gave you food even though they have little themselves. One must be kind to others. It isn't optional."

They parted from Reuven, who was going back to his home near the lake, and started on their way. They walked the entire morning. Though the sun was drying the mud, their shoes and the donkey's hooves were caked with it, which made the going slow.

"Hey, Monkey!" Pigsy shouted.

"What now, Idiot?"

"I had a brilliant idea!"

"Right. Let's hear it," said Monkey.

"Let's shave Master's donkey."

Everybody stopped and stared at Pigsy.

Xuanzang finally said, "You haven't always been well behaved or polite, but you have always been reliably stupid. What are you talking about?"

"If we shave the donkey, then we'll have four bald donkeys traveling together, instead of three!" [Editor's note: bald donkey 秃驴 is a derogatory term for Buddhist monks.]

Even Xuanzang smiled at this. "I was wrong. You are also unreliable in your stupidity."

Our band of travelers advanced on, Monkey leading the way, followed by Eight-Rules Pigsy, the Foreign Guide Bear, and, finally, on his donkey, Xuanzang, the Tang monk.

Our Monkey chattered, "Where are we going next? Where to? Where to?"

Bear called out from behind, "Peki'in!"

The entire entourage stopped.

"Northern Capital?"

"A Chinese city?"

"We are thousands of *li* away from China!"

Bear laughed.

"No, not China, just a nearby village. A famous mystic once lived in a cave nearby."

Cave was a trigger-word for Xuanzang. "Cave?! Not again!"

Monkey tried to reassure him. "Master, don't worry, don't worry! They only have regular caves here, not demon-caves."

They continued on their way. They walked along a mountain ridge, then made their way downhill. Now they were making their way adjacent to a rocky stream. Bear stopped and called out to Monkey and Pigsy, "Come back here and see the cave!"

Monkey and Pigsy came back, but they couldn't see the cave.

"Where's the cave?"

"Right here!"

Pigsy grunted, "Cave? That's not a cave! Just a crack between the stones."

"Nevertheless, tradition says this is the cave, and that Rabbi Shimon and his son hid in here for many years."

Pigsy grunted again.

Xuanzang admonished him, "Pigsy, one should be respectful of other's traditions, even if they appear strange to us."

"Strange? A mouse couldn't hide in that crack, let alone two men!"

Dear Monkey! He couldn't resist a challenge.

"Old Monkey will find out what's really in this cave!"

Before anybody could say a word, he shook himself, and turned into a mosquito. First, he jumped onto Pigsy, and gave him a proper bite on his snout, then he jumped into the crack.

"Ouch!" shouted Pigsy, but our old Monkey just giggled.

The crack was narrow, even for a mosquito, but Monkey flew on, and the crack eventually widened out to a broad cave with a sandy floor.

THE SECOND JOURNEY

He shook, turned himself back into his normal simian form, and looked around. The cave was lit by two oil lamps. There was a pile of clothing on the sand, along with two human heads. One of them was speaking to the other, explaining in esoteric terms the Yin-Yang, female-male nature of the one god.

"Just as they unite above unto one, this also unites below, in the secret of one, in order to be with them above, one in correspondence with one. For the Holy One, blessed be He, who is one above, does not sit on His Throne of Glory, until She also becomes in the secret of one like Him so it would be One in One. Thus, we have established the secret of "God is One and His Name One…" The words hung in the air for a second when Monkey's presence became known. One of the heads asked him. "Who are you? How did you find us?"

"I am the Great Sage Equal to Heaven, otherwise known as Monkey. I've come here with my master, the Tang Monk Xuanzang. We were told of this cave. It was too small to enter, so I turned myself into a mosquito so that I could explore."

"What were you told of this cave?" asked the head.

"That many years ago a sage and his son hid in here. But who are you? I have found many things in caves, but talking heads are not usually among them."

"Talking heads?"

"You, and your partner there."

"Partner? That's my father."

His father understood what the problem was. "You misunderstand. We aren't talking heads. I am Rabbi Shimon son of Yochai, and this is my son."

"I am very happy to make your acquaintance. Still, you do appear to be lacking bodies."

"Ah. We have been hiding here for eleven years. We hide our naked bodies in the sand most of the time, and only wear our clothes for a short time each day, during our prayers, so they won't wear out. We have no way to get new ones."

"What do you eat?" asked Monkey, "Or drink?"

"There's a spring and a carob tree further down in the cave. Some light filters in, so the tree is all right, though the fruit gets tiresome after a decade or so. You can't pick and choose your miracles."

"That's for sure! But Old Monkey is wondering, who are you hiding from?"

"The Romans!"

"But the sages outside aren't hiding from them," said Monkey.

The two heads looked at each other for a moment. Then the son replied, "You are from a different place, or time. For us, it is death to go outside."

"I am from the East, a different place for sure. But here is here. And now is now. I think."

"Don't be so sure. How did you get in here?"

Monkey explained again. "I changed myself into a mosquito, and flew in."

"A talking monkey who can change himself into a mosquito should carefully consider what reality is. Go outside and look around."

Monkey turned himself back into a mosquito and flew outside. His friends weren't there. The stream was dry, the air was hot, and half the mountainside was a mass of charred wood. He flew back inside the cave and changed back to his normal shape. "You are evil demons, playing games! Where are my friends? Where's my master?! You aren't the first demons who've tried to eat him!" He admonished the heads.

"Demons? Do we look like demons to you?"

Monkey considered this. He could see they were regular humans, not demons. But where did his friends go? What kind

THE SECOND JOURNEY

of trick were they playing? Unless they are telling the truth — but then how was he to reunite with his fellow travelers?

"I will believe you for now. But tell me, why are you here? What happened?"

"Continue down the cave," said the older sage, "and you will see."

Old Monkey didn't see much choice in the matter, since going out of the cave wasn't going to get him anywhere. Besides which — he wasn't afraid of caves. Brave Monkey! Magic clouds weren't for caves, so he ran down the cave as fast as he could.

As he soon discovered, this was a magical time-travel cave. As Monkey advanced further into the cave, he visited earlier times.

Our dear Monkey stumbled into a study room. He quickly shook himself, and turned himself back into a mosquito, so he could observe without being seen. Nobody looks at a mosquito, until after they're bitten.

There were three sages in the room. Shimon, a younger version of the sage he had spoken to earlier, Yosei, and Judah. They were discussing politics and the nature of their trouble began to take form for Monkey. He learned their names as the conversation went along. Soon a fourth man joined them, also Judah, but called 'Judah, the son of converts'.

Judah said, "What a fine nation these Romans are! They've built markets, bridges, bathhouses!"

Yosei was silent.

Monkey was waiting for the trouble. And it came.

Shimon said,

"They built all that for themselves!"

"Markets, so they can place their whores there!"

"Bridges, so they can collect tolls!"

"Bathhouses, for their own pleasure!"

The meeting dispersed. Trouble was brewing. Too many people had heard what Shimon said. Our mosquito-Monkey waited silently on the ceiling, carefully avoiding the spider webs in the corners.

Sure enough, the next morning word had gotten out.

Judah was elevated in status.

Yosei was exiled to the north.

And a death sentence was set for Shimon.

Monkey watched Shimon and his son hide in the study hall cellar. His wife brought them food and water every day. So how did they end up in that cave? He sat and waited for the events to unfold.

A few days later Shimon got nervous. More and more soldiers were searching for him, and he was afraid that they would question his wife, and that would be his doom. So, they ran off in the middle of the night to that cave.

Monkey followed them back to the cave.

Shimon's head greeted him, "You understand now?"

"Yes."

"Fine. Now leave us to our studies."

The two of them went back to their esoteric discussions.

"That they bring me an offering" ... as we have learned. What makes it an offering? It is in the secret of Gold, because it is nourished originally from there as it is the lower Gvurah that comes from the side of Gold. Even though She comes from the side of Gold, She perseveres only by the side of silver, which is the column."*

This sounded like Daoist teachings to Monkey, but he needed to leave and search for his friends. Suddenly a voice came through the crack in the stone and echoed deep in the cave.

"Who will tell Shimon Bar Yochai that the Roman Caesar has died and it is safe to come out?"

Monkey emerged from the cave and stood as a mosquito on the man's hand.

"I will tell them!"

"And who are you?" asked an old man.

"I am Monkey, the Great Sage Equal to Heaven! Who are you?"

"I am Elijah. If a mosquito can talk, then it can tell Shimon and his son that the danger has passed."

Our dear mosquito Monkey flew back into the cave and told Shimon and his son what he had heard. They extracted themselves from the sand, got dressed, and moved towards the cave entrance.

"Old Monkey can turn into an insect and leave the cave, but how can they do it?"

As the two walked, the cave sighed, and the opening widened for them. Monkey followed them out. His friends hadn't returned. There were still burned trees on the mountain, but there was also the fresh green of new growth. A man with an ox was plowing a small field next to the stream.

Shimon was incensed. "How could he waste his time with everyday activities? He should study the Scriptures, the Way and the Mystical Truths."

As soon as the words left his mouth, his eyes turned a deep red color, and a beam of fire destroyed everything he looked at. In a few seconds the man was a pile of cinders, and the ox was roasting over a burning bush. Shimon looked up, and cooked birds fell from the sky.

Monkey had seen demons do this kind of trick in the past, but didn't expect it here. "It's a shame that I'm a vegetarian. I would enjoy the meat, but we can't let this sage destroy everything!"

Dear Monkey! He stood in front of the cave and blocked Shimon's view, so he couldn't cause any further damage. Shimon shot fire bolts at him from his eyes, but Monkey had been tempered in the alchemical brazier of Lao Tzu, the Daoist immortal, for forty-nine days, so it had no effect on him.

They heard the sound of rolling thunder, and the sky opened up. Monkey could see an old sage leaning over the hole in the sky. It was Olam-Tzu, World-Master. Our Monkey had known him as a kind, helpful god, but now he was angry.

"You have come to destroy my world?! Go, return to the cave!"

The sky closed again, but our Monkey saw the World-Master wink at him just before it did. Monkey followed Sage Shimon and his son back into the cave. The cave narrowed behind them. Soon they were back at the sandy floor, and the two sages took off their clothes, buried themselves in the sand again, and resumed their esoteric discourse...

"...Surely for these reasons, Elijah has been delayed above, where he is confined. And he does not descend to you because he would have come down with wealth for you..."*

Just then the oil lamps went out. The cave was pitch black, but Shimon and his son continued.

"...but he is confined above and descends not, as your poverty is in reality a redemption for Yisrael. Hence, the Messiah says, 'Until a poor man comes,' as the verse says, 'and by his injury we are healed.'*

Then, silence. Monkey waited. Nothing. Total darkness and total silence.

This Sage Shimon was a dangerous fellow. Monkey was glad that he wasn't traveling with them.

"Old Monkey can't see or hear anything. I hope this cave isn't a monkey-dissolving gourd! How can I leave here? My diamond eyes need at least a little light to see by!"

He thought for a moment, shook himself, and with a few words of incantation, turned himself into a bat, a divine mouse!

It took a few seconds for our Monkey to get used to his new senses. Then his night bat-senses showed him that the cave was empty. The sages were gone, as were the oil lamps. All that was left was a smooth sandy floor. He flew towards the entrance, but the tunnel grew too narrow. He could tell that the opening was there, since there was a slight breeze of cool fresh air, but there was no way to get out.

A Buddhist Monkey learns how to wait, and our Monkey knew how a divine mouse needs to wait. He found a convenient spot on the ceiling, hung upside down, and took a nap. When he awoke, he could still feel the breeze, but it was now a warm breeze. Monkey guessed that it was daylight outside, and that a little light would filter in through the crack. He shook himself back into a mosquito, and sure enough, there was just enough light for him to find his way out.

There, in the sunlight stood his friends, Eight-Rules Pigsy, the Tang Monk Xuanzang, and Foreign Guide Bear. Even the donkey was waiting for him there.

"Monkey, my simian disciple! What did you find in there?"

"Sage Shimon and his son. It is a long and complicated tale."

Pigsy laughed.

"Silly Monkey, didn't you hear what we were told? Those sages lived many generations ago. The only cave they could be in is a burial cave!"

"If Master Tang wasn't here, my rod would teach you what I saw," Monkey said.

"But I am here. If Monkey says he saw them, I believe him. If they lived many generations ago, they won't be able to join us as teachers. Still, the world is often not what it appears on the surface. Let's continue on our way. Peacefully."

Let's leave our heroes for a moment, and see what Sage Elisha and Sage Akiva are up to.

Master and Disciple

The morning study session was over. The students had all left the study hall to eat lunch, some with their families, and the others with the families they were boarding with. Elisha often ate with Akiva, as his home was closer, and Elisha wasn't married. Rachel had prepared a simple lunch of boiled vegetables and beans, as she did every Tuesday.

Elisha and Akiva sat at the table, eating with spoons.

"Elisha, you know that we eat this simple food once a week, to remind us," said Rachel.

"Yes, it reminds you of your humble beginnings," he said.

Akiva started reminiscing. "Rachel's father was wealthy. Not a bad man, but like many, he was blind to the potential hidden in simple people. We married without his permission, so he disowned Rachel. The two of us slept in a haystack, rather than in her father's mansion. We thought we were poor."

"Thought you were poor? You were."

"So we thought. Then one day, a man knocked on the door to our haystack. Or he would have, if we had a door. He told us that his wife had given birth, and asked if he could take some hay for her to rest on, to make her more comfortable."

"So poor is a relative term."

"Yes, one man's cave can seem like a palace to another."

"Speaking of which," said Elisha, "we saw some palaces

when we visited the Orchard."

"Palaces? Huts."

"That's what you saw. I saw palaces and treasuries."

"That's odd," Akiva replied. "You come from a wealthy family. A hut should look like a simple hut to you. And like a palace to me."

"I saw a palace. Not a hut that was a palace in my eyes. And not just one palace. Dozens of them. And treasuries."

"Elisha, you didn't go into The Orchard drunk, did you?"

Elisha was hesitant to sound critical of Akiva. There were already legends about him. He was said to have been illiterate until the age of forty, and by perseverance, brains and willpower studied and became the leading sage. Simon the son of Shimon told a parable about this:

> There was a stonecutter who worked in the mountains. One day he took his pickaxe and went to live on the mountain. He'd swing at the rocky mountain, and break off small chunks of rock. People stopped by and asked him, "What are you doing?"
>
> "I'm tearing up this entire mountain, and throwing it into the river."
>
> "Can you really do that?" they asked.
>
> "Yes," he answered.
>
> He kept digging away, until he reached a large rock. He got a crowbar under the rock, loosened it, and tumbled it down into the river. He reached a larger rock, and did the same.
>
> This is what Akiva did to the other sages. As it is written:
>
> *He putteth forth his hand upon the flinty rock; He*

THE SECOND JOURNEY

*overturneth the mountains by the roots.**

The best way to approach a touchy subject with a master is to refer to something he has already said.

"Akiva, you said that some are blind to the potential hidden in simple people. Some can be blind in other ways."

"It's the Orchard, Elisha. The deep truth is there. No room for blindness."

"I saw the same as you. At first."

"And then?"

"What were we not to say? What did you tell us when we left the chariot?"

"Don't say 'Water, water!"

"Ben Azzai tricked me into saying "Water, water". And my eyes opened."

"Ben Azzai, may he rest in peace."

"May he rest in peace," Elisha repeated, then smiled. "You know what he said about you?"

"What?"

"All of the sages are like the dry peel of a head of garlic to me, of no weight, no importance, except that bald guy."

Akiva smiled. "He had a sharp tongue. And a sharp eye. Unlike you. You said those words, and were blinded."

"I was blind, until I said, 'Water, water'. Akiva, at first, I saw what you saw. Simple, wise old men, farmers and shepherds living in huts, who knew the hidden wisdom and secrets of the Upper Realms. More or less what I expected to see. For some reason, I started getting thirsty. Physically thirsty. I didn't expect physical needs would be felt in The Orchard. That's when Ben Azzai offered me some water. Offered, then withheld. Until I said those words."

"He deliberately set you up for that?"

"We'll never know. He died a few days later." Elisha said. "But he's not the issue. I know what I saw. The Orchard was filled with palaces, huge structures made of shiny green stones. And there were heavenly beings everywhere. The people that you spoke to were not humans. Certainly not normal humans like you and me."

Akiva was confused. "You mean they were angels? Not a surprise to find them in The Orchard."

"Not angels. Immortals. Divine beings. They reminded me of how the Greeks describe their gods."

"Elisha, Elisha. You and your Greeks! They will be the end of you. What do you know of their false gods? Why do you waste your time with their pagan stories? Is it not written

> *Know this day, and lay it to thy heart, that HaShem, He is G-d in heaven above and upon the earth beneath; there is none else.**

"There is none else," Elisha pondered. "Yes I know, after all,

> *Their idols are silver and gold, the work of men's hands. They have mouths, but they speak not; eyes have they, but they see not.* *

"But do they really worship the idols? Or are they just images, symbols of something else?"

Akiva's bald pate was getting red, a sure sign of suppressed anger. "It makes no difference. There is only one god. The rest is a figment of your imagination."

"I know what I saw."

"Elisha, who are you going to believe? The Holy Teachings, or your eyes?"

THE SECOND JOURNEY

"I know what I saw."

"So why didn't I see it?"

The only answer Elisha had was that Akiva was blind. But he couldn't say that outright. Not to Akiva. Besides which, maybe Akiva was right. Who was to say that Akiva was the blind one? Maybe he, Elisha, was hallucinating. Maybe 'Water, water' put him in some kind of trance.

The best way to defuse the conversation was to turn to something normal.

"Akiva, we have been eating boiled vegetables. Do you still maintain that we should say the full grace after meals, even though we did not eat bread?"

"Of course. As you can see, I remember what it was like to be poor. One should thank God for a full meal, even if the meal was boiled cabbage."

We will leave our sages discussing the fine points of traditional prayers, and return to our travelers. Where did our heroes go next? Let's find out in the next chapter.

Patience

A timid man cannot learn
An impatient man cannot teach.*

Our travelers continued on their way. Monkey led, Bear walked alongside the mounted Xuanzang, and Pigsy brought up the rear. Bear explained where they were headed.

"This town is home to a famous sage, Hillel. He is called 'Prince of Israel' and is a great teacher. He is known especially for his great patience. No one has ever managed to make him angry."

Our Monkey immediately saw the challenge. "No one? Only because he hasn't met Old Monkey yet."

"Disciple, behave yourself," admonished Xuanzang.

"Oh, I will only ask him a few questions. How about a little bet, Idiot Pigsy?"

Pigsy took him up on it. "Monkey, you are no match for these foreign sages. I'll bet. How about four hundred of these Persian 'zuz' coins?"

"It's a deal!"

"You two are gambling? Right in front of me?"

"Not a gamble, Master, not a gamble, a sure thing! This Sage Hillel will lose his cool inside of five minutes when he meets old Monkey, The Great Sage Equal to Heaven!"

THE SECOND JOURNEY

They passed through a wide valley. The stream to their left had overflowed its banks and they were forced to detour through the still-brown fields. Here and there they saw a few green shoots, and there were red flowers scattered in the open spaces. Bear, their guide, pointed to a town on a hill to their right, "That's where we're headed."

It was a small town with wide main streets built in the Roman manner. The roads were paved with rectangular stone blocks. The buildings were erected with the same gray stone, the roofs thatched with palm fronds. They walked past a small amphitheater, and noticed the aqueduct that brought water to the town from a nearby spring.

Bear showed them a public building with a mosaic floor. It showed a lady's face made of small stones, with eyes that appeared to follow you around the room.

Xuanzang noticed as well. "Magic?"

Bear explained. "No, just an artist's trick. Come, we need to find lodging."

"Where does Sage Hillel live?" asked Monkey.

"We'll pass his house on the way."

Sure enough, a few minutes later Bear pointed out the house.

"Let us take a break. Master, you can sit on this stone bench. I'll finish my business here in a few minutes. Pigsy, better get your money ready." Pigsy just grunted in response.

Now the day they arrived was a Friday, the Sabbath eve, and Hillel was washing his hair. Our Monkey went to the entrance of Hillel's house and in a rough voice called out, "Who here is Hillel, who here is Hillel?"

Hillel wrapped himself in a dignified, purple-striped robe and went out to greet him, "My son, what do you seek?"

"I have a question to ask."

"Ask, my son, ask."

"Why are the heads of Babylonians oval?" Monkey asked.

"My son, you have asked a significant question. The reason is because they do not have clever midwives. They do not know how to shape the child's head at birth."

Monkey thanked him and returned to his fellow travelers.

"Did you succeed?"

"Not yet! Not yet!" laughed Monkey. "Let's wait until he goes back into the bath, then we'll see!"

He waited a while, then went back to the house of Sage Hillel.

"Who here is Hillel, who here is Hillel?"

Again, Hillel wrapped himself and went out to greet him, and said, "My son, what do you seek?"

"I have a question to ask."

"Ask, my son, ask."

"Why are the eyes of the residents of Tadmor bleary?"

Hillel answered calmly. "My son, you have asked a significant question. The reason is because they live among the sands and the sand gets into their eyes."

Monkey thanked him and returned to his fellow travelers.

"Did you succeed?"

"Not yet! Not yet!" laughed Monkey.

"Let's wait until he goes back into the bath, then we'll see! One more time should do it!"

He waited a while, then went back to the house of Sage Hillel.

"Who here is Hillel, who here is Hillel?"

Again, Hillel wrapped himself and went out to greet him, "My son, what do you seek?"

"I have a question to ask."

"Ask, my son, ask."

"Why do Africans have wide feet?"

"My son, you have asked a significant question. The reason is because they live in marshlands and their feet widened to enable them to walk through those swampy areas."

Monkey saw that Hillel was not upset in the least.

He said to himself, "Old Monkey will get him yet!"

"I have many more questions to ask, but I am afraid lest you get angry."

Hillel pulled the robe closer around, Now Monkey got angry. He resisted the urge to reach for his compliant rod, and just asked, "Are you Hillel whom they call the Prince of Israel?"

"Yes."

"If it is really you, I hope there aren't many more like you among your people!"

Hillel answered calmly. "My son, for what reason do you say this?"

"Because you made me lose four hundred zuz!"

"Learn patience from me, and be careful of your spirit. Avoid situations of this sort, as a truly patient man like me will make you lose four hundred zuz on such a bet, and another four hundred zuz if you try it again. No matter what, I will not get upset."

We do not know what was happened to them next in this town; let's find out in the next chapter.

No-Work Day

After Monkey failed to irritate Hillel, he returned to find his friends waiting on the same stone bench he'd left them at. Our dear Monkey knew he'd have to suffer Pigsy's barbs.

"Finally met your match! A foreign sage, no less!"

Monkey knew he deserved the ridicule after losing his bet, but nevertheless, he was fuming inside. When Idiot Pigsy started singing a little ditty with the words, "It's so easy to win four hundred!" steam was visibly blowing out of his monkey ears. Xuanzang couldn't fail to notice.

"Disciple Monkey! You've achieved true merit, and you've been taught a lesson in patience by Sage Hillel. It is time to leave your anger behind."

"Yes, Master. I know it. I know it. But it is hard for Old Monkey."

Pigsy snickered. Xuanzang admonished him, "You are no better, Pigsy. You know how to behave yourself, now do it.

Pigsy stuck his snout into his cloak out of embarrassment.

Xuanzang had a thought, "Monkey, you found Sage Hillel is a most patient man."

"Too patient! Too patient."

"That is a sign of a good teacher. I wonder if we could convince him to return to the Tang lands with us."

"Master, I don't know. These foreigners are very attached to

THE SECOND JOURNEY

their land and their people."

"Even so, we should ask him."

With that, our Monkey led Sage Xuanzang back to Hillel's house and once again called out, "who here is Hillel, who here is Hillel?"

"My son, what do you seek?"

"I have no more questions, venerable sage. I have brought my master, Sage Xuanzang, to meet you."

Hillel turned politely to Xuanzang, who said, "Sage Hillel, we are travelers from far to the East, we seek wisdom in your lands. My disciple has already learned from you, at some expense to himself."

"Yes, some lessons come at a cost. Though knowledge is the one thing that can be bestowed as a gift, and yet retained for oneself. How may I help you, honored visitor?"

Xuanzang made his bid. "Though your people mostly live in this area, there are some who have found their way far to the East, to the lands of the Tang Emperor. They seek a teacher, for their last teacher died a few years ago."

Hillel thought for a moment before answering. "This is our land, the center of our life, but our people are scattered to the four winds, to Egypt, Rome, Persia. Everywhere. I did not know that they had reached so far away. Are you sure?"

"These people are called the 'Sect Who Extract the Sinew'. Their temple has no idols, just scriptures in your language. I did not know of them either, until someone brought me this." Xuanzang reached into his sleeve and extracted the leaf with the foreign characters, the leaf that had triggered this journey.

Hillel carefully took the leaf. A quick glance was all that he needed, "Yes, those are our brothers." He remained thoughtfully silent for a moment before speaking:

"It will be hard to find a scholar who will go there to help them. The more established sages, like myself, have too many teaching responsibilities right where we are; the younger sages would have to take their wives and children on a long, possibly dangerous trip to an unknown land; and the very youngest are not qualified and will wonder how they are to find wives in this far off land."

Xuanzang was disappointed. "I have been sent to find a teacher, I cannot return home empty-handed."

"I understand. I regret that I don't have much advice. If you wander around our lands long enough, perhaps you will find someone who is both qualified and willing. There are many scholars here; there may be some who want to travel out of curiosity, or because they are looking for a change in their lives."

This was not the help Xuanzang was hoping for, but he thanked Hillel, bowed, took his leave, and returned to find his friends standing near the same bench, ready to leave.

Bear had some important news for them.

"It's Friday today, the Sabbath begins at sundown. We must make haste to find an inn to stay in and prepare for the Sabbath Games. It should be interesting."

"Sabbath?" inquired Xuanzang.

"Games?" Monkey wanted to know.

Bear explained. "The Sabbath is a holy day of rest. No work allowed."

Xuanzang nodded. "Ah, it's a No-Work Day."

Bear smiled, "It is far more complicated than that, as you'll soon find out. But you can call it No-Work Day, if you like. Which brings us to the Games."

Our dear Monkey was jumping up and down in excitement. "Yes, the Sabbath Games! Can I compete?"

Bear scratched his head, "Maybe in principle. But the rules are complicated."

THE SECOND JOURNEY

Pigsy had to chime in. "Rules, you say? Monkey is not one for rules!"

"He's right. Old Monkey isn't good at rules. But neither is so-called Eight-Rules Pigsy."

"No, I can barely follow eight normal rules, let alone hundreds of foreign rules. Old Idiot Pigsy will never remember them."

Xuanzang was curious, "Is it a sports event? A legal event?"

"Hmm, a bit of both."

"Ah, like Confucius' playing the ball game Cuju. Hard to imagine."

"You will see," Bear answered.

They found an inn, unloaded their belongings in the room and hurried off to the games.

There was a crowd gathered in a small street. Houses with balconies lined both sides of the street, and ropes cordoned off an empty section in the middle.

Bear, their Foreign Guide, gave a low whistle, "It's the Domain Game! This should be fun."

He turned to his companions, saying, "It's like this: We're not allowed to carry things around on the Sabbath or move them from a public area to a private one, or the other way around. So, they've set up these two houses with balconies as private areas, and the goal is to get an object from one house to the other without violating the carrying rules."

"Who are the judges?"

"Ah, that's the interesting part. You'll see."

A player climbed into one house where he was handed a pomegranate. He threw it from the balcony of one house to the balcony of the other. The crowd shouted. The judges held out their thumbs—three up, two down. Then a vigorous argument started.

"It was above the height limit!"

"No, it wasn't!"

"Who cares? Throwing doesn't work! When it flies through the air, it's as if it rested on the ground!"

"You and your 'as ifs' "

Xuanzang was confused, "Why did he throw it? What's the argument?"

"One is not allowed to carry from one 'domain' to another. If you walk while holding something, that's clearly carrying; but, if it's thrown through the air, that's a matter of debate. Sooner or later, they'll start arguing about the minimum size required for something to be considered a significant object."

After a while it quieted down. Monkey looked at Bear, who gave a short nod.

"Try it, and let's see what happens."

Monkey picked up a date, ran up the stairs, and threw it across the street.

"No transgression! It was too small!"

"Too small my foot! It was a whole date!"

Most of the judges nodded in approval.

"Where did it land anyhow?"

"Who cares!?"

The judges were getting more and more excited.

"He can do whatever he wants, he's not one of us!"

"Oh yeah? Who told him to play, huh? Whoever told him about this game is at fault for whatever he does!"

"Yeah, but he's a monkey!"

"So what?!"

After a while it calmed down. Monkey took another date, took a bite out of it, and tossed it across. All five thumbs were up. Bear shouted up to him:

"It's too small to qualify as a significant object! Well done!"

Somebody threw a cake of dried figs up to our Monkey.

THE SECOND JOURNEY

He wound up his arm and gave the fig cake a mighty heave towards the second house. As he let go of the figs, Pigsy let out a tremendous burp and distracted Monkey. The throw was off, and the fig cake hit the opposite wall and stuck there.

A tremendous roar from the crowd, and endless bickering among the judges.

"The wall is part of the house."

"So what? The figs are on the outside of the house!"

"Fools! The outside of the house has a special status. It's not in or out, it's hanging in the air."

"Yeah, but it'll eventually fall off."

There was no conclusion. Somebody handed Monkey a ceramic jug; a poor quality, local piece that couldn't be remotely compared to the fine Tang vases back home. Monkey bit off a hair, whispered "change" so that the hair turned into a copy of the jug, dropped the jug behind him, and spun around to give the fake jug a mighty throw across the street. When it was halfway across the street, he shouted "change!" again, and the jug turned into a dove that simply flew away. The judges all held up their thumbs.

"He didn't complete the action," one of the judges explained.

The crowd applauded. Nobody seemed to care that the jug had turned into a fowl. Since the jug had been picked up and started moving, but it never got put down, the transportation process was incomplete; something our Tang friends did not know.

"Old Monkey has a lot to learn about these foreigners. They aren't easily impressed."

Just then a ram's horn sounded. Inside of two minutes the street emptied out. Bear called them over, "The Sabbath is starting in a few minutes. Everybody has gone home. We should go to the inn."

Space was found in the inn courtyard for their donkey, and our band of travelers ascended to their shared room on the second story. They washed themselves from a small basin of water and changed into clean clothes in honor of the approaching Sabbath rest day. Xuanzang put on the brocade cassock that Emperor Taizong had given him years ago.

Bear led them to the synagogue, a low stone structure with a wooden roof supported by two rows of tall columns. Rows of a dozen wooden benches faced the central table, while an ornate cabinet at the southern end held the Holy Scriptures. Xuanzang recognized the layout from the temple in Kaifeng. They sat on the back bench near the entrance where Monkey and Pigsy attracted a few curious glances, but eventually, everybody got down to the business at hand; talking. Everybody was talking, some very loudly. Xuanzang tried to make out what they were saying, but it was all jumbled up.

"Bear, what kind of prayers are these?"

Bear laughed. "Prayers? No, not yet. Just gossip. It's... tradition. To be more exact, it's prohibited, one should not be gossiping at all, let alone in a holy place. Yet everybody does it. Even the sages."

He nodded towards a group of bearded sages at the other end of the prayer hall, who were deeply engaged in a discussion of some sort.

"They live with this tension of doing something they know they should not do?" Xuanzang asked.

"Yes, of course. Don't you? We have a huge respect for tradition and rules, but also just a tad of disrespect."

One of the sages got up, walked to the central table, and pounded on it with his fist a few times. The room grew silent.

Bear whispered. "They're getting ready for prayers now."

"Will they read from the Holy Book?" Xuanzang asked.

"Not tonight, only in the daytime."

Xuanzang nodded and glanced at Pigsy and Monkey, who were easily bored. They seemed okay. The evening prayers were short. Once they were done, one of the sages got up to the front of the hall to deliver a short lesson about the details of The Way.

There was a special ceremony at the beginning and the end of the Sabbath day, and similar ceremonies for festival days.

The special day always began at sundown, and a prayer was said before the festive meal. The prayer included a prayer or blessing for the special day, a blessing for the ceremonial wine, and, if it was a festival, a blessing thanking God for helping us live to see this day. Three blessings in all.

The Sabbath or festival ended at the following sundown, or a little after, when it was really dark out. And again, there was a ceremony involving wine, but this ceremony also included a lit candle, to symbolize that the holy day was over, and one could now light a fire. If a holiday starts on Saturday night, then you had to include all the parts of both ceremonies, since the Sabbath just ended, but a new festival had just started. But in what order?

So, the discussion began, with the eldest sage explaining the case under discussion.

"When a holiday starts right after the Sabbath, we have to say several blessings, which we'll indicate by letters. One on the wine, which we'll call W, E for the end of the Sabbath, C for the end-of-Sabbath candle, B for the beginning of the holiday, and L for life, that we were able to reach this day. In which order should these prayers be said?"

"Abaye?"

"W B L C E."

"Rava?"

"W B C E L."

"Rav?"

"W B C E!"

"Bear, what is all this about?" Xuanzang inquired.

"Those are letters in our alphabet. I hope you'll learn them soon. Each letter symbolizes a word that starts with that letter. Wine starts with W, Candle with C, End of a day with E, blessing for the Beginning of the day with B, Life with L."

"So many opinions about the order of these things?"

Bear laughed quietly. "I rather suspect that we aren't done yet."

"Hang on, Bear—we've had W B L C E", "W B C E L", and now "W B C E". What happened to L for Life?"

Bear scratched his head. He was so used to the sages arguing, that he often didn't pay much attention to the details. He tapped on the shoulder of a young sage in the row in front of him. The sage turned around. He had a wispy black beard.

"Excuse me?"

"Yes?" said the sage.

"Why are some of the sages including 'Life' in their lists, and others don't?"

"Ah. Some of them are referring to the last day of Passover, which is the tail end of a holiday, not the first day of a holiday. So 'Life' isn't relevant in that case.

Bear couldn't resist asking. "By the way, in what order do you think it should be?"

"I am an unlearned man. I don't dare have an opinion on such matters."

The young sage turned back to face the center of the room, while Bear explained to Xuanzang.

Xuanzang understood, but realized that this explanation in itself was twisted.

"That means that they are arguing about the details of a case, but half the sages are talking about one case, and the rest about another.

To this Bear had an unsatisfactory answer. "It doesn't seem to bother the other the sages."

The discussion continued.

"Rabba?"

"W E C B."

"Levi?"

"B C W E!"

The orderly discussion broke down. A group of sages in the far corner shouted out "B W C E". Mar, son of Rabbana, who sat next to Pigsy, yelled that the order is "C B W E". A Sage named Marta said in the name of Rabbi Jehoshua that the proper order is "C E W B".

Xuanzang was getting a headache.

Monkey shouted out "C E W B!"

Xuanzang was shocked.

"Do you have any idea of what this is really about?"

"No," chuckled our dear Monkey, "but they're having such an enjoyable time, I thought I would help!"

Nobody paid much attention to Monkey, or to anybody else for that matter. After a while, they all dispersed and went home for the Sabbath meal, continuing to argue as they went.

Xuanzang was confused. He turned to Bear, "Isn't there one way? A correct way? It's not like some are disciples of Kong-Tzu, some of Lao-Tzu, and others of the Buddha. You only have one tradition here."

"Ah, we all follow the same way, but disagree on a few minor points. Well, many minor points, actually, and, come to think of it, quite a few major ones too. In the end they'll decide on the proper Way, but the alternate ideas will stay around, you never know when they'll be useful. As the saying goes, 'There are seventy faces to the Way'."

"Master, Old Monkey knows it. It's a warrior's pleasure to play with weapons and joust to see who is more skilled. And foreign sages battle with words. It's their pleasure!"

"I may yet learn something from you, my simian disciple." Xuanzang smiled.

"As we foreigners say: "who is the wise one? The one who learns from every man." And every monkey as well, if I may be bold enough to add to the old saying. By the way, I've organized a nice treat for us. As honored foreign guests, you'll join Rav Nachman and his wife Yalta for dinner tonight."

We don't know what will happen at the Sabbath dinner; let's find out in the next chapter.

WINE

Our Foreign Guide, Bear, had arranged for our friends to eat the Sabbath meal with Sage Nachman and his wife, Yalta. Xuanzang and Monkey were pleased, but not as excited as Pigsy. He was so ecstatic he could only utter a series of porcine grunts and squeals.

Bear laughed.

"Yes, there'll be plenty of food. Not all vegetarian, but our hosts will make special food for you."

"Is Lady Yalta a good cook?" Pigsy asked anxiously.

"She doesn't cook, her servants do. She is a royal descendant, practically a princess. Sage Nachman, on the other hand, makes a point of preparing some of the Sabbath food himself, in honor of the holy day."

It was a short walk to Sage Nachman's house. They were ushered in and led to a dining room.

Sage Nachman explained, "If there were just two or three of us, we would sit or lean on couches, in the Roman style. But there are too many of us here tonight, so we'll sit around the table."

Xuanzang was seated to the right of Sage Nachman, with Bear, Monkey and Pigsy seated next to him. Sage Ulla, was also an honored guest, and sat on Sage Nachman's left. Sage Nachman's wife, Lady Yalta, wearing an embroidered dress, sat at the far end of the table.

The meal began with Sabbath prayer said over a cup of wine.

Servants then brought jugs of water out for everybody to wash their hands. Sage Nachman asked Ulla to say the prayer over the loaves of bread. Our Monk Xuanzang folded his hands and quietly recited his own prayer. The loaves of bread were then torn to pieces and distributed to everyone at the table.

Xuanzang spoke to their host, "Kind Sage, you have prepared the type of feast we are accustomed to back home. How did you learn of our eating habits?"

"Your guide, Bear, told me that you don't eat meat. And the secrets of Eastern cooking are known in this part of the world, as are your tea and silk."

"I forget that though few travel in search of scriptures or wisdom, many travel for trade and money," said Xuanzang.

"How are you impressed with our part of the world so far?"

"I have been in many places. People are both the same and different everywhere, but, I have never been in a land where the sages enjoy arguing as much as your people do. In the Tang lands, since the days when Sage Confucius walked the land, everybody knows their place, and everybody knows the rules. Here, everybody obeys the rules, but there are many opinions as to what the rules actually are. In all my travels, I have never seen a people so fond of arguing."

"It's true. But these are all arguments within the family." Sage Nachman answered.

"Family?"

"Extended family", Nachman explained. Everybody is descended from the same ancestor long ago."

"Oh! A clan! A very large one, but a clan nonetheless."

The meal went on. Even Pigsy had his fill. Finally, it was time for the thanksgiving prayer after the meal. Sage Nachman asked Ulla to say the prayer and passed him the traditional cup of wine. Everybody was silent while Ulla thanked their God for their meal, only answering "Amen" occasionally. Monkey wanted to do so as well, but he wasn't sure when was the correct time to say it, so he waited for Ulla to finish. When Ulla was done, he said the blessing over the wine, drank from the cup, and passed it to Sage Nachman. Sage Nachman sipped a little, and said, "Ulla, please pass the cup to my wife Yalta, as it is auspicious for childbearing."

Ulla didn't want to bother. "Women have no need for such a blessing," he said. "They are blessed indirectly, through their men, according to what Rabbi Yoḥanan said numerous times — 'The fruit of a woman's body is blessed only from the fruit of a man's body,' as it is stated in the Bible, "and He will love you, and bless you, and make you numerous, and He will bless the fruit of your body," 'your' being in the masculine gender."

Lady Yalta, being royalty, was not pleased with this in the least. Her face turned red, she clenched her hands, set her jaw, and stomped away from the table.

All were shocked. Monkey recognized a warrior gone berserk when he saw one. Even he'd be afraid to face her in this mood.

Every person has a warrior's berserk side buried inside. In some, it is buried very deep, in others, it lies in a shallow pit, always ready to jump out. The Buddha's teachings can bury it very deep indeed, deep enough that it shrinks and dies. Perhaps the teachings of Hillel can accomplish the same.

Xuanzang got up, "Maybe with my teachings I can calm her down. Such anger is not good for the soul."

"Master, you have never been in such a rage yourself. Let Old Monkey try, I know what anger is."

Monkey left the room and looked for Lady Yalta. He didn't see her, but he could hear her stomping downstairs. He followed her into the wine cellar. A lamp had been lit down there before the Sabbath to allow the servants to bring up wine. With his diamond eyes he could see Yalta clearly even in the dim light; she was a demon now, not a lady. She was kicking one of the barrels in the bottom row. It took a few kicks, but she managed to break one of the staves, and the barrel collapsed, flooding the cellar floor with wine. She started kicking a second cask but turned when Monkey gave a loud whistle.

He held a barrel stave out to her; she stared at him before nodding and accepting the stave. Monkey picked up another one and glanced at her; again, she nodded, then roared. Monkey gave out a yell, and the two of them ran up and down between the barrels, smashing them as they went. Monkey lost count, but there were hundreds of smashed barrels; they were knee-deep in wine, and you could get drunk just from the smell.

Meanwhile, back upstairs, everybody else sat frozen in place, listening in shock to the roars of rage and the shattering of the barrels. Finally, Sage Nachman said to Ulla, "Send her another cup, perhaps it will calm her down."

Perhaps, Sage Nachman did not know his wife very well, or perhaps he wanted to teach Ulla a lesson. We will never know.

Ulla poured another cup and gave instructions to the servant.

"Give this wine to Lady Yalta and tell her that all of the wine from this bottle counts as wine of blessing; although you did not drink from the cup of blessing itself, you may at least drink from the same bottle."

The servant took the wine, as instructed, and found Yalta standing next to Monkey, knee deep in wine, panting, and still holding the stave. He gave her Ulla's message and reached out to hand the cup of wine to her. She hit the cup with the stave and sent it flying. Then she spat and gave him a message for Ulla, "From beggars like Ulla, one gets meaningless words, and from rags one gets lice!"

The servant turned and ran up the stairs. Monkey bowed

to Yalta, "Well done, Sister!" he said, and joined his comrades upstairs.

Thus ended an otherwise delightful Friday night meal.

Xuanzang sighed. His dear Monkey, Sun Wukong, had learned much on their previous Journey, but perfection was hard to achieve. Nor did any of the sages present at this unfortunate meal seem likely candidates to accompany our travelers home as teachers from a far-off community; Ulla had triggered such anger in Yalta, and if Nachman had been wiser, the entire situation could have been avoided. Even if he did want to convince Nachman to return with them, he would undoubtedly bring Yalta along, unleashing a Western version of Monkey on the innocent citizens of Kaifeng.

A proper Buddhist never despairs, because a proper Buddhist never has hopes. Yet Xuanzang had another Buddhist quality — compassion. He had compassion for the blue-hat people of Kaifeng, and he really wanted to find them a teacher. This entire Journey was for that goal, and so far he'd had no success.

The four of them made their way back to the inn and went to sleep.

In the morning, Bear woke his companions and they returned to the synagogue for the morning prayers. Xuanzang was pleased to see that they read from the Scriptures, but there was one point during the prayers that confused him.

"Bear, why did some of the men go to the front, cover their heads and chant something? Everybody was very quiet when that was happening."

"Those were the priests. They were blessing everybody. A blessing written in our scriptures, the Torah."

"Priests? Xuanzang asked. "They don't look like priests. They don't look any different from anybody else."

"Generations ago they dressed in special clothing in the

temple, but now that the temple is gone they wear the same clothes as everybody does."

"So how do they become priests?"

Bear explained. "It's hereditary. They're born into the priesthood."

"Hereditary going how far back?"

"A millennium and a half, more or less."

Xuanzang nodded, "That would be the early Zhou dynasty, or maybe even late Shang."

"I wouldn't know," said Bear. "It predates our own kingdoms. The priesthood started when we left Egypt, we were slaves there for centuries."

"You don't behave like slaves."

Bear laughed, "I guess not. I rather suspect that we didn't behave like slaves even when we were slaves."

The prayers finished and the congregation dispersed. Everybody was headed home for lunch, the second Sabbath meal.

We don't know what will befall our travelers at lunch; let's find out in the next chapter.

Karma

Our Tang Monk Xuanzang, and his disciples Monkey and Pigsy, were spending the Sabbath day in the same small town. They left the prayer hall with their Foreign Guide, Bear.

"Rav Nachman has arranged for us to eat lunch at his friend Sheshet's house," Bear explained, "he just told Sheshet that we were foreign dignitaries, he didn't tell him any details about you."

"Dignitaries? Master may be dignified, but I'm not! Nor is Pigsy!" Monkey said.

"You are dignitaries because you represent a far-off kingdom, not because you are dignified. Sheshet won't judge you by your appearance, because he can't see."

"A relief for Pig! Even on our first Journey people thought I was ugly. Here, though they've mostly been polite, it is still plain that they don't like the clan of hogs!"

As they walked, Xuanzang noticed that narrow alleys, bounded by stone walls, led off the main street. Most of the alleys led to courtyards around which clustered several houses. Xuanzang recognized this from other places he had visited. Many of the household activities, such as cooking and clothes washing, took place in these common courtyards.

But there was something odd about this area. Some alleys were dead ends, others were open at both ends. There was one that led to a large pit. Each alley opening had a different marking. One had a straight beam going across it, another, a crooked beam. One had boards on the sides, another was raised a step above the main street, and so on.

"Bear, what are these alleys?"

Bear stopped a passerby who explained, "Ah, this is the Test Neighborhood. I'm surprised you have not heard of it. The sages test different ideas of how to define alleys, courtyards and such; for the Sabbath rules, you know."

"And for arguments, no doubt," Bear added

The passerby laughed and went on his way.

They followed Bear down an alley with boards nailed to the walls every few handbreadths and stepped through a broken section of the wall to enter Sheshet's courtyard.

"Is our host so poor that he can't afford to fix the wall?" Xuanzang asked.

"No, it's just a Sabbath test section. Regular gates don't generate enough arguments."

Sheshet's servant met them at the door and ushered them inside. Sheshet was seated in the dining hall, hands folded on his lap. "Welcome, honored guests! Welcome!

"Who do we have here? A gentleman from the hog family…a frisky monkey…a religious man from the Far East, and a large local man."

Xuanzang stood still and remained quiet, but Monkey couldn't restrain himself, "Bear! You were teasing us! Telling us nonsense about Sheshet!"

"What nonsense?"

"That he can't see."

"But he can't." said Bear.

"So how did he…?"

Sheshet interrupted with a laugh.

THE SECOND JOURNEY

"I am blind, but you introduced yourselves as soon as you walked in the door."

Our travelers looked confusedly at each other. Sheshet nodded towards Pigsy.

"We don't eat pigs here, but some of our neighbors do, so the smell is familiar; but, from the sound of your hoof-steps you clearly walk on two feet. Your friend is either a monkey or a child who can't keep still; I can hear his fur rubbing on his coat as he walks, so he is not a child. Your master is silent and walks slowly, obvious signs of a scholar; add to that the unmistakable sound of silk clothing and I know you are either extremely wealthy or come from the land of silk."

Monkey wasn't convinced, "Silence is a sign of a scholar?"

Xuanzang answered, "Do not speak—unless it improves on silence."

Sheshet replied, "Speak little but do much, and receive all men with a pleasant countenance."

"Silence is an empty space; space is the home of the awakened mind," said Xuanzang.

"I grew up among the sages, and in all of my days, I have found nothing better for a person than silence." Sheshet said.

"Know from the rivers in clefts and in crevices: those in small channels flow noisily, the great flow silent. Whatever's not full makes noise. Whatever is full is quiet." Xuanzang added.

Sheshet replied. "A time for reaping and a time for sewing; a time for silence and a time for speaking."

The two men bowed to one another and remained silent. The others dared not speak, for it would break the spell. And who would want to be called 'not full'?

The servant broke the spell, "Will Master and the gentlemen like to eat lunch now?"

Sheshet nodded and the servant led them to the dining hall.

As they walked, the two sages chatted.

"I see that in your lands, far to the East, your ideas of wisdom are similar to ours."

"In some ways they are, though your fellow sages seem to enjoy argument far more than we are used to." Xuanzang noted.

Sheshet laughed. "Argument is a national pastime; the sport of the wise. Personally, I prefer the calmer forms of that sport, though there are some who view it like a gladiators' contest."

"Your people are scattered all over the world."

"Indeed, they are," Sheshet replied. "I understand they are all argumentative to one degree or another.

"Have you ever considered traveling to far-off lands to teach your distant brothers?"

"Travel? I manage fine here; I know where everything is. A man with my vision isn't meant to travel far."

They reached the dining room and the servant indicated where each man should sit. He brought out bowls and spoons for all, followed by a huge pot of steaming food.

Sheshet explained. "This is a special Sabbath meal. We call it Hamin, it means hot, or maybe we should call it a hot pot."

"Why is it special?"

"We do not cook on the Sabbath, so the food is prepared ahead of time, and left overnight on hot coals. It cooks slowly and has a special taste; some say it has the taste of Heaven."

Pigsy knew about food. "Where we come from, most food is cooked quickly."

"This pot is usually a mix of vegetables, beans, meat and rice, but I heard that you eat a vegetarian diet, so this week we made it without meat."

"What will you eat?" asked Xuanzang.

"I will eat the same food as my guests. And do not worry, this is a new pot, it has never been used for cooking meat."

Sheshet made a blessing over the wine, then they washed their hands and shared the bread. The servant ladled large portions of the Hamin into each bowl. They all ate slowly, except Pigsy, who had finished his bowl before the servant had finished serving everyone. His bowl, needless to say, was refilled over and over again, while Xuanzang and Sheshet exchanged words of wisdom.

"How can you weigh a large elephant?" asked Xuanzang

"Load it on a boat and draw a line to mark how deep the boat sinks into the water. Then take out the elephant and load the boat with stones until it sinks to the same line. Finally, weigh the stones."

"When is a cupful of water more than the water of the ocean?" asked Sheshet.

"A cupful of water given in compassion to one's parents or a sick person brings eternal merit, but the water of an ocean will someday come to an end.

Sheshet nodded. "I see that there is indeed wisdom in the East. Perhaps your disciples can teach me something as well?"

"Monkey, would you like to share some wisdom with us?"

"Old Monkey spent many years with different masters, but I never had the patience to learn anything of the mind properly, only the wisdom of the body, traveling on magic clouds, changing, fighting with my compliant golden-hooped rod. That sort of thing."

"And you, Sage Pig?"

"Oh, I'm an Idiot. I know nothing except how to eat, carry a load, and wield my nine-pronged rake. I barely know my own name."

"And what name is that?"

"The Bodhisattva calls me 'Heavenly Tumbleweed,' but most call me Eight-Rules Pig."

Sheshet was curious, "Why do they call you Eight Rules?"

"Right view, right thought, right speech, right behavior, right livelihood, right effort, right mindfulness and right concentration."

"Eight indeed. Eight that are quite lofty goals. Do you accomplish all of these?"

"I am an Idiot Pig, I can only try."

"We all can only try. But Xuanzang, my apologies for not pronouncing your name properly, does your teaching provide the rules of society, what must be adhered to by the community?"

"We teach universal compassion, but our rules are for the individual, not the community." Xuanzang explained.

"What, then, is the source of the community rules in your lands?" Sheshet asked. "There must be some order if humans are to live together in peace."

"Those are the teachings of Confucius. He lived about a thousand years ago."

"Ah, maybe in the time of Ezra the scribe."

"Your earliest Sage?" Xuanzang asked.

"No, that would be Moses."

"An elderly sage? Carries a shepherd's staff? Stutters?"

"Yes, but how…?"

"Most questions should be answered clearly and honestly, but some are best answered with silence."

Sheshet remained silent for a few moments. "One sometimes wonders if we, the sages of today, will be remembered a thousand years from now."

"One cannot know such things. One can only do his best."

"Who was the founder of your faith?" Sheshet asked.

"The Buddha."

"I assume he was the first of your teachers, just like Moses was ours."

"First teacher, but not the first Buddha. The fourth, actually. Ah, I see you are confused. 'Buddha' is a title for those who have achieved enlightenment but is also the name of our first teacher. There are destined to be a total of one thousand Buddhas."

"Different than our Thirty-Six Righteous Ones. There are always thirty-six. If one dies, another is born. But some say that the Thirty-Six are all of us, and that anyone who does a good deed is of the Thirty-Six at that moment. So, there are always people doing good things somewhere."

"We say that anyone can become a Buddha, but that there will only be one thousand total, for all time."

They went back to eating their Hamin, which was cooling off. In the meantime, Eight- Rules Pigsy had applied Right Concentration and Right Effort to finish twelve bowls. Sheshet had noticed the constant clicking of the spoon on the bowl, as well as the slurping sounds of Pigsy eating.

"Master Eight-Rules Pig, how much have you eaten?"

"Twelve bowlfuls, my kind host."

"In your lands, do you have a word for future payment for today's actions?"

"Of course," said Xuanzang. "You mean Karma, every action has an effect."

Sheshet smiled, "There is a special karma for those who eat too much Hamin at once."

"And what is that?"

"Some questions are best answered with silence."

Xuanzang bowed his head in understanding. What a shame that Sheshet wasn't willing or able to travel. He would have made a fine teacher in Kaifeng. They finished their meal, listened to Sheshet say the grace afterward, eventually returning to their inn for the night.

"It is common to rest on Sabbath afternoon, especially after eating Hamin." Bear explained. They lay down, and napped quietly, except for Pigsy, who snored loudly.

An hour went by, and Pigsy's snores had turned into groans. Monkey lay in his bed and listened.

"Idiot, be quiet! No one can sleep!"

"I'm in horrible pain! I think the Hamin's Karma has caught up with me."

"So soon?"

"My stomach is exploding. This will be the end of Old Pig. Maybe I'm pregnant again!"

"Nonsense, Idiot. Just indigestion."

Pigsy stopped talking and let out a groan. Xuanzang rose and came over to where he lay, "Pigsy, what is it?"

"Remember when we drank from that river and got pregnant? This is worse. I won't make it. Pray for my soul. If I must be reincarnated, may it be in a better form."

Xuanzang looked at Monkey.

"Monkey, how much of that Hamin did you eat?"

"Most of a bowlful."

"And how do you feel?" asked Xuanzang.

"A little heavy in the stomach. That food digests slowly. And a little gassy."

"I feel the same, Xuanzang, said Pigsy, how much of the Hamin did you eat?"

"Eighteen bowlfuls, Master."

"You were warned about the karma after twelve bowls, yet you ate six more?"

"Yes, Master. And now I will die."

Pigsy stopped speaking and went back to groaning, clutching his stomach. Xuanzang considered for a moment. Pig's belly did look much larger than usual. Maybe he really was pregnant. Maybe they should go back and ask Sheshet for advice or an

THE SECOND JOURNEY

antidote. Pigsy screamed in pain, they heard a loud ripping sound, followed by pathetic whimpering.

"Monkey, he's an idiot pig, but he is my disciple! He's being ripped apart from inside! What shall we do?"

Our dear Monkey laughed, "Master, do you smell anything?"

"A horrible smell! His guts are exploding!"

"The only thing exploding are his farts, Master. Let's move him outside, or we'll all suffocate." Xuanzang could only agree with Old Monkey's diagnosis of porcine flatulence, so they proceeded to drag Pigsy outside. Bear heard the racket and got up.

"What are you doing?"

Monkey laughed. "Idiot Pigsy needs a ninth rule: 'don't eat too much'! He ate eighteen bowls of Hamin, and now we need to move him outside, so we don't die from his gas."

Bear roared with laughter, grabbed the whimpering hog around the waist, picked him up, and stomped outside. He let Pigsy down gently under the shade of a tree.

"By sunset he'll have worked his way through the worst of it. Eighteen bowls! We should call him 'Eighteen Bowls' instead of Eight Rules"

"Old Monkey will call him 'Eighteen Farts.'"

Xuanzang gave him a look that could freeze the blood of any immortal monkey. "You are right, Master. No new names for Pigsy. He has enough already."

Bear agreed.

"Everybody has enough names already. We have to stay here till nightfall, when the Sabbath is over, so we can only start traveling again tomorrow morning."

We don't know what further adventures our travelers will encounter; let's find out in the next chapter.

BANDITS

On Sunday morning, after the Sabbath, our travelers gathered in the inn courtyard to prepare for their departure. Xuanzang sat stop his noble donkey steed, accompanied by his two disciples, Monkey and Pigsy. Bear, their Foreign Guide, joined them as well.

Their few belongings were packed and loaded onto Pigsy's shoulders. The donkey carried some provisions, but was not overloaded, as he had to carry Xuanzang as well. As they were leaving, a local sage approached and asked if he could join them.

Bear explained, "It's Master Yochanan, the son of the blacksmith. A very well-known sage. He wants to go to Tiberius and thus must head in the same general direction as we. It's dangerous to travel these roads alone; too many bandits and murderers around."

One of our travelers was quite pleased. "Old Monkey will finally have a chance for some exercise! My Compliant Rod will turn some bandits into meat patties!"

"Careful, there are those who would like to sacrifice us to their goddess. Not as meat patties, but we won't feel too healthy even if we're just cut up into pieces and tossed on a fire."

They started on their way, Sage Yochanan walking next to Monk Xuanzang.

"Sage Yochanan, you didn't pack anything for this journey."

THE SECOND JOURNEY

"I don't own much."

Xuanzang sighed, "I, too, should have few possessions; just my simple clothing and my food-begging bowl. Unfortunately, I have become famous in my own land, and was showered with gifts before this Journey. I expect we'll lose our excess possessions before we complete this mission."

"I had possessions, an inheritance from my parents. A small house and fields. I sold them all to support myself while I studied. I exchanged what God created in six days for what it took him forty days to deliver."

"Sage Yochanan, what does that mean?"

"Our tradition is that God created the physical world in six days, then rested on the seventh day; that is why we rest on the Sabbath, the seventh day of the week. But the Torah, the Teachings, took longer. Sage Moses ascended Mount Sinai and remained for forty days before he returned with the Torah."

"Sage Moses? Elderly gentleman with a rough shepherd's staff? Has a speech impediment?"

"Yes! Xuanzang, how did you know that?"

"Sages must know one another.

"One who speaks wise words, even if he is of the nations of the world, is called a wise man."

"Sage Yochanan, it is an honor to join you on this trip."

They continued on their way, chatting wisely of this and that, as sages are wont to do among themselves. Xuanzang wondered if he had finally found the teacher he was looking for.

They traveled without incident for a few days, and after traveling a hundred *li* came to a marshy area dense with trees and thorny bushes. They meandered through the marsh, trying to stick to the drier parts. Occasionally they crossed small streams. The going was slow, and their shoes, feet and hooves were weighed down with mud. Nobody complained, but the only happy traveler was Pigsy, who was happy as only a pig in mud can be.

Suddenly, dozens of bandits emerged from the woods. Xuanzang and Sage Yochanan were terrified, and in their confusion tried to flee. Unfortunately, the bushes were far too dense, making escape impossible. Monkey viewed these Western Bandits as a minor nuisance and changed his Compliant Rod to be the length of a man. He and Bear charged at the bandits, with Pigsy trailing close behind. They were about to drive off the raiders when their leader, a priest wearing a red robe covered with crane feathers, tossed a magic net over them, and they were immobilized, like flies trapped in a spider's web.

The bandits ordered them to take off their clothes so they could search for gems and jewels. Xuanzang was going to have his wish fulfilled, all of his worldly possessions would be taken from him. Though it did not end there, the bandits had further plans. Being worshippers of the Indian warrior goddess Durga, every year they would find a handsome man of good quality to be offered as a sacrifice to the deity to pray for happiness and blessing.

Upon seeing that both our Tang Monk and Sage Yochanan were handsome in appearance, they looked at each other with pleased expressions. "The season for the sacrifice to the deity is drawing near, and we could not find a suitable man. Now we have found two men with a nice and refined appearance. It is auspicious for us to take them both as sacrifices!"

Xuanzang was worried, "I would not dare begrudge this filthy and ugly body of mine as a sacrifice to the deity, but I have come from a far distance with the intention of learning the wisdom of the West. If you gentlemen kill me before my intention has been fulfilled, it will, I am afraid, be inauspicious for you."

A wicker chair was brought forth for the leader. He sat and

fanned himself with a crane feather fan.

"A sacrifice we need, and a sacrifice you will be."

Everybody begged for mercy on behalf of the two sages. Bear even volunteered to substitute for them, but the bandits would not consent. The bandit leader sent his men to fetch water and clear the ground in the marsh to prepare an altar. He ordered two men with their swords unsheathed to lead the sages to the altar.

To the bandits' amazement, Xuanzang showed no sign of fear. Sage Yochanan was not as calm but appeared resigned and braced himself for the inevitable. Feeling that he would not be spared, our Tang Monk said to the bandits, "Please grant me a little time, so I may die happily and with an easy mind."

Then he concentrated his mind on the Tusita Palace and meditated on Maitreya Bodhisattva, praying to be born in that place, pay homage and make offerings to the Bodhisattva, and to receive the Yogacarabhumi Sastra from him. Then he would be reborn to enlighten these people and make them practice superior deeds and abandon all evil actions.

Xuanzang had met many Daoist priests in Tang lands and during his travels, so he realized that the bandit leader had the appearance and behavior of a Dao Immortal. Sage Yochanan had no way of knowing this, but seeing how calm Xuanzang was, decided to use the few moments left to him to review his learning of the Way.

"If two people are grasping a cloak, one says, "I found it!" and the other says, "I found it!," or one says, "It's all mine!" and the other says, "It's all mine!", and they each swear they don't own less than half of the cloak, then they split the cloak. One says, "It's all mine!" and the other says, "It's half mine!", the one who says, "It's all mine!" swears he doesn't own less than three quarters and the one who says, "It's half mine" swears he doesn't own less than one quarter, then the former takes three quarters, and the latter takes one quarter."

Xuanzang worshipped the Buddhas of the ten quarters and sat in meditation, concentrating his mind on Maitreya Bodhisattva. While he was in contemplation, it was as if he had ascended Mount Sumeru and transcended the first, the second, and the third heavens, seeing Maitreya Bodhisattva at the Wonderful and Precious Terrace in the Tusita Palace. In this moment, he had forgotten all about the bandits.

Yochanan continued:

> "If two men were riding on an animal, or one was riding and the other was leading the animal, and one of them said, "The animal is all mine," and the other said "It's all mine," they each swear that they don't own less than half of the animal and they split it. If after the case is settled, they both admit to the other's claim, or, if there are witnesses, they can split the animal without an oath."

Pigsy and Bear were wailing and weeping, while Monkey gnashed his teeth in anger and frustration. Suddenly a black wind rose from the four quarters, flattening the trees and blowing leaves and dust into the air. The superstitious bandits, greatly frightened, asked, "From where does this foreign sage come?"

Bear explained, "This is the monk Xuanzang from the Tang Empire in the East, seeking wisdom in our lands. If you kill him, you will have committed a deadly sin. The windstorm shows that our God is enraged; it would befit you to make a quick repentance."

The bandits were fearful and begged for pardon one after another. They prostrated themselves before the Tang Monk, but he was unconscious of them. When they touched him, he opened his eyes and asked, "Is it time now?"

"We dare not harm the teacher. May you accept our repentance?"

Xuanzang accepted their apology and told them that evil deeds such as killing, thieving, and worshipping improper deities would cause one to suffer pains in Hell in the future. "Why should you sow the seeds of suffering for an unlimited time just for the sake of a corporeal body which lasts no longer than a fleeting moment, like the lightning or the morning dew?"

The bandits prostrated themselves and apologized, saying, 'Our thoughts were erroneous and upside-down. We did what we should not do and served the deity whom we should not serve. Had we not met this teacher, we would have never heard such inspiring instructions! From today onward we shall stop this banditry career!'

Their leader presented his crane-feather fan to Xuanzang, asking, "May I be your student and disciple?"

"Each man should follow the customs of his own people. May I suggest that you study with Sage Yochanan here?"

"Sage Yochanan, you are the most beautiful man I have ever seen. If you were a woman, I would marry you today!"

"What is your name, reformed bandit?" asked Yochanan.

"Shimon."

"Shimon. Shimon of Lakish? The student who became a gladiator?"

"That's me. Your foreign companion has convinced me to return to my studies."

"Join me," said Yochanan, "and you can marry my sister; her beauty will not disappoint you!"

Shimon and Yochanan left together, discussing the intricate details of the Temple incense recipe. Xuanzang was again disappointed by his search for a teacher. The rest of the bandits dispersed back to the homes and families they hadn't seen for many years.

We don't know what our travelers will encounter when they leave the marsh; let's find out in the next chapter.

Mother

"Do you have many marshes here, in the far West?" Xuanzang asked Bear.

"A few, Xuanzang. This is mostly dry land, but there are marshes here where the streams drain into the lake, and along the coast, where the hills block the flow of water to the sea."

"The Tang lands of the East are large, and we have many marshes. They attract both mosquitoes and bandits, much like here. The day may yet come when either the bandits or the mosquitoes will challenge the Heavenly Mandate itself."

"There is much to be said for stability, but there is little of that in our world." Bear replied.

"Where are we headed now?"

"There is a sage you should meet," said Bear. One who is wealthy, generous, and kind. I am sure that you will find some of the wisdom you seek from him."

"Very good! I am learning your wisdom, but I feel like I am missing something."

"We are meeting the most famous sages, what can be missing? Where else can I take you?"

"I am learning to speak your language, but I am not learning to read it. I owe a debt to the blue-hat people of Kaifeng. They don't need scriptures; they already have them. They need help in understanding them. I can understand your spoken language, but I can hardly read, let alone help to interpret your scriptures."

"I can teach you the basics as we travel, and maybe we will encounter a sage who can help you further. It is hard to read or write while we walk, but we can find time when we stop to eat. It will take us a couple of days to reach Sage Tarfon's town, we can begin our lessons this evening."

A few hours later they saw a small farmhouse in the distance. It was built of local gray stone, as was nearly everything in this foreign land, with a ladder leading up to a flat roof. As they approached, they saw that it was surrounded by a low stone fence, and that a few goats and hens were wandering in the otherwise neat yard. The farmer came out to greet them, "Forgive me for not coming out to meet you!"

He brought them into his courtyard. He had a thatched hut set aside for travelers, and brought out bread, wine, and vegetables to the courtyard for them.

"Excuse me for being impertinent, but where are you from?"

"These gentlemen are from the East, from the Empire of the Tang. I am Bear, originally from the Samarkand area, I now serve as their guide."

The farmer lifted his eyebrows. "Empire of the Tang? That must be very far away."

Xuanzang explained, "It is indeed far away. I am a local student, looking for wisdom in far-off lands."

"You are a very modest man, clearly an experienced sage rather than a mere student. The other travelers are your students?"

"Students, or perhaps disciples. They have traveled with me in the past."

"They have an unusual appearance."

Monkey had the answer to this. "We have round heads pointing to Heaven, and square feet walking on Earth. We have nine apertures and four limbs, entrails and cavities. In what manner do we differ from other people?"

Their host laughed, "The main difference is that you are wiser and have a sharper wit than most people. Welcome! I apologize for not inviting you to join me for my meal. I will be eating with my old mother. She needs to be slowly and carefully fed, and the presence of strangers, no matter how illustrious, may disturb her."

Monkey replied, "Centuries ago, before I was a Great Sage or Equal to Heaven, I was seeking the secret to immortality. I heard a woodman singing of a great teacher who could grant me the knowledge of that secret. I ran to him and asked if he knew.

"Oh, I don't know the secret!" he answered. "That song was taught to me by a Daoist immortal. He can teach you the secret."

"If you are a neighbor of the immortal, why don't you follow him in the cultivation of the Way? Wouldn't it be nice to learn from him the formula for eternal youth?" Monkey asked.

"My father unfortunately died, and my mother remained a widow. I had no brothers or sisters, so there was no alternative but for me alone to support and care for my mother. Now that my mother is growing old, I can't do more than chop two bundles of firewood to take to the market in exchange for a few pennies to buy a few pints of rice for the two of us."*

"So, I came to know the secret of immortality while he took care of his old mother. I am very proud of myself. My Master will tell you that I am sometimes quite arrogant. But when I remember that woodcutter, I know that he was the better person, mortal though he was."

"What of your own mother?

Monkey shrugged. "I have no mother. I was born from a stone egg."

Their host was taken aback, but collected himself, "I must go to my mother now. Maybe we will speak further in the morning."

Our travelers thanked him profusely as he took his leave.

Xuanzang pondered what they had just heard.

"Bear, filial piety is not limited to one land."

"Of course not, Xuanzang. It is correct and natural in any land and in every language."

They went to sleep in the thatched hut. Xuanzang and Bear spent their night thinking of their mothers, while Pigsy and Monkey, who did not have mothers thought instead of the Bodhisattva Guanyin, who was as close to a mother as they ever had.

They got an early start the next morning and wound their way uphill along mountain paths while the sun was low. A rustling sound followed by the appearance of a huge wild boar, startled Xuanzang, but it was simply a large pig, and it wasn't interested in them. Since the Tang travelers were all vegetarians, and their guide Bear did not eat pork, they weren't interested in it either.

Finally, they reached the highest point of the mountain range and started walking downhill. These Western mountains were small, practically hills when compared to the Snowy Mountains they had crossed on their first Journey. They eventually reached a flat plain that stretched towards a sea in the distance.

"What is that sea?" Xuanzang asked.

"We call it The Great Sea," Bear replied. "Many nations surround this sea, and hundreds of trading ships travel along these coasts; even your Tang silk reaches islands in the middle of this sea."

"It looks so peaceful."

"It isn't always, Xuanzang. Sometimes there are storms, the violence of Nature, and sometimes the violence of men, invaders, sea battles."

Xuanzang sighed, "It is the same everywhere. Men lack compassion and kill each other. They blame the gods, but it isn't the gods who raise the spear. Men should have compassion even for the tiny ant, let alone their fellow human; and even if the human is a pig or a monkey." Monkey and Pigsy chuckled, and they continued on their way.

"Do you see that manor in the distance? That is Sage Tarfon's house."

"It looks like a small city."

"He is very wealthy."

As they drew closer, it became clear that the small city surrounded a small palace. Bear led them through the town to the gates of the palace. Two unarmed guards stopped them. Bear was going to explain who they were, but Xuanzang decided to test his knowledge of the language.

"Sirs, we are travelers from the Tang lands of the East, who have come from afar to study the wisdom of the West. I am the monk Xuanzang, and these unusual-looking fellows are my loyal disciples, Monkey and Eight-Rules Pigsy. We have come here to meet Sage Tarfon."

Pigsy clumsily bowed, while Monkey leaped in the air and spun around.

The guards were expressionless as they watched this, but finally smiled at Monkey's antics.

"Welcome! Judging from your accent and your companions, you have indeed come from far away! Sage Tarfon is usually in the courtyard this time of day, keeping his old mother company."

As they walked into the courtyard, Pigsy spoke quietly to Monkey, in their civilized language, "Did you notice? The guards had no weapons!"

"Either Sage Tarfon has no enemies, or these guards don't need weapons."

The center of the courtyard was paved with flat, gray stones and was large enough to play cuju in. Stone benches were scattered along the edge of the enclosure, while vines grew toward the sky on wooden trellises. Water flowed in narrow channels through the middle of the courtyard, and colorful fresco paintings covered the walls of the courtyard. It was hard to believe people so remote from Tang lands enjoyed such luxury.

Xuanzang nodded towards a bearded man who was walking across the courtyard, an elderly woman on his arm. He wore a white blanket with purple stripes, in the Roman toga style, with blue and white fringes dangling from the corners.

"That must be Sage Tarfon. We will have to wait until he finishes with his mother. I dare not interrupt."

The sage led his mother around the courtyard, occasionally helping her over the water channels, or guiding her around rough spots in the paving. Various servants walked around quietly, performing their duties. There was no sign of the cooking and laundry that normally takes place in a courtyard. Xuanzang presumed that there was another courtyard in back where such activities took place.

As they watched, Sage Tarfon's mother caught her sandal on the edge of the water trench, and the strap across her foot broke. Sage Tarfon knelt and tried, without success, to fix it on the spot. One of the servants ran off, presumably to get another pair of sandals. Sage Tarfon remained on his knees in front of his mother; he placed his hands on the ground with his palms up. She looked at him, nodded, and stepped on his palms.

Thus, an odd walking performance started. Tarfon moved his hands, step by step, with his mother's feet on his hands. None of the servants or workmen paid much attention to what was happening. They made their way halfway across the courtyard before a servant ran up with a different pair of sandals.

"Bear, what did you make of this?"

"Sage Tarfon is known for his care in honoring his mother."

THE SECOND JOURNEY

"He is not a young man himself." Xuanzang noted.

"That does not negate his obligation to her. Did you notice something else?"

"Only that nobody was surprised at this. Even his mother wasn't surprised."

"Yes, Sage Tarfon's behavior is known and expected," Bear paused before adding, "I think you can meet him now."

Sage Tarfon washed his hands in the water channel and dried them on a cloth that a servant had brought to him. He walked over to greet his guests, "Please excuse me for not greeting you earlier."

Xuanzang bowed. "We saw that you were busy with your mother. "Those who practice filial piety will be born again into the way of blessing."

"I don't know about 'born again', but I do know that the day is short, there is much to do, the workmen are lazy, the reward is great, and the landowner is pressing them."

"You press your workers?"

Sage Tarfon laughed, "I don't really own anything. The reference is to the Holy One."

"The World-Master? The one who sits on a sapphire block?"

"World-Master, yes, it is he who owns everything, and we all work for him. But how do you know about the sapphire block? Have you read our scriptures?"

"Where we come from, the Tang Empire in the East, one needs to know the Jade Emperor. In this part of the world, one needs to know the World-Master. One of my goals for this trip is to learn how to read and understand your scriptures, but it's slow going. While I have gained some wisdom on this journey, I have made only limited progress with regard to reading your language."

"If you are as studious as you seem, I am sure you will succeed."

"I do hope to learn your language and more about your traditions. But I will never be as knowledgeable as your own sages, who have grown up with your traditions." Xuanzang answered.

"You are sage in your own traditions. There is no need for you to become a sage in ours as well," Tarfon replied.

"Some of your people live in our lands. They are in need of a teacher. I will make a poor teacher for them. And I have my own Buddhist duties to attend to, teaching and translating."

"So you are looking for a sage to return to your lands? Just as you are busy with your duties in your land, so our sages are busy here. It will be difficult to find one who will be willing to leave his work here and join you."

A servant ran up to the sage, and hurriedly whispered a few words.

"Oh. I've just heard some bad news. One of my colleagues is very ill. All of the sages are gathering to pray for him, but I cannot go, I must stay here with my mother."

"We'll go. Perhaps the prayers of travelers from the East will be of some help; and you will gain great merit for your filial loyalty."

"I only do what is my duty."

They bid the sage farewell and continued on their way.

"Bear, who is this sage who is ill?"

"He is known as 'The Master', though his name is Master Judah. He lives further north. It will take two days to reach his home. I hope we won't be too late."

The two days passed uneventfully. They traveled on the coastal Roman road and found that many others were walking the same path as they. When they reached The Master's house, this became clearer; his house was nearly as large as Sage Tarfon's, and his courtyard was even larger. The courtyard was

THE SECOND JOURNEY

filled with sages and scholars of every age and shape; and they were all praying for Master Judah's health.

"Master, we don't know their prayers! How can Pigsy and I help here?"

"Just recite whatever sutras you can remember, Monkey."

"Shall I go and...?"

"Monkey, it is best that we don't interfere with things here too much. If the Master is destined to live, he'll live. If not, then he will not. Don't go down to Yama in the realm of the dead and 'fix' his records, as you've done in the past. These people have their own realm for the dead, so you won't find their records with Yama."

Monkey recited the Sutras he had learned, while Pigsy recited his eight rules, as that was all he knew. Bear joined the sages in their prayers, and Xuanzang prayed as well. After a while they realized that the crowd wasn't static. People were slowly filing into The Master's house, then coming back out to the courtyard. Bear explained.

"There's an obligation to visit the ill, and there's a belief that each person who visits the ill takes away a small part of the sickness away with him."

As they spoke, they found themselves drifting into the house. Xuanzang signaled his disciples to be quiet and just follow the line that was snaking in and out of the sickroom.

The Master was lying in bed, propped up on some cushions. His face was thin, and a sickly yellow color. His eyes were closed, and he was breathing laboriously through his open mouth; each breath an infinity of effort. There was no doubt that he was going to die soon. Xuanzang realized that he should be dead, that it was only the endless prayers that were keeping him alive. The sages in the courtyard had accumulated great merit, and their prayers were preventing The Master from being freed of his suffering. If they stopped even for a few seconds, The Master would immediately die. It was unlikely that a Western Sage could achieve Nirvana, but surely, he had great merit and would reenter life in a good form.

Once they were outside again, Xuanzang looked around the courtyard. During normal times, it was probably quite neat, but with the sickness and the crowds, it had accumulated some refuse. Sure enough, there were some empty clay jugs piled up in a corner. Xuanzang knew what needed to be done. There was enough suffering in the world, without adding onto it this way.

He called Monkey over, and quietly explained his plan.

"I'll do it! I'll do it."

Dear Monkey. He ran over to the pile of jugs, picked up the largest one he could find, and scrambled up a ladder to the roof of the house. He waited until there was a gap in the crowd, and dashed the jug down into the courtyard, where it shattered on the paving stones. The sages were momentarily startled. The prayers stopped, a cold wind blew over the crowd, and the prayers were replaced by lamentations.

Bear led them off to a far corner of the courtyard, hoping that they could escape condemnation from the gathered sages. At first, there were a few glances in their direction, then one by one sages approached and asked to speak privately with Monkey. Monkey went under a small archway, so they could speak with him quietly. Xuanzang watched Monkey carefully, but Monkey kept his cool, merely nodding as the sages spoke to him.

Finally, the discussions ended, and Monkey returned to his companions once again.

"What was it?"

"It is all right Master! It's okay! They were thanking me. They knew it was time but they did not want it to happen."

"Yes," Xuanzang sighed, "if they knew of the Buddha's way,

perhaps they wouldn't have needed you to break the spell of their prayers."

Bear wasn't convinced of this. "Suffering and death are part of life. No teaching can change that."

Xuanzang explained with a story:

> "Once there was an ugly woman. She married late in life and only had one child, a boy. Her husband was older, and died, leaving her a widow with only her son, who was everything in her life.
>
> "One day, the son got sick and died as well. The woman was heartbroken and so, she went door to door, seeking someone or something to bring her son back to life. Nobody could help her, until finally someone directed her to the Buddha. She went in anguish to the Buddha and told him her tale.
>
> "'Please, please bring my son back to life.'"
>
> "'I can easily bring your son back to life, but first you must bring me a mustard seed.'"
>
> "'A mustard seed?'"
>
> "'Yes, that's all that's needed. But you must bring it from a house that has never seen sorrow.'"
>
> Needless to say, there was no such house. Suffering is universal."

"That's what I'm saying. Suffering is universal. There is no 'cure' for it," Bear said.

"Bear, there is."

"What? How?"

"All suffering is a result of desire, of uncontrolled craving. You are attached to your body, you crave it, so if your body suffers, you suffer. You crave your family, your friends, so, if they suffer, you suffer. If you remove these desires, these obsessions, from your heart, you will have found the way to escape the cycle of suffering."

"Have you succeeded in doing this?" Bear asked.

"I believe so."

Bear thought for a moment. "If your disciple Monkey was destroyed, would you suffer?"

"I shudder at the very thought, which shows that despite my many years, I have not yet trained my heart completely."

"I do not want to train my heart. God wants us to feel emotion, to love, knowing that love can lead to pain. I can understand your vegetarian diet, and your concern for animals. Maybe not for the ants and moths, but certainly for the horses and donkeys of this world. Compassion is good, but to avoid passion? Not for me!"

Our travelers left the mourning sages behind them, and resumed their Journey, we don't know what wisdom they will acquire next; let's find out in the next chapter.

Letters

Our Guide, Bear, led our travelers away from the lamenting sages. He was followed by Sage Xuanzang on his donkey, Pigsy, and Old Monkey.

After some hours of walking, they came to a small stream and sat on rocks in the shade of a large tree.

"Let's get started on our reading lessons," Bear suggested to Xuanzang.

"I'll be glad to. I'm not sure that my disciples are interested."

"Old Monkey would like to try. I've already picked up some knowledge."

"These language lessons aren't for an Idiot Pig. I'll never learn it."

"If I can learn it, so can you!"

The voice was sudden and unfamiliar. The four of them looked around, but there was nobody else there.

"I'd expect you to know about talking animals!"

It was the donkey!

Monkey and Pigsy were in shock. Xuanzang admonished them, "Surely you, my loyal disciples, are aware that beasts can attain humanity through self-cultivation."

"You're right! You're right," said Monkey. "It's just that it is rare to meet such people, especially in these Western lands."

"I know it's true. How can a pig walking on two legs think

otherwise? But what was Donkey before he joined us? Our last horse was the White Dragon Prince, and he had swallowed our first horse in one gulp!"

"Don't worry, before I became a person, I was a regular donkey."

Bear scratched his head, "If you're a person, do you follow the Way?"

"I am a vegetarian, as are all donkeys. If my owner follows the Way, then I also refrain from work on the Sabbath day."

Bear appraised the donkey, "Yes, that's true, it is written that one's animals rest on the Sabbath as well. When did you attain humanity?"

"Many years ago."

Bear was suspicious, "how many? More than a thousand, perhaps?"

If a donkey could blush, this one would have. As it was, he hung his head and replied, "Yes. More than a thousand. And yes, I am that donkey."

Bear thought for a moment, strode closer to the donkey, grabbed it, and lifted it over his head like it was a tiny chick. "The truth now! Are you that donkey? If you utter even half a lie, I'll bash your head into the ground and end your short miserable life, right now."

"It's not short! It's long!" The words tumbled forth, "God who brought him forth out of Egypt is for him like the lofty horns of the wild-ox; he shall eat up the nations that are his adversaries, and shall break their bones in pieces, and pierce them through with his arrows."

Bear gently put the donkey down, "he's telling the truth. No other donkey would know the exact words of his master Balaam."

"Master Balaam? You know the donkey's master?"

THE SECOND JOURNEY

"Not personally, Sage Xuanzang. It was a long time ago. My people were once slaves in Egypt. They miraculously escaped and made their way through the desert to this land, but some of the peoples that they ran into on the way tried to stop them. Mostly through battles, but one tried to have a sorcerer-sage curse my people. That sorcerer-sage was Balaam. He was not successful and ended up blessing our people instead."

"How is our donkey person connected to this story?" asked Xuanzang.

"Ah. In some ways he could see better than the sorcerer-sage Balaam, and the World-Master opened his mouth so he could warn Balaam."

"So, this wasn't simply self-cultivation. Donkey, how did you achieve immortality?"

"I have lived a long time, but I do not know if I'm truly immortal. I guess we just need to wait and see."

Xuanzang nodded. "Talking animals are common in our little group; maybe we should move on to the reading lesson?"

"Excellent idea. We've gotten used to talking monkeys and pigs. There's no reason to have a talking donkey disturb our lesson."

Bear drew three characters in the sand with a pointed stick.

"These are the first three letters of our alphabet; their names are: Aleph, Bet, Gimmel.

"Old Monkey's seen them! Many times! They aren't characters! They're sounds! But I can't remember them! They don't mean anything at all, just scratches in the dust, like a chicken would make."

"What do the characters in your land mean?" asked Bear.

"Each one is a word. Each one has a meaning all to itself."

"You have a character for each word? How many characters are there?"

"Thousands!"

Bear scratched his head. "I have heard that our letters were once symbols of words. Aleph was a drawing of an ox, Bet of a house and so on. But over time the pictures became simplified, and they no longer mean words; they signify sounds."

"Does every sound have a letter?"

"Yes. There are twenty-two letters, and…" He trailed off, "No, that isn't true. Some letters can mean different sounds, depending on how they are used. And the letters aren't sounds by themselves, they have to be combined with the breath-sounds to actually be sounds. Like Bet can be Ba, or Be, or Bu.…"

Xuanzang understood, "you need at least two letters for each sound then; one for the beginning of the sound, and one for the breath part. So, which letters are for the breath parts?"

Donkey knew.

"It's a little difficult. It took me 200 years to finally understand. They cheat. There are no letters for breath-sounds. You have to guess or know what the word you're reading is, and then you fill in those sounds yourself."

"I'm just an idiot pig, but if you need to know what the word is before you can read it, what was the point in writing it in the first place?"

"After a while it flows naturally. Let's get started, and you'll see."

Bear wrote three different letters in the sand. Xuanzang peered at them.

"The first looks like our word for 'mountain', Shan. The second looks like the word for 'water', Shuǐ. The third doesn't look that familiar. Maybe like 'down', xià. So, we would read this as 'mountain-water-down'. Maybe a waterfall? But we would be wrong of course. What does it mean?"

"The letters are sounds, so we have SH M R. This is the 'root'

THE SECOND JOURNEY

of the word, which has to do with watching or guarding. The exact meaning depends on the missing breath-sounds. So, it could be 'guard', 'guarded', or 'he guarded'. If you add one or two letters, it could change the meaning, to "I guarded', or 'you guarded' and so on. It sounds complicated, but the rules are straightforward. It won't take you long to learn."

Xuanzang had some experience with languages.

"No, it doesn't seem difficult, as far as languages go. It is sobering to think that the way we write the Tang language is much more difficult to learn."

They studied their letters for a little while longer, then continued on their way. Donkey was given more respect now that he was recognized as a person.

We don't know what they will learn next; let's find out in the next chapter.

Skip

Our friends continued along their way. Monkey took the lead, with his shrunken Compliant Rod hidden behind his ear. Our Tang Monk Xuanzang followed behind on his talking donkey, while Bear, the Foreign Guide, walked next to him. Eight-Rules Pigsy, our unique 'Idiot', brought up the rear, his nine-pronged rake over one shoulder and the excess baggage on the other.

Spring was in full swing. This land was soft with gentle mountains and fertile plains:

> *Lo, the winter is past, the rain is over and gone;*
> *The flowers appear on the earth; the time of singing is come,*
> *and the voice of the turtledove is heard in our land;*
> *The fig-tree putteth forth her green figs, and the vines in*
> *blossom give forth their fragrance.*
> *Song of Songs*

Xuanzang's mind was filled with questions about the endless arguments of these western sages. There had been a hint that sometimes things could get awfully bad, but nobody had said a word beyond that. Donkey might know more than people realized; nobody pays much attention to people in the background. If a sweeper can go wherever he likes, where could a donkey go, and what would he hear?

His thoughts were interrupted by Bear.

"It is almost time for Pessach."

"Pessach?"

"Our spring holiday."

"Oh, that's not unusual. There are spring holidays in every country between here and Xi'an." Xuanzang said.

"That makes sense. Here it is more of historical holiday than a nature festival. We celebrate our ancestors' leaving Egypt many generations ago."

"In the land of the Tang, we also venerate our ancestors."

"I've heard of ancestor worship," said Bear, "But it isn't like that at all. It's more about remembering our past, remembering where we came from."

"Egypt—you've told me about that. I've heard the story from an old shepherd as well."

"Curious. The man who led us out of Egypt was an old shepherd. Not much of a hero figure, but that's who he was."

"In some ways that makes for a better story. Less bloody, anyhow," said Xuanzang.

"Oh, there is plenty of blood and death in the story; even a miraculous plague, and the Egyptian Nile River turning to blood."

Xuanzang shuddered.

"It was a long time ago. Though we've had plenty of bloody events since then, I'm afraid. As they say:

> *"Such is the human condition, but it's a condition we bring upon ourselves. Men prefer sorrow over joy... suffering over peace!"*

"Not just humans! Not just humans! All people do this!"

Xuanzang sighed. "Yes, it's a sorry state of affairs, Old Monkey, but it's true of all people, whether human, Pig, or Monkey. It is true of many gods and demons as well."

"Our Pessach starts in two days. We'll reach a town this evening, we can spend the holiday there."

"Bear, what does 'Pessach' mean?"

"It means 'skip over' or 'pass over'. Our God brought down a terrible plague unto our enemies' houses but skipped over our houses."

"Oh. Your god didn't seem so cruel to me."

"Cruel? Maybe just. Anyhow, Xuanzang, what would you know of my god?"

"Let's just say that I have met a number of gods and shepherds in my time."

Our travelers continued on their way. Soon they saw a small town. Our friends from the East waited outside the town, while Bear went ahead and made holiday arrangements for them. "One of the Sages in this town will host us over the holiday. We will join him and some of the other sages at the Seder."

"Seder?"

"A special meal. You'll see. In the meantime, there are many preparations!"

Pigsy was hoping there would be plenty of vegetarian food at the special Seder meal, but he noticed Monkey keeping an eye on him, so he only grumbled quietly to himself.

Their host had a second floor in his house that was set aside for guests. They put their luggage down, made sure that Donkey was taken care of in the stables, and went out to see how the town got ready for the holiday.

The preparations seemed mostly centered around cleaning. Xuanzang knew of this custom, "everybody is sweeping out the old year's bad luck now, to make room for the new year's good luck?"

"Close, but not quite right. On this holiday we don't eat leavened bread, bread that has risen. We bake special flat bread that is not allowed to rise. So, we must dispose of all the leavened bread in our houses. That's why everybody is busy cleaning; they're trying to find bits of old bread that may still be hiding in their houses."

They passed by a small house. A woman was standing in the doorway, broom in hand, looking pleased with herself. Clearly, she had completed her cleaning, and removed all the old bread from her house.

Just then they heard loud shouting from a nearby alley. A group of sages, moving quite rapidly considering their advanced age, ran around the corner shouting. A white mouse ran in front of them, carrying a small piece of bread in its mouth. It ran right under the woman's legs. She shouted, let loose a curse that Xuanzang was glad he didn't understand, and ran after the mouse.

Soon enough, the mouse ran out of the house once again. Fortunately, the bit of bread was still it its mouth. Unfortunately, this was a different mouse, a black one. Was it the same piece of bread? Well, that was a matter for the sages to discuss, a discussion they were already vigorously engaged in. The woman, in the meantime, was vigorously engaged in heaping curses on the sages, which they pointedly ignored.

"Bear, what is this all about?"

"The mice are specially trained by the sages, to create interesting situations for them to discuss. Now they are debating whether one can assume that the bread is the same bread, even though the mice are clearly different mice. If it's the same bread, the house is clean. If not, they'll have to clean it again. My guess is that the sages won't be able to decide, and the woman will get over her anger and go clean again."

Sure enough, the woman went back inside with her broom, and the sages wandered off, still debating the issue.

After checking in on Donkey, Bear, Pigsy and Monkey lay down on mats to sleep. Master Xuanzang stayed up, reading the Mahaprajnaparamita Sutra by the light of a single oil lamp. He hardly noticed Pigsy's loud snoring as he'd become so used to it. Soon he was overcome by fatigue and dozed off with his head resting on the reading desk. Though his eyes were closed, he remained half-conscious, able to hear the continuous sighing of the dark wind outside his window.

Xuanzang was woken by a knocking at the door. Shuddering in fear, he opened the door to their room. What ghost or demon would be there this late at night?

It was merely a group of elderly sages.

"We want to check your rooms, to see if there is any leavened bread there."

"No! Shimon, I told you a hundred times! There's no need! They are foreigners, their bread doesn't count."

"But the room isn't theirs! The owner isn't a foreigner!"

"The room is theirs, at least for the next few days, they're renting it."

Xuanzang had enough experience with the local sages to know that they would be arguing until the morning, unless they got distracted by some other issue. He gently shut the door, blew out the lamp, and went to sleep.

Our friends woke up the next morning to the smell of smoke.

Xuanzang was panicky. "Monkey! What's on fire? Do we need Princess Iron Fan to help us put out the fire?"

"The tribe of hogs knows how to smell! It's burning food! Burning bread."

THE SECOND JOURNEY

"I'll go out and check!"

Dear Monkey! He swung out of the window and onto the roof to look around. There were small fires in every courtyard, each surrounded by small crowds of people, tossing scraps of bread into the fires.

Monkey swung back into the room to report. Bear had woken up as well and was yawning loudly.

"The smoke? Nothing to worry about. They're just burning the leftover bread before the holiday."

After breakfast, they wandered around the bustling town. The holiday started that evening, so the open-air market was packed. Though the main street was fairly wide, they could hardly move for the crowds. Pigsy and Monkey attracted a few curious looks, but most were too busy to even notice them.

The street was lined with vendors. Some had set up tables out of boards on trestles, while others had spread colored cloths on the pavement. Each vendor specialized in one type of item. One sold nuts, pistachios and walnuts, piled up high on a table, another root vegetables, orange carrots, white parsnips and red beets. Vendors spread greens on mats.

Xuanzang noticed something odd.

"Bear, why so much lettuce?"

"It's used as part of tonight's ceremonial meal. As is that flat bread that you see."

Indeed, there weren't any vendors selling buns or cakes. Just round, thin, flat breads.

Xuanzang noticed that Bear was steering them past certain alleys.

"Why are we avoiding that area?"

"You are vegetarians. You have compassion for even the moth and the spider. I think it best that we avoid the meat-selling district on a busy holiday eve."

"Old Hog won't mind! I'm a vegetarian now, but I used to have a cannibal's diet!"

"That may be true, but this Tang Monk thanks you. I can eat with those who eat meat, but the sight of piles of raw meat would be too much for me."

They spent some time in the market, and much to Pigsy's delight, many of the vendors offered samples of their wares. Towards the edge of the market they found tables piled high with dried herbs and spices, and further out, stores that sold everything from ceramic dishes and jugs to wooden toys. Our Monkey was enamored by the tiny carved animals, but resisted the urge to buy one. What use has a wandering Buddhist monk for such possessions?

Xuanzang was the first to notice.

"Bear, what's happening? The market is emptying, though it's still early afternoon."

"People are going home to get ready for the holiday. There's a lot of cooking and preparations to do. We should go soon as well, and bathe and get dressed for the special meal."

Bear led them back to their inn so they could wash and change into clean clothes. They were going to join a number of sages for the holiday meal, at Sage Meir's house.

Sage Meir had cleared out a large room for the meal. There were small tables set around the perimeter, with a narrow couch by each one. Sage Meir sat at the head, with the other sages at tables on either side. There was a table for Sage Meir's wife, Bruriah, who was considered a wise and learned woman, a sage in her own right. They had set up two larger tables as well, with benches to sit on. One for our Tang friends, and the other for a group of five or six children.

The meal started with the wine blessing, just as it had on a Sabbath. Following the blessing, carefully laid out plates were brought out, each with a variety of vegetables and sauces. Xuanzang noticed that the other tables had a small bone on them as well, but they had skipped the bone in honor of their vegetarian guests.

The tables were carried away, even though the meal wasn't over, then brought back again.

"They do strange things, just to keep the kids awake and interested."

Xuanzang nodded at Bear's explanation and tried to follow the discussion. The Sages were telling the story about the Exodus from Egypt. They spoke of how their ancestors were slaves, and Moses led them to their freedom through a series of miracles, while cursing the Egyptians with ten plagues. This went on for a while, so Pigsy and the children were getting hungry!

The discussion turned to the miraculous crossing of the Reed Sea. The sages spoke of when Moses lifted his shepherd's staff, and a wind blew the water aside, so the People could cross the sea. This was considered the greatest miracle of all, greater than all the ten plagues put together!

The question was, how much greater? It was written that God's finger caused the plagues, and that God's hand caused the Sea to split. So simple arithmetic says that the splitting of the Reed Sea was worth fifty plagues. Except that the plagues themselves could be counted as multiple plagues, in which case you could get two hundred total, or two hundred fifty, or...

Fortunately, the sages ended their discussion. The flat Matza bread was brought out, a few prayers were chanted, another cup of wine was drunk, and finally, they could eat.

It was a huge meal, plenty of vegetarian food too. Even Pigsy couldn't complain. They had already drunk two cups of wine as part of the ceremony, and wine was the drink of the hour while the meal was served. Soon Pigsy, his stomach full, and his wine cup filled and emptied, many times over, was sound asleep.

In the meantime, and over more wine, the sages continued their long, learned discussion of the miraculous crossing of the Red Sea.

Dear Monkey! He should have known better! Five hundred years ago he got drunk at the Heavenly Banquet, with disastrous results. Havoc in Heaven! Our Old Monkey got drunk again here in the West, but he did not stumble into Lao Tzu's alchemical workshop. He simply fell asleep on the table, right next to the snoring Pigsy.

Monkey was floating on his magic cloud, and saw Moses standing in front of the sea, the people and their sheep were crowded behind him. He landed next to Moses, right on the edge of the sea.

"Hello, Sage Moses!"

"Hello, flying ape. Have we m...met?"

"You don't remember? We met in your heaven, when Master Xuanzang helped you with those angels?"

"I don't recall..."

Moses closed his eyes for a moment.

"Ah. That d...didn't happen yet. But it will. So, in a way we have met before, even though we haven't."

Monkey scratched his hairy head and decided to give up on trying to understand. "What are you doing here with all these people and the sheep?"

"These are the People of Israel, all twelve tribes of them, and all their sheep, Moses explained. "They were slaves in Egypt, and our God brought plagues upon the Egyptians, until they were forced to let my people go."

"Plagues?" asked Monkey.

"Yes, the water in their river turned into blood, frogs overran them, and eventually they had a day of complete darkness and a night of death in each home. Then we were pursued by the Egyptians; they had changed their minds, and we were stuck at this sea. I was supposed to wave my staff at the sea. Then a strong wind would blow from the east, and the waters would part, and we'd all just walk through."

"So, wave the staff! Wave the staff!"

"I did, I did. It doesn't work! Maybe the power in the staff has been used up?"

"Where does the power come from?"

"I don't know. It was a regular wooden pole, until the World-Master told me it could do all these miracles. My brother's staff became magical, too."

"Olam-Tzu? Your god? He seems quite reliable..."

"You know him?"

"We've met! We've met. Old Monkey meets gods all the time!"

Moses scratched his head, then turned towards the sea, and gave the staff a desultory wave. Nothing happened. "See? The staff lost its power!"

"Maybe somebody switched it on you, and that is a fake one?" Monkey suggested.

"Not likely, but who knows?"

"Try my staff! Try it!"

Our dear Monkey held out a needle-seized compliant rod.

Moses looked skeptical, until Monkey gave it a shake, and it was the same size as Moses' staff.

Moses took a deep breath, waved the rod...and...

Nothing. Nothing at all. He handed it back to Monkey. Another shake, and it was the size of a needle again, and tucked behind his ear.

The people were getting restless and some were complaining; their leader had gotten them out of Egypt, but they were going to die right here, next to the sea.

"We need that east wind. The staff is supposed to do it, but it's stopped working. I even tried my brother's staff, but it was useless as well."

"You need wind. Wait! Wait! Old Monkey knows what to do!"

He mounted his magic cloud, and went to the Palm-Leaf Cave, on the Jade Cloud Mountain.

"Princess Iron Fan! Princess Iron Fan! It's your grandfather, Old Monkey!"

The princess came out.

"You, again! Wherever you tread, trouble follows! Go! Before I break my swords over your head or blow you back to your Flower-Fruit Mountain!"

Monkey chuckled. "The past is past, and the now is now. Leave the past behind, but now, help a people far away. They have need of your fan."

"I should trust the words of a lying ape?! You damn trickster! What people?"

"People far away, Lady Iron Fan. In the West beyond the West. Slaves escaping their masters."

"You expect me to 'lend' you my fan? You, the thief who stole Lao Tzu's elixir pills?!"

"Don't lend! Don't lend! Come with me, you can do the fanning!"

"Does the Bodhisattva Guanyin know about this?"

"She sent me to accompany the Tang Monk to the West beyond the West, but she does not know of this fan-mission. Must I go get her?"

Princess Iron Fan knew that Guanyin had a soft spot for Monkey and would certainly support his mission. "I'll not risk giving you the fan. But I'll go with you to take care of your little problem. What is it that you need to blow?"

"Water! Water! We have to dry up a lake."

THE SECOND JOURNEY

So, Princess Iron Fan joined our Dear Monkey on his magic cloud, and the two of them flew back to Moses and the trapped people.

Moses was there waiting for him, and he was worried. The murmuring among the tribes had turned into a roar. Something had to happen, or they throw him into the water, and then they'd get slaughtered by the Egyptians too.

Dear Monkey! He whispered a few words to Moses, then went back to Princess Iron Fan, and the two of them rose above the sea on his magic cloud. Moses held his staff in two hands and raised it dramatically over his head. The crowd quieted down at this. Monkey nodded at the Princess, who waved her magic fan twice, and the East wind rose.

The wind blew the water aside, and the people and sheep started crossing the seabed. As it is said:

> ...*caused the sea to go back by a strong east wind all the night, and made the sea dry land, and the waters were divided.*
> *And the children of Israel went into the midst of the sea upon the dry ground; and the waters were a wall unto them on their right hand, and on their left.*
> Exodus

Moses was relieved.

"Thank you, Monkey Monk from the East. I really needed that help."

Monkey and Princess Iron Fan waited until the last of the Children of Israel had crossed the sea. In the meantime, the Egyptian pursuers had reached the sea and began crossing as well. The Princess folded her fan, and the wind stopped. The water rushed back into the sea, destroying thousands of the pursuers.

"Old Monkey will get into trouble over this. So many killed in the water! This is not the True Fruit!"

He took Iron Fan back to the Palm-Leaf Cave, mounted the magic cloud, and woke up with his head on the table. He lifted his head and looked around. The children were all sleeping, as was Pigsy, who was snoring loudly as usual. Xuanzang and the Sages were still discussing some scriptural verses and trying to connect them to the Exodus.

> *O my dove,*
> *that art in the clefts of the rock, in the covert of the cliff,*
> *let me see thy countenance, let me hear thy voice;*
> *For sweet is thy voice, and thy countenance is comely.*
> *Song of Songs*

"Old Monkey's head hurts too much to follow these foreign sages. I no longer know what's a dream and what's real."

The festive Seder meal ended with the chanting of some foreign sutras, and the drinking of even more wine. Monkey and Bear had to practically drag Pigsy back to the Inn when they finally finished.

We do not know what will happen to our friends next; let's find out in the next chapter.

The Other

Our friends woke up late the following morning; only Xuanzang woke up before noon. There was a whole chorus of snoring, led by the renowned soloist Pigsy, accompanied by Bear, their Foreign Guide, and our dear Monkey.

In all the years that Xuanzang had known Monkey, he had never heard him snore, but snoring is only human…and simian, as it turned out. Xuanzang idly wondered whether Donkey was also snoring. Putting that thought aside, he started his morning meditation. When he was finished, his companions were still sleeping. Rather than wake them, he went to check on Donkey.

Donkey was quietly eating some hay.

"Good morning, Donkey."

"Good morning, Tang Monk."

"You are talkative this morning, Donkey. Usually, you don't say anything at all."

"I was hoping to speak with you."

"About?"

"About your reading instruction, Xuanzang. Bear is helping you."

"Yes, we haven't gotten very far, but he's been very helpful."

"I think Bear would be happy if somebody else would take over your instruction."

"Why? He's been our guide in so many things!"

Donkey took another mouthful of hay, chewed, and finally swallowed. Our Tang Monk waited patiently, as that is one of the things monks do best.

"Bear is afraid that he will be embarrassed. He doesn't read very well."

"He's being very helpful now."

"That's because you're just beginning. The ancient scriptures are written differently. The words are different, the grammar is different; he has trouble with that."

Xuanzang knit his brows "How can you possibly know that?"

"Take it from the Donkey's mouth. I have heard him read scriptures."

"Who could teach me? Monkey and Pigsy don't know how to read your language."

Donkey took another mouthful of hay and chewed slowly.

Xuanzang waited.

Donkey swallowed and took yet another mouthful.

Xuanzang waited.

"I know how to wait."

Chew. Swallow. Hay.

"On the other hand, you will likely outlive me. And you have a ready supply of hay, while I will need to eat sometime today. So, who will teach me?"

Chew. Swallow. Hay.

Xuanzang started reciting the Prajñāpāramitā Sutra—the perfection of wisdom sutra. After only four thousand lines, he understood.

"You intend to teach me?"

Donkey swallowed his hay.

"Yes. It took you long enough. I'll have a stomachache tonight from overeating."

"Why didn't you just say so?" asked Xuanzang.

"Because a good teacher forces his student to think."
"So, you are a sage!"
"No. More of a wise-ass."
"How will we tell Bear?" Xuanzang wondered.
"Just tell him. He'll be relieved, not angry or insulted."
"You may be right. After all, I've never known a talking donkey to be wrong.

"Bear prepared a small student's scroll for me, with the letters and some simple words. Can we go over it now, Donkey?"

"Of course. I can't do much in the way of writing, for obvious reasons. So, Bear will have to remain your address for that."

Xuanzang went up to their room, took his practice scroll out, and went back down to the stables. "I wanted to ask you something, Donkey."

"Ask, my son, and you will be answered."

"Your sages are, to be polite, argumentative."

"One might say that…"

Xuanzang went on. "Has there ever been an argument that has gotten completely out of control? Or a sage who's gone too far?"

Scholars have long debated whether a donkey can sigh, but this donkey certainly did. Then he went back to his hay.

Chew. Swallow. Hay.

Chew. Swallow. Hay.

Now it was Xuanzang's turn to sigh, "I guess not all questions can be answered. Let's get on with the reading lesson."

He read out loud to Donkey, who corrected him as he went.

As they were reading it the second time, Bear showed up.

"There you are! I thought we'd lost you! I guess you just ran off to escape the snoring. I'm glad I don't snore."

Xuanzang looked at him but didn't say anything.

"I see Donkey is helping you with your reading."

"Yes, I hope you don't mind."

"Of course not. I'm not such a good teacher anyhow. I don't have enough patience."

"Donkey here is very patient. He chews his hay slowly and gives me time to think, but he can't write, so I'll need to impose on you for that."

"You haven't tried writing yet?" asked Bear.

"No, but there's no reason to put it off."

"Maybe tomorrow. Writing is prohibited on the Sabbath and holidays."

Xuanzang sighed, "In my youth I memorized hundreds of sutras, but today I find it difficult to remember a handful of foreign rules."

Bear laughed, "Far more than a handful!"

Donkey's ears perked up. "It sounds like your friends are waking up."

They hadn't noticed the buzz of the snoring in the distance, but now that Donkey pointed it out, they realized that it had stopped. Soon they heard the sound of distant bickering.

Xuanzang sighed.

"People can change. My disciples changed during our last Journey. They found the True Fruit. But some bad habits are permanent, perhaps the only permanent things in this world."

The rest of the day went smoothly enough. Pigsy ate too much of the flat bread with honey and had a stomachache, but he was always eating too much of something, so nobody paid him much attention.

At the end of the day, they joined the owner of the inn in the end of holiday blessings, similar to those at the end of the Sabbath. Bear explained the situation to them.

"This is a seven-day holiday. The first day is a complete no-work day, like the Sabbath. Well, almost, I'd better not get into

THE SECOND JOURNEY

details. The next few days are half-holiday days. So, we can work, if really needed, or travel. The important thing is that we don't eat leavened bread this entire week. In principle *you* could, since you are foreigners, but everybody would appreciate it if you didn't, they'd rather not have leavened bread around."

"The flat bread is fine, but it gave me a tummy ache," Pigsy complained.

"Everything gives you a tummy ache, you don't know when to stop!" Monkey chided.

Xuanzang glared at his disciples but didn't say anything.

The next day they got up early, bought a supply of flat unleavened bread, and continued onwards. After they'd traveled for a couple of hours, Monkey asked to stop to relieve himself. They all thought it was a good idea, except Donkey, who didn't bother with any sort of modesty in these matters. Monkey stepped behind some ruins and left a bubbling pool of monkey urine at the base of an old pillar.

You will recall that Monkey had once thought to escape the Buddha Tathāgata with his magic cloud, and when he had gotten far enough decided to 'leave a kind of memento' ... and with a total lack of respect he left a bubbling pool of monkey urine at the base of the first of five pillars. The pillar, as we all know, turned out to be one of the Buddha's fingers.

Xuanzang walked a little further into the woods and relieved himself behind a bush. He then noticed an elderly man hiding behind a tree and eating. He walked over and waited till he was noticed.

The gentleman was sitting on a rock, eating a thick chunk of bread. Much thicker than anything they'd eaten on this holiday. He was clean shaven, in the Roman style, and wore a new toga, one without the traditional fringes in the corners. Yet he didn't look Roman, and he didn't look comfortable. And why was he hiding in the woods to eat bread?

Finally, the man looked up and started. "Who are you? You're not from here."

"Venerable sir, I am Xuanzang, a Tang monk from the East."

His new acquaintance looked relieved, "Ah. Good. I didn't want to be noticed by anybody local."

"Are you a fugitive? Why would a Roman be a fugitive?"

"Fugitive? In a way I am, because I'm not Roman. I'm..."

Xuanzang waited.

"Where did you say you are from?"

"The Tang Empire, many months travel east of here. I've come with two of my disciples to learn the wisdom of the West."

"What kind of disciples? Where are they?" The stranger asked.

"They're on the road, waiting for me. One is Monkey, known as the Great Sage Equal to Heaven. The other is Eight-Rules Pigsy. We also have a local guide, whom we call Bear."

"You come from the far reaches of the Earth, with a monkey and a pig as disciples! Perfect! The world is a marvelous and random place."

"Why random?"

"There's no judgment, and no Judge. The world just carries on in its insane way."

"Who are you? " Xuanzang asked. "Why do you speak this way?"

"You are considered a sage in your own lands, right? Even your monkey is a Great Sage. I was a sage here as well. Among the greatest of them. I had wisdom, knowledge, respect, students..." He trailed off thoughtfully.

"We've met many sages here. None of them mentioned you."

"They wouldn't, monk from the East. I'm the man that one doesn't mention."

"The man that one doesn't mention. We had heard hints, but nobody would say anything concrete."

"When they do mention me, they call me 'The Other'. I wouldn't be surprised if you ran into one of my students. Maybe Meir, he lives not too far from here."

Xuanzang nodded. "Yes! We ate the Seder meal with him."

"He's the only one who still pays attention to me. I taught him most of what he knows, and he's the leading sage of the younger generation."

"A wise man who doesn't abandon his teacher."

"Yes, I like to think so." said The Other.

"You said, 'There's no judgment, and no Judge.' Why do you say that?"

"There is a verse in our scriptures:

> *If a bird's nest chance to be before thee in the way, in any tree or on the ground,*
> *with young ones or eggs,*
> *and the dam sitting upon the young, or upon the eggs,*
> *thou shalt not take the dam with the young;*
> *thou shalt in any wise let the dam go,*
> *but the young thou mayest take unto thyself;*
> *that it may be well with thee, and that thou mayest prolong thy days.*
> *Deuteronomy 22*

A few years ago," The Other continued, "I was visiting a town near the Sea of the Galilee. I saw a local man climb a date palm to raid a bird's nest. He didn't shoo away the mother bird, he just grabbed the eggs out from under her."

"Thus, going against your Scriptures, and showing a basic lack of compassion." Xuanzang added.

"Exactly. So, this fellow did it wrong and walked away carrying the eggs back to his family. Shortly afterwards, another local climbed up a different tree, shooed away the bird as he was supposed to, carefully removed the eggs, and climbed down. Just as he reached the ground, a viper bit him. He died in horrible pain."

Buddhists know how the world worked.

"Life is pain. There is pain and suffering everywhere. Death around every corner."

"I knew that all along but had not ever really faced this fact. Only when I saw that our Scripture lies did I fully grasp the reality of suffering; and how foolish the teachings of our Scriptures really are."

"Truth is hard to accept. But it does not mean that one ought to abandon all of the ancient traditions."

The man sighed, "It meant that to me. I am the renegade, The Other. I always will be."

Xuanzang had to ask. "Can you go back? Return to your traditions?"

The sage sat quietly, then spoke, "A voice came out from heaven: Return, rebellious children. All, apart from The Other."

The Other sat with his head bowed. Xuanzang stood quietly. He knew when to be still, and how to be quiet This Other seemed familiar, but he didn't recall meeting him before. It would come to him, if he waited long enough. Then he heard quiet footsteps coming through the woods. The Other looked up.

"It's Meir. He's the only one who knows where I am."

"Master! Master! Oh. I thought you were alone. I see the Tang Monk is here with you."

"Yes. I wouldn't worry about him. He has no part in our internal squabbles. Xuanzang, you have met Meir; he persists in looking for me and asking me questions about the finer points of our traditions, though I've told him repeatedly not to."

"Master, you know what Rabbi Hanina, the vice-chief of the priests, says. Can we derive from his words that we may burn clean priestly gifts together with unclean priestly gifts on Pessach?"

"Yes, now stop pestering me."

"You know I won't stop, Master Elisha."

Xuanzang's Buddhist equanimity collapsed. "Elisha?"

"Yes, that's my real name. You have heard of me?"

Xuanzang was confused. He knew Elisha, but as Ben Zoma, not as Xuanzang. How could he explain this to Elisha?

Elisha turned back to Meir.

"I'm no longer your master, and you are the only one who calls me by my real name." The man known as The Other, who was once known as Elisha, turned to Xuanzang, "I expect that one's disciples in your far-off land are better behaved than they are here."

Xuanzang was about to answer when they heard a loud thrashing coming through the brush, "Master! Master!"

Pigsy was first, and he was the cause of most of the noise: stomping through the brush with his rake over his shoulder. He was followed by Old Monkey who chuckled as he pranced along behind Pig. Bear lumbered slowly behind, followed by Donkey.

"These are your disciples?"

"The two poorly behaved ones are my disciples: Eight-Rules Pigsy and Monkey, also known as the Great Sage Equal to Heaven. The rather large gentleman there is our local guide, known as Bear. The donkey is…Donkey."

Elisha, looked at the little group, "so, we have a human named Bear, a talking magic Pig, and a chattering Sage Monkey. The only animal who doesn't speak here is the donkey; and I wonder what tales he would tell if he could."

"Yes. One must wonder." Xuanzang nodded.

"After all, Man has no advantage over the beasts, it is all in vain," The Other quoted.

"This is your own thinking?"

"Mine, but also Scripture:

> *For that which befalleth the sons of men befalleth beasts;*
> *even one thing befalleth them;*
> *As the one dieth, so dieth the other;*
> *Yea, they have all one breath; so that man hath no pre-eminence*
> *above a beast for all is vanity.*
> *All go unto one place; all are of the dust, and all return to dust.*
> *Who knoweth the spirit of man whether it goeth upward, and the spirit of the beast whether it goeth downward to the earth?*
> Ecclesiastes 3

Xuanzang thought for a moment, "These are your own Scriptures? It is not something borrowed from some other travelers from the East?"

"It is our own, though some would prefer not to admit that. Since you have a small zoo traveling with you, I gather that you also don't see much difference between man and beast."

"None at all. A beast can improve itself through self-cultivation much as a man can. After all, the Bodhisattva Guanyin's goldfish, through self-cultivation, became the Great King of Numinous Power!"

This was hard for Elisha to understand; with furrowed brow he asked, "How is that possible?"

"He was a goldfish reared in her lotus pond. Every day,

THE SECOND JOURNEY

he would float with the current to the surface to listen to her lectures, and slowly, gradually, he acquired his powers through his self-cultivation. Unfortunately, he used his powers for evil and became a demon who ate children. He was going to eat me as well. The Bodhisattva herself had to come and rescue me; she turned the demon back into a goldfish."

"Strange things happen in your land."

"Strange things happen everywhere, Sage Elisha, you just need to keep your eyes and ears open, and you will see them."

Monkey was keeping his diamond eyes open.

"Master! Master. This is Elisha, Elisha from the Orchard!"

Xuanzang tried to stop Monkey, but he was too late.

"Monkey, how do you know me? I have never met you."

Xuanzang sighed. "Sooner or later, I would have had to tell you. We were in The Orchard with you."

"No, I was there with only Akiva, Ben Zoma and Ben Azzai. Four of us, altogether."

Xuanzang bowed. "I must mention my faults today. Ben Zoma and Ben Azzai were not with you in the Orchard. They were asleep in the study hall. Monkey and I took their place."

"I don't understand."

Xuanzang struggled to find the words. "My disciple Monkey has…special skills. Magical abilities."

"He's a sorcerer?"

"Maybe that's the word. But a playful, well-meaning sorcerer."

"How did he trick me into thinking Ben Zoma and Ben Azzai were in the Orchard with us?"

"You would have to ask him for the details. He makes a sign with his fingers, and whispers a spell. Beyond that, I don't know."

"If you were there, Xuanzang, tell me what we saw."

"What we saw, or what Akiva saw?"

"Maybe you really were there. Tell me, what words were we

not supposed to say?"

"Water, water." Xuanzang replied.

Elisha shook his head. "This seems impossible, yet true."

"And what about you? You are hardly recognizable. You are a sage, and must have many students, yet you look completely different."

"I once was a sage, and I used to have students. Disciples such as your own; but they are all gone...except for Meir here, who is too loyal to admit to reality."

"Loyalty is a fine thing! After all, Lord Guan was loyal till the end to Liu Bei...you don't know anything at all about this, do you?"

The Other shrugged. "No, not at all. It's all...Sanskrit to me."

"Curious turn of phrase."

Elisha sighed. "When you know Hebrew, Aramaic, Greek and Latin, the phrase one can use to plead ignorance is quite limited. At least around here. I could have said,'It's all Tang to me.'"

"All Chinese; Tang is the dynasty." Xuanzang corrected.

"My ignorance is as wide as the sky...If I lived in your land, maybe I could learn the language."

Xuanzang was silent, but our dear Monkey couldn't resist: "Come with us. Come with us!"

"Come with you? To the land of the Tang?"

"Yes. Yes!"

"What would I do there?" Elisha asked.

"What do you do here?" Monkey replied.

"Not much these days. The Jews have rejected me, except for this loyal fool Meir. The Romans want to use me as an example, the ancient traditions have caused them a lot of trouble over the generations; I don't want to be used by them. Heaven says I can't return, Jews say I don't belong, I won't be a tool for the pagan

Romans... What do I do here? Not much, I survive in the empty space between Heaven, Jews, and Romans."

Xuanzang liked Monkey's idea, "So join us. Come with us to the land of the Tang. There is something you can help with there."

"I doubt that I can be of much help to anybody anymore. Even to Meir, though he insists on getting my advice."

Meir had been waiting, not very patiently, for a chance to ask The Other a question, "Rabbi Elisha, may I ask one more question?"

"Yes, oh pestering one."

"On the Sabbath, do we consider all the roofs of a town to be a single domain, or is each one its own domain?"

"What do you think?"

"Um, perhaps all the roofs of a town are considered a single domain, provided no roof is greater than or equal to ten handbreadths higher or lower than any of the neighboring roofs?"

"Sounds good to me. You know that your opinion will be seriously considered, no matter what it is, anything with my name attached to it will be stricken from the record."

"Not entirely true."

"True enough."

Xuanzang brought them back to his idea, "I have learned patience and can listen to many hours of your learned discussion of the Sabbath rules. Yet, I suspect that the discussion can go on for days, perhaps even until the end of time. So, I should like to remind Sage Elisha here of my suggestion."

"To go with you to the other end of the world? To the Tang kingdom?"

"Yes."

"What will I do there?"

"My blood brother, the Great Tang Emperor, will honor you as a foreign guest and as my companion; you will be a great sage and a teacher again."

"Sage? Teacher? Who would I teach? There are none among the Tang lands who would be interested in my knowledge."

"You'd be surprised," said Xuanzang.

"If I tried leaving, somebody might follow me and try to bring me back."

"Don't Worry. Don't worry. Old Monkey has a plan!"

The Other was skeptical, he turned to Xuanzang, "how do his plans work out?"

"My eldest disciple is, after all, the Great Sage Equal to Heaven. His plans are very intelligent plans, carefully thought out."

The other smiled. "You are forgetting that I am a sage as well. You didn't answer my question."

"Well, he is the Great Sage Equal to Heaven, and his plans are carefully thought out; but, much as I admire his capabilities, I must say that events don't always follow his plans."

"It's a simple plan, a simple plan. It will work!"

"He's also quite persuasive."

"What's the plan?" Elisha asked.

"You will die. Then no one will chase you!"

Elisha and Xuanzang looked at each other. "Monkey, I hope there is some explanation for this! Surely you don't mean to smack Sage Elisha with your rod and turn him into a meat patty!"

Monkey chuckled, "This is the trick of 'die and disappear'. Fake Elisha will be sick. Meir will come to pray for him. He shall die, we will bury fake Elisha, and the real one will come with us!"

"How will you make a fake me? How can you fool anybody?" The Other asked.

THE SECOND JOURNEY

"You don't know Old Monkey. Watch."

He pulled off one of his hairs, gave it a shake, and shouted 'change!' Suddenly, there were two Sage Elishas standing next to each The Other.

Elisha One raised his hand, Elisha Two mimicked him.

"Ah," said Elisha One.

"Exactly," said Elisha Two.

Monkey explained. "This is how Master Xuanzang and I became Ben Zoma and Ben Azzia. This time I used hairs. Then I used ourselves."

Meir was concerned, "How will I know which is which?"

"Ask a question. Only one knows the answer."

"If one steals a cow, or a slave; years later the cow or slave has grown old, and thus lost considerable value, does the thief pay back the original value, or the current value?"

Both of the Elishas answered together, "Meir, why are you asking? You know the answer to that."

"Sage Monkey, that didn't work out very well."

"No matter. No matter. I know which is which. We'll take the real sage; you'll bury the fake sage. All will be well."

Elisha looked at Xuanzang, who remained silent. Bear had nothing to say. Pigsy was excited, "Good plan, Elder Brother, Good plan!"

The Other was still concerned. "How will I travel with you? In these countries I am known."

"Don't worry! Don't worry! Monkey will shave your head! You'll wear a monk's robe and carry a begging bowl. No one will guess! No one will guess!"

Elisha thought, before slowly speaking, "They will all believe that I had died, so maybe this could work. Donkey, what do you think?"

Donkey bit off a bit of grass and chewed. Real Elisha stared at

Donkey. Donkey stared back, then continued chewing. Donkey knew that Elisha suspected him, but he wasn't going to reveal his secret. Not yet.

"So, a Journey to the East, with friends I just met, and a mysterious goal. Better than moping about here for the rest of my days. I'll die. I'll go."

He stomped his foot on the ground.

"I live. I die.

"I live! I live!"

Stomp. Stomp.

Fake Elisha joined in, and now they alternated in the chant.

Stomp. Stomp.

"I die! I die!"

"I live! I live!"

"I die! I die."

Now monkey started stomping as well.

"This is the hairy man.

This is the hairy man!

"Who summons the sun and makes it shine!"

The Elishas again:

"I live!"

"I die!"

Soon they were all stomping and shouting in rhythm.

"To the West!"

"To the East!"

"To our home!"

"To the Unknown!"

Xuanzang banged his monk's staff on the ground as he joined in the chant. Even Donkey got caught up in the rhythm and stomped the ground with his hind legs. Finally, Xuanzang stopped banging his staff and they all gradually calmed down.

Bear pointed out that they didn't have much daylight left,

THE SECOND JOURNEY

so they needed to get moving. Sage Meir took the fake Sage Elisha off towards a nearby farmhouse, where he would 'get sick' and 'die'. Monkey shaved Sage Elisha's head while Pigsy rummaged through the luggage, finding him suitable Buddhist garb. Eventually, they were ready to go.

"New clothes, new haircut, I'll need a new name as well." Elisha pointed out.

Xuanzang thought for a moment before speaking, "'Zhixing, 智行. It means, 'Travel-for-Wisdom.'"

Our awakened friends continued on their way. We will leave them for the time being and see what happens to Sage Meir and the ersatz Elisha.

Meir led his Elisha to a nearby farmhouse. "I know the family here. They will take care of 'sick Elisha', even though he has left the community and most call him 'The Other.' You need to look sick now."

Dear fake Elisha. No sooner than the words 'look sick' were uttered did his color fade until he was nearly white. He was shivering with fever, and a rash covered his face.

"Good, but don't overdo it. We need you sick now, don't die too fast!"

Old man Abraham came to the door. Nobody knew just how old he was, he had been old as long as anybody could remember, "Meir! I haven't seen you in...oh! You've brought Elisha, he doesn't look well."

"He's sick, I found him this way in the woods. I don't know where else I can take him."

"Bring him in, Meir."

Sage Meir and Old Abraham dragged Fake Elisha into the house and laid him on a bed.

"Sarah, prepare some broth! We have a sick man here." Abraham called to his wife; she saw what was happening and went out in the courtyard to draw water and add wood to the cooking fire.

"Meir, any idea how long he's been like this?"

"No. I saw him four days ago, and he seemed fine, so less than four days. More than that I don't know."

"He has a fever. Do you know what to do for that?"

Meir thought for a moment. "As a remedy for an internal fever, let him bring seven handfuls of beet leaves from seven furrows. Let him cook them with their dirt and eat them; and let him drink from Eder leaves mixed with beer or grapes grown by trellising the vine on a palm tree soaked in water. Can you arrange that?"

"Beets are no problem. I'll have to ask around for the Eder leaves. We will do what we can. Come back in a few days to see how he's doing. If he takes a turn for the worse, we will send someone to tell you."

There wasn't much more for Meir to do there, so he headed home to face his next challenge, Bruriah, his wife.

We do not know how Sage Meir will deal with his wife; let's find out in the next chapter.

Wife

We were telling you about Sage Meir, who had left the fake sick Sage Elisha at Old Abraham's house, while the real Sage Elisha joined Xuanzang and his disciples on their journey.

He had to return home and face his wife now. What should he tell her? Strange as life had been, recent events were far beyond normal experience. If he, Meir, was a normal sage, and his wife was a normal woman, there was no way he could tell her the truth. Women were notoriously unreliable, and any secret you'd tell them would inevitably slip out, in the market or by the local spring, and spread through the community.

But he was not your average sage. Though he didn't let it go to his head, he knew that he had a special status; if anybody else had stayed connected with a teacher like Elisha, they would have been ostracized long ago. Meir, on the other hand, was met with understanding. Bruriah, too, was far from your average woman. She was famous for her wisdom and was considered a sage in her own right, though nobody would actually call her 'Sage Bruriah'.

Bruriah could keep a secret, and Meir was not good at acting. He was surprised that he got away with it at Old Abraham's house. Maybe having a sick 'Elisha' with him distracted the old man. In any case, he wasn't going to be able to pull that off with Bruriah.

Bruriah met him at the door. She was a middle-aged, small, slight woman. She wore a long gray dress with a wide light blue sash around her waist and a matching blue scarf on her head. Blue and white fringes dangled from the corners of the sash.

"Meir! Oh, What's wrong?"

"My teacher is sick."

"Elisha? Is it serious?"

"He looks pretty bad. I left him with Old Abraham."

Bruriah looked at Meir. Meir looked back. She spoke, "You must be very upset. Come inside where we can talk about it."

They went inside, and sat at their table, far away from the door. Bruriah brought two cups of wine and a few dried figs. They ate and drank silently for a few minutes.

"Meir, what is it really?"

"If I'd married a stupid woman, then I'd be able to keep secrets."

"Yes, but then you'd be bored out of your mind. What's really going on?"

Meir scratched his head, "I'm not sure that I believe it myself. Remember our guests for the Pessach meal?"

"I'm not likely to forget; it is not often that we have monkeys, pigs and foreign monks here for the holidays."

"Well, they ran into Elisha, and convinced him to return home with them. He's headed east, to whatever far off place from which they come. He's not sick."

"You'll miss him, but it may be better for him. If it is not Sage Elisha, then who is sick?"

"Well, Elisha One is well, and going to the East; Elisha Two is sick and dying in Old Abraham's house."

"Elisha Two is a fake, to cover Elisha's escape?"

"Exactly. That Monkey is a sorcerer; he chewed off a piece of his hair and turned it into a second Elisha. The hair is covering for Elisha. It will get sick and die. I'll bury it and weep, but my tears will be for my teacher whom I may never see again."

"So, Elisha will be dead, and Elisha will go to a place where he isn't an outcast. All in all, it seems like a good solution."

"Yes, I suppose it does. I'm a little nervous for Elisha, though. He doesn't know those travelers at all."

"We know them. A strange group, I'll admit, but they were well behaved—making allowances for Mr Pigsy's appetite. Their master is a wise man. I'm sure they'll take care of him."

Meir nodded and sat lost in thought.

Two days went by, with normal activities. Meir and Bruriah went to the study hall to discuss the finer points of traditional property law. Some sages felt uncomfortable with a woman in the group, but most had convinced themselves that she wasn't really a woman, at least when it came to wisdom, and as such had managed to ignore the elephant in the room.

On the third morning, Meir answered the door to a breathless child who had clearly run some distance, "Sage Meir, your Master is very sick!"

Meir knew what that meant; he had to go. The Fake Elisha would be dead by the time he arrived. He wondered if Monkey would want his hair back, but that was no concern of his. Now he was an actor in a play. As was Bruriah.

"Bruriah!"

"What is it?"

"Elisha's taken a turn for the worse!"

"You had better go right away!"

She ran inside and quickly put together a pack of food and a water skin, and Meir ran off with the child.

Bruriah sighed, "The things you do for love!"

In the meantime, Meir hurried with the child until they reached Old Abraham's house. Abraham met them at the door and shook his head.

"I am too late?"

"Yes, he stopped breathing a few minutes ago..."

Meir sighed, "I feared as much. The responsibility to bury him lies with us. There isn't anybody else."

He tore his toga, from his neck down to his heart, as a sign of mourning.

"Are you okay?"

"I don't know. I think it will hit me later. Keeping busy with the burial will help right now."

Old Abraham nodded, "We won't be able to use any of the burial catacombs around here. Nobody will want him near their ancestors. We can dig a grave at the edge of my field."

"It should be a few cubits away, in the woods. We'll mark it clearly and lay a ring of stones around it, so people don't accidentally come near it and become impure...who would have thought, years ago, when I started studying with him, that this is how it would end? The student has honor and respect, and the teacher is buried in a hidden corner, with only one to mourn him."

"His teaching lives on in you."

They walked together through the field, Meir carrying a shovel over his shoulder. Abraham pointed out the area he had in mind. Meir started digging. The ground was sandy, but hard-packed and the work was difficult. As he dug deeper, he ran into roots that crisscrossed the grave. Each one had to be cut and removed. By the time the pit was deep enough, it was early afternoon.

They carried the dead 'Elisha' to a small shed. The two of them poured water over the body, then wrapped it in a plain cloth. They jury-rigged a stretcher from an old blanket and carried the body across the field to the waiting grave.

"Meir, Elisha is far lighter than I'd expected."

Meir was surprised that it weighed as much as it did, since it was just a monkey hair, but of course he couldn't say that. "I guess he was sick longer than we knew. There should have been hundreds of people at his funeral, not two."

They reached the grave and lay the body on the ground. Meir climbed down, and Abraham helped slide the body into the grave. Meir straightened the body, then climbed out, where he helped Abraham fill the grave with the now loose soil. It didn't take long.

"It's no Cave of the Machpela, but it will have to do."

The Cave of Machpela, you may know, is the ancient burial cave where the original Patriarchs had been buried two thousand years earlier.

Meir went about collecting rocks to pile up on top of the grave. There never would be a proper monument erected over it, but there should be some form of a marker. They stood next to the grave for a moment. Abraham chose some verses from the Book of Psalms:

> O thou that dwellest in the covert of the Most High, and abidest in the shadow of the Almighty;
> I will say of HaShem, who is my refuge and my fortress, my G-d, in whom I trust,
> That He will deliver thee from the snare of the fowler, and from the noisome pestilence.
> He will cover thee with His pinions, and under His wings shalt thou take refuge; His truth is a shield and a buckler.*

"Abraham, do you think God will forgive him?"

Abraham gave the only answer one could give, under the circumstances. "That is for God to know. We can only hope."

"I think that in the end, he wanted to return, but that voice from heaven dissuaded him."

"Return, rebellious children. All, apart from The Other," Abraham recalled.

"Yes. I wish we'd see some sign that he has been forgiven."

"It's getting late. You need to get back to Bruriah before it gets dark."

"Yes. We should go."

Just as they were turning to go, a puff of smoke emerged from the grave, and a cool breeze swept over them.

"Maybe that's your sign?"

"I will take it as such," said Meir.

They turned and left.

Let's leave Sage Meir alone on his way back to Bruriah and rejoin our band of travelers.

Xuanzang, our Elder Tang Monk, now had Pigsy, Monkey, Bear, Donkey, and the New Tang Monk, Elisha, also known Travel-for Wisdom, as companions.

They had been delayed on their trip, so they ended up camping out. Bear built a fire and they all slept around it, wrapped in their blankets.

They rose with the sun. Elisha helped Pigsy pack up their belongings, while Monkey scampered up a tree to have a look around. Xuanzang didn't see Bear around, then noticed him contemplating a tree trunk. He walked over. Bear motioned him to be quiet. Xuanzang looked carefully. There was a tiny spider on the smooth tree trunk. The early morning sun struck it a sharp angle, so there was a magnified, stretched-out shadow of the spider on the tree. A giant shadow cast by a tiny creature.

THE SECOND JOURNEY

Xuanzang waited patiently till Bear turned towards him. "Amazing, I have never looked at a spider so closely before."

"The spider's shadow is what you saw. Often we understand things only by seeing their shadow."

"Now I remember. When I was a child, I would sometimes crush a fly, rather than shoo it away. I would even torture flies, like kids do, until one day my teacher saw me doing that, and said, "Let's see you make a fly." At the time I didn't pay him any attention; but now I understand."

"I heard your sages say that there is a list of things that Man does not know: The day of his death, the day he will be consoled, the depth of justice, and what is in the heart of another man."

"Yes, I have heard that as well, Xuanzang, though I think the list was longer."

"Probably. They are wrong about at least one of those. Sometimes, one can know what's in the heart of another man.

Bear spoke, "My heart, in this case."

Xuanzang was silent.

"Wonder at God's creation, and compassion for both the fly and the spider. Even though the spider traps and eats the fly. Sometimes I can be read like a book."

"Easier than a book." Xuanzang went back to his disciples, who were finishing the travel preparations. Bear needed some time alone to contemplate things.

We don't know how their journey will progress; let's find out in the next chapter.

CROSSING

It was time to head back East.

Travel-for-Wisdom Elisha walked next to our Tang Monk, Xuanzang, who rode his occasionally articulate Donkey. Bear walked slowly behind them, lost in thought, while Pigsy followed with the spare luggage and his nine-pronged rake. Our Monkey scampered ahead of our friends, chattering and jumping on rocks.

Though they were traveling uphill, the going wasn't difficult. They were on a Roman road, and the Romans knew how to build roads and bridges so they would last. The road meandered through a valley, next to a ravine. As they approached a bend in the road, Monkey, who was still scampering ahead, came back to his companions.

"There's a city ahead! It looks like a good city! No monsters or tricky monks there."

"Let's go! We need some food. I'm hungry!" Pigsy cried.

Elisha wasn't too excited, "I know I'm a monk now, but somebody may yet recognize me. And there has been some trouble here in recent years; many rebellious people dwell in this city, perhaps it is best not to spend too much time here."

Xuanzang thought for a bit. "Travel-for-Wisdom and Pigsy will come with me. We'll go up the mountain on the left and find a place to rest. Monkey, you can go with Bear to get some food in this city. We'll wait for you." With that, Monkey and Bear headed into town.

The town gates were open, and farmers were leaving the town as the market was closing for the day. Our travelers hurried off to the market to acquire some food before it completely emptied; they had managed to buy some bread and dried fruit, when Bear had an idea, "Let's get some wine."

They went into a tavern, ordered some wine, and sat down. The tavern was crowded with merchants who needed to moisten their throats after a long day of haggling. Throats get moistened, and tongues get loosened. Our travelers sat in silence and listened to the conversations unfolding around them.

"Did I ever tell you…?"

"Yep. A thousand times, Grandpa!"

"Once I saw a day-old antelope that was as large as Mount Tabor. You know how big Mount Tabor is? It's forty *li* high. The length of the animal's neck was three parasangs, and his head stretched another parasang and a half. It cast feces and dammed up the Jordan River."

"Oh yeah? I've seen a frog that was as large as the fort of Hagronya. How large is the fort of Hagronya? As large as sixty houses. A snake came and swallowed the frog. A raven came and swallowed the snake and flew up and sat in a tree. How strong is that tree, which can bear the weight of that raven?"

"Every word he says is true. I saw it too. If I hadn't been there and seen it, I wouldn't have believed it."

"Uh huh. Once we were traveling in a ship and we saw a fish. A mud-eater insect had sat in its nostril and killed it. It washed up on shore, and sixty districts were destroyed, sixty districts ate from it, and the other sixty districts salted its meat to preserve it. And they extracted three hundred flasks of oil from one of its eyeballs. When we returned there after the twelve months, we saw that they were cutting beams from its bones, and they had set out to rebuild all those districts that had been destroyed."

"Sure. Once we were traveling on a ship and we saw a fish upon which sand had settled, and grass grew on it. We assumed that it was dry land and went up and baked and cooked on the back of the fish, but when its back grew hot it turned over. And were it not for the fact that the ship was close by, we would have drowned."

Monkey couldn't resist. "Right. Once, we needed to cross a wide river. An old turtle, scabby-headed and white-shelled, spoke with us and offered to carry us over. We all crossed on his back together—three people, a horse and our luggage. The turtle trod on the surface of the water as smoothly as if he were walking on level ground."

"Impressive! Once we were traveling on a ship and we saw a fish that took its head out of the sea, and its eyes had the appearance of two moons, and water scattered from its two gills like the two rivers of Sura."

Dusk approached and the tavern started emptying out, as the city gates were going to close soon. Bear and Monkey left as well and climbed up the hill to find their companions.

Are you wondering what had happened to Travel-for-Wisdom, Pigsy and Xuanzang in the meantime?

Our friends climbed halfway up a gentle mountain and followed a path that led around the mountain top. They'd found an olive grove and settled down on some rocks to wait and rest.

Xuanzang noticed an odd rock structure. "Travel-for-Wisdom, do you see that enclosure below us? Like a low rock wall? It's pretty big, but irregularly shaped. It looks like a shoe or a sandal...The walls are just piled-up fieldstones. There's a big pile of rocks at one end. It appears this was all done on purpose. But why?"

Travel-for-Wisdom hesitated, but a new arrival saved him from answering, "Somebody's approaching up the hill."

"Don't worry! Don't worry! I've got my rake handy! Where's that monkey with our dinner?"

A man approached them slowly. What did he look like, you ask?

He had two lame legs,
And walked slowly with two walking sticks,
He had an old wide-brimmed leather hat,
Sun wizened face,
And a short gray beard.

He was clearly no threat to them. Xuanzang greeted him.

"Hello, venerable sir! We are travelers from the Tang lands in the East, come to visit your lands in search of wisdom."

"Welcome! Welcome! May I join you?"

"We are those who left the family. We have no possessions at all." Xuanzang replied. "These rocks are certainly not ours. Please sit and rest with us."

"They call me Adam, like the first man."

"The equivalent of our Fuxi, the first man in eastern lands. I am Xuanzang, a Tang Monk. Here is my disciple, Eight-Rules Pigsy."

"One rule around here is to not eat pigs, so he doesn't have much to worry about."

"I know! I only worry what I am going to eat, not whether the others will eat me."

Adam turned to Elisha, "And you are?"

"I am Travel-for-Wisdom. I have another name, but I left it behind."

"We are all traveling for wisdom, in a way. Not too quickly, in my case."

"You've been hurt?"

"It's an old battle injury."

Xuanzang had seen many temples, monuments and stupas in his time, and he was curious about the odd formation below them. It was so irregular in shape that it seemed unlikely to be an animal pen. "What is that odd wall down there for? Some local agricultural practice?"

"I've hobbled across much of this country. There are five or six of these as far as I know. All about this shape, and all abandoned. I think they were ancient places of worship."

"We've been here for a few months now and have yet to see anything like it," replied Xuanzang.

"They're all in remote areas. Sides of mountains, foothills off the main road."

Just then Bear and Monkey showed up, "We're back! We're back! We heard some wild stories back there! And we have food, Old Pig!"

Monkey noticed their newest addition, "Who's our guest?"

"Adam. I guess you can call me Walks-for-Knowledge, or Limps-for-Knowledge. We've been looking at that odd enclosure on that flat area below."

Monkey peered at it with his diamond eyes. It looked like rocks piled up after clearing a field, or a sheep enclosure, but there was an aura.

"Was there a temple here once? A very long time ago, but a powerful temple? I still sense it."

Travel-for-Wisdom sighed, "Not a temple; a holy site. The original altar was here."

"Original?"

"It's been kept secret, handed down from sage to sage." Travel-for-Wisdom answered.

THE SECOND JOURNEY

"For how long?"

Travel-for-Wisdom shrugged, "at least a thousand years." Nobody was counting. Nobody was telling. It is Joshua's altar. As it is written:

> *Then Joshua built an altar unto HaShem, the G-d of Israel, in mount Ebal, as Moses the servant of HaShem commanded the children of Israel, as it is written in the book of the law of Moses, an altar of unhewn stones, upon which no man had lifted up any iron; and they offered thereon burnt-offerings unto HaShem, and sacrificed peace-offerings."**

Adam and Bear stared at him. They both asked the same question: "altar? Where?"

"It's there, under that pile of rocks. When they stopped using it, they didn't want to destroy it, so they covered it."

They camped out under the olive trees that night and slept calmly.

We don't know what will befall our friends as they return to the East; let's find out in the next chapter.

GIANT

The next morning, Travel-for-Wisdom Elisha woke up at sunrise. Pigsy and Bear were still sleeping, but Xuanzang and Donkey were awake. They had gone downhill, out of the olive grove, to catch the warmth of the early sun.

Or so Travel-for-Wisdom thought.

There is something holy about the early morning. One hears only the birds and the wind. He didn't want to disturb the morning peace, so he walked quietly down to the monk and donkey. He heard voices as he approached. One was Xuanzang's voice, as he struggled with the foreign words; but somebody was teaching him. Whose voice was that? He stopped. It wasn't possible, but it was true. He should have realized. Talking monkey-person, talking pig, why should the donkey be silent? The only talking donkey he knew of was older than that altar, but who else could it be?

Only one way to find out; he drew closer to the pair. Donkey was the teacher, Xuanzang the student. He quietly asked the question: "What have I done to you that you have beaten me these three times?"

Donkey froze, and slowly turned his head, "It's that obvious?"

"Not really. I was wondering, and then I saw you two together now, and I guessed. How old are you?"

"Donkeys don't know how to count."

THE SECOND JOURNEY

"Or speak, or read, for that matter."

"Exactly."

Travel-for-Wisdom smiled, for the first time in many years.

"Smartass ass!"

"Donkeys don't know how to smile either."

Xuanzang didn't see a formal ceremony, but he knew that The Other and Donkey were now blood brothers. He expected Travel-for-Wisdom to refer to Donkey as Elder Brother now.

In the meantime, everybody else had woken up. Bear was cooking a vegetarian breakfast, while Pigsy packed up their supplies. Xuanzang watched them, and then realized something; he walked over to Bear, who said, "Just some boiled vegetables. I'm trying to bake some flat bread too. We can eat it on the way."

"Good. Thank you. I haven't been paying much attention until now, but have you changed your eating habits?"

"You are asking if I am a vegetarian now? No. I'm not. I just haven't eaten meat in the past few days. Nobody else in our group eats meat, so it was easiest to adopt your diet."

"When our ways part, you will go back to eating meat?"

"Maybe. We shall see. I'm getting used to it, and we will remain together for a while yet."

"True."

The other travelers joined them for breakfast, and they got on their way. The path wound around the ancient enclosure and led them downhill to the main road that headed east towards the sun.

"The way of the going down of the sun. This road is in our scriptures," Travel-for-Wisdom explained.

"Travel-for-Wisdom, the road goes East. Not "going down of the sun."

"Ah, Sage Monk, it depends on which end you start at, doesn't it?"

Soon they joined the main road, which again ran parallel to a riverbed. As they progressed, they left the cool mountain air behind, and entered the annoying heat of the valley. The sun rose higher and higher in the sky, and the annoying heat was replaced by an oppressive heat. By the time the road flattened out, they were all sweating like hogs, except Pigsy, who was sweating like a horse. Soon their water gourds were empty.

"Bear, where can we get water?"

"Venerable monk, I am not familiar with this area."

Donkey solved the problem. "I've been wandering around here for a couple thousand years. There's a spring up ahead, you can see the green of the vegetation there already."

"What would we do if our donkey couldn't speak?"

"He would lead us to water anyhow, as did my horse in the desert many years ago."

"He Haw!"

Old Monkey chuckled, but they were all glad when they reached the spring. Ages ago someone had cut into the rock to improve the water flow and built a stone basin to collect the water. They drank their fill and filled up their water bags before continuing on their journey. Their way turned south and the heat rose further.

"Don't worry, there's water up ahead."

They trusted Donkey now, and sure enough, by late afternoon it started cooling down, and they saw a small village surrounded by green orchards. Small water channels ran through the orchards, and there was a khan, a simple inn for travelers. As it was getting close to sunset, they decided to spend the night. Pigsy hid his snout, Donkey kept quiet, and Monkey tried to remain unobtrusive. They ate the vegetarian bread that Bear had prepared that morning and were preparing for sleep when they heard sounds in the courtyard.

THE SECOND JOURNEY

"I'll go! I'll go! I'll check what the noise is!"

Monkey left but did not return.

Xuanzang was getting anxious. They waited. And waited. Then waited a bit more.

"We haven't run into any demons or monsters on this Journey. But now it seems like we have, and a formidable one, if it is keeping Monkey so busy."

Pigsy grabbed his rake. "Don't worry! I'll go help Elder Brother."

He stepped outside. The sounds continued, but neither Monkey nor Pigsy returned. Then the remaining travelers heard a gasp, the gasp of a small crowd.

"Should we wait? In the past, whenever I went somewhere on my own, it only made things worse."

Bear and Travel for Wisdom looked at each other.

"It doesn't sound like a battle. It's entertainment, if I'm not mistaken. Bear, what do you think?"

"Entertainment, and good entertainment, if it has kept the attention of those rowdy disciples for so long. Let's go see!" Our friends went out into the courtyard. Bear and Travel-for-Wisdom had to practically pull our apprehensive Tang Monk along. But soon he was relieved.

There was a small bonfire in the middle of the courtyard, and a group of men sat enthralled, listening to a storyteller. Our Monkey and Pigsy were there as well. Xuanzang had never seen Monkey sit so still for so long. Old Monkey once told him:

> "I'm quite capable of performing such difficult feats as kicking down the sky or overturning wells, stirring up oceans or upending rivers, carrying mountains or chasing the moon, and altering the course of stars and planets. But where could I, tell me, acquire the nature to sit still? Even

*if you were to chain me to an iron pillar, I would still try to climb up and down. I can never manage to sit still."**

But here he was, mesmerized by a story!

"So, the Philistines stood atop the mountain on the one side, and Israel stood atop the mountain on the other side; and there was a valley between them. A champion from the camp of the Philistines came out. His name, Goliath of Gath, six cubits and a span tall. He had a brass helmet on his head, and he was clad with a coat of mail; and the coat weighed five thousand shekels. He had brass greaves on his legs, and a brass javelin between his shoulders. The shaft of his spear was like a weaver's beam; and his iron spear's head weighed six hundred shekels; his shield-bearer went before him."

The storyteller paused. Not a sound could be heard, except the quiet crackling of the fire.

"He stood and challenged the armies of Israel. 'Choose a man and let him come down to me. If he is able to fight and kill me, then will we be your servants, but if I prevail against him, and kill him, then shall ye be our servants, and serve us. Give me a man that we may fight together!' When King Saul and all of Israel heard those words of the Philistine, they were dismayed and afraid.

"Remember little David? He was the son of Jesse, of Bethlehem in Judah, who had eight sons; the three eldest sons followed King Saul to the battle; Eliab,

THE SECOND JOURNEY

Abinadab, and Shammah. David was the youngest brother and worked as a shepherd for his father.

"Meanwhile, the Philistine giant drew near morning and evening, and challenged Israel for forty days. And Jesse said unto David his son, 'Take this parched corn, and these ten loaves, and carry them quickly to your brothers in the camp.'

"Look at young David! He rose up early in the morning, left the sheep with a keeper, and went to his brothers as his father had commanded him.

"What did he see? Israel and the Philistines were in battle array, army against army. Dear David! He left his baggage with the baggage keeper, ran to the army, and greeted his brothers. As they were speaking, look! The enemy champion, the Philistine of Gath, Goliath by name, came out again from the ranks of the Philistines, and shouted his challenge as he had done for the past few days.

"The men of Israel when they saw the giant, all fled, shaking in fear. And the men of Israel said, 'He's come to taunt us again, but the brave man who kills him, will be enriched by the king with great wealth and receive the hand of his daughter in marriage.'"

Most of the audience knew the story well, yet they sat and drank in every word. To Monkey and Pigsy, this was a new story, and they didn't want to miss anything. They knew where this was going. David was going to turn that monster into a meat patty. Not with a nine-pronged rake or a Compliant Rod, but with some surprising weapon. The storyteller continued:

"Young David spoke to the men nearby. 'What shall be done for the man who kills this Philistine? Who is he, that he taunts the armies of the living God?' So, the men told him—riches and the king's daughter, as David had already heard.

"But Eliab, his eldest brother, heard this and was angry. He said, 'Why did you come here? And who's watching the sheep back home? I know how naughty you are, you've come to see the battle.' And David said, 'What have I now done? It was just a few words!' So, he turned away, and asked another and all the men told him the same thing.

"Rumors spread quickly, and soon they reached King Saul, who ordered that David be brought to him. And David said to Saul, 'No fear! No fear! I, your servant, will go and fight this Philistine.'

"King Saul said to David, You can't fight him, you're just a youth, and he has been a warrior since he was small. But David said, 'This servant kept his father's sheep; and when a lion or a bear came and took a lamb, I went out after him, and smote him, and saved it right out of his mouth; then I caught him by his beard and killed him. I destroyed both the lion and the bear; this Philistine shall end up like them, for he has taunted the armies of the living God.'

"King Saul was impressed, and he didn't have any other choice, since none of his heroes were willing to go up against the giant. So, he said to David, 'Go, and the LORD shall be with thee.' With that, Saul clad David with his clothes, put a brass helmet on his head, and covered him with mail armor.

"Dear David! He tied his sword on top of it all and

tried to go out, but he could barely move! 'I can't go with these; I'm not used to them.' So, he took them off. Instead, he took his staff in his hand, and chose five smooth stones out of the brook, and put them in his shepherd's bag, and held his sling in his hand."

Monkey knew what would happen. He thought it would be a magic shepherd's staff, but it was the sling! A magic sling!

"The Philistine came closer and closer to David, his shield bearer in front of him. When he saw David, he laughed at him, David was young, and had a fair complexion. What did the giant say?"

Everybody knew what he would say, but they waited expectantly.

"'Am I a dog, that you meet me with sticks and stones? Come here, and I will feed you to the birds and beasts!'

"But our dear David had an answer. 'You come with sword, spear, and javelin; but I come to you in the name of the God of the armies of Israel, whom you have taunted. We'll see who will feed the birds and the beasts!'"

The storyteller paused, and the audience held its collective breath. Monkey was gripping his Compliant Rod, which was now the size of David's shepherd staff. Pigsy was squeezing his rake's handle as tightly as he did when fighting demons.

"When the giant Philistine arose and approached David, David ran straight towards him! He put his hand in his bag, took out a stone, slung it, and smote the Philistine in his forehead; and the stone sank into his forehead. The giant collapsed on the ground!

"David prevailed over the Philistine with a sling and with a stone.

"He smote the Philistine, and slew him.

"But David had no sword!"

"No sword, but no problem. He ran, stood over the Philistine, took the giant's sword, killed him, and cut off his head. The Philistines saw that their hero was dead and fled in panic."

Everybody sighed in relief, though most had heard the story many times, and even Pigsy and Monkey knew where this was headed.

They slept uneventfully that night.

We don't know what happened to our friends on their way home. Let's find out in the next chapter.

Bath

As was often the case, Xuanzang woke up just before sunrise. Bear and Travel-for-Wisdom were still sleeping, but there was no sign of Monkey or Pigsy. He wandered out of the khan, worried that they were up to some mischief. His disciples could easily get bored. Though they had found the True Fruit, and been rewarded by Buddha in the Eastern Heaven, they still needed excitement, and there were few opportunities to bash in the heads of demons and fiends on this journey.

There was only one main street in the village. Xuanzang walked down it, admiring the sunrise over the mountains to the east. He wondered how the translation work was coming along back in Xi'an, then caught himself; those who sought enlightenment could not entertain homesickness. He heard some splashing in the distance, followed by some grunts and squeals. What were those disciples up to?

Pigsy and Monkey had found the village's source of water. There was a long aqueduct leading down from the foothills. Besides bringing water to the village, it made a wonderful waterslide for the mischievous Tang disciples. Xuanzang sighed. They would muddy up the villager's water, but the mud would settle out. Best to let them have their fun.

By the time Xuanzang got back, Bear and Travel for Wisdom were up, and getting ready for the days travel. Bear knew how hot it could get later in the day.

"Oh, there you are. We should get an early start, and eat on the way. It gets hot very quickly here. Where are Pigsy and Monkey?"

"I expect they'll be here soon."

Sure enough, the two disciples showed up, dripping wet. Travel-for-Wisdom started asking why they were wet, but our wise Tang Monk signaled him to be quiet. They filled up their water bags and continued on their way.

By mid-morning they were all sweaty again, but the air was so dry that the sweat dried immediately, leaving large salt stains on their shirts. Pigsy and Monkey had forgotten their early morning bath by now. They were only hoping that their water supply would hold out.

Pigsy realized it first. "We're almost there. I can smell water! Lots of it!"

"I still can't see it, even with my diamond eyes."

"Keep walking. You'll see. You'll see!" Pigsy promised.

They walked around a small hill, and there it was.

Bear explained: the City of Dates.

Our friends had reached the ultimate oasis. One of the hottest and driest places on earth, but with ample fresh water flowing down from the uphill springs. A well-maintained network of channels directed the water to gardens and orchards. Date palms grew everywhere. Merchants sold fresh dates, as well as cakes of dried dates. There was a palace further up, closer to the water sources.

"Master, let's avoid that palace." Monkey said. "It has a bad aura."

"Does a demon or monster live there?"

"A human, a monstrous human. An evil king. Some bad things happened there."

THE SECOND JOURNEY

"We have no need to go there." Bear said. "Even Pigsy will find a way to satisfy his hunger with fruit, without begging from an evil king. Xuanzang, it's close to noon now, too hot to travel. We can wait here a few hours, then continue when it cools off, or we can stay overnight."

"Are there any sages here that we should meet?"

"No. This city is famous for other reasons. As the poem says:

> "Known for its trees, Famous for its past, Remarkable for its priests:
> Known for its trees
> The city of date palms,
> Thousands of trees
> Their feet in water, their heads in the sun's furnace
> Famous for its past -
> The gateway to the land
> For those who left Egypt
> Its walls fell to the sound of Joshua's horns
> Remarkable for its priests -
> The ones who bless
> The ones who get a tithe
> Half of all the priests reside in this town."

Our Monkey was intrigued, "They attacked this city with musical instruments?! That's a skill I want to learn."

Pigsy laughed. "Monkey—you've used musical instruments for battle! Remember the bells that you stole from the demon Sai Tai Sui, on Qilin Mountain? One bell rang out fire, the second rang out smoke, and the third rang out a sandstorm."

"Yes, but those were not mortal bells, those were bells forged by Laozi.

Xuanzang shuddered at the memory of demon Sai Tai Sui.

"Bear, did magic horns blow down the walls of the city?"

"They were just hollowed-out ram's horns. Seven of them, cut off of regular animals. They had to circle the city each day for seven days, and on the seventh day, they circled it seven times, blew the horns, and the walls fell."

"So, there was magic, even if the horns were just plain horns." Xuanzang pointed out.

Bear shrugged, "Magic, or the World-Master's help, or both. This was a long time ago, it's in our scriptures."

"Maybe it was priest-magic. Like our Daoist priests."

"No record of that. Anyhow, our priests just do temple rituals. They're not known for their magic."

Pigsy was still thinking about music. Not that he was a musical pig, but... How about those golden cymbals, Monkey? They were almost the end of you! Even the twenty-eight constellations sent by the Jade Emperor couldn't help you."

"One did! One did! Gullet the Gold Dragon saved me that time!"

"You had a lot of help on our Journey." Pigsy recalled.

"Yes,
I disturbed with arms the royal court.
I disturbed, too, the Peaches Feast,
Wrath I incurred when I stole Laozi's pills,
To make a long story short,
I was nothing but trouble
Until the Buddha tamed me,
And Guanyin sent me to seek merit.
But the seeker of merit will always get divine help
No matter how rebellious his past."

Travel-for-Wisdom, formerly The Other, sighed. "Maybe that's true in the Tang lands, but here the seeker of merit often finds nothing but pain."

Xuanzang replied, "My disciple has special favor in Heaven, and a protector in Guanyin. The rest of us mortals are subject to suffering, whether we live in the East or West. I see no reason to stay here tonight. Let's rest and eat some dates. We can cool off in one of the pools and then continue on our way."

There was a public pool on the side of the road. Travelers were cooling themselves off in it, still wearing their robes. The robes would dry in no more than a few minutes once they came out.

Our Tang travelers availed themselves of the pool. Bear and Travel-for-Wisdom dumped a few buckets of cool water on Donkey before joining them.

Pigsy settled gratefully in the cool water.

"All that's missing are a few maidens to keep us company."

"Disciple, will you ever leave your carnal desires behind?" Xuanzang scolded.

"Master, younger brother Idiot has forgotten who those bathing beauties really were: spider fiends!" Monkey reminded them all.

Xuanzang shuddered at the memory.

"Between them and their Daoist priest friend, we were nearly finished! Poisoned!"

"You're right, Elder Brother. Pigs prefer the good parts of memories and forget the bad parts."

Xuanzang couldn't help getting philosophical. "Not just pigs. All people try to forget the bad of the past, but there is always a new evil waiting around the corner. Only true enlightenment can free us from this suffering."

"I'll go find some food. That's one pleasure I am still allowed." With that, Pigsy left the pool. The water level dropped briefly, but soon rose again as fresh water flowed in from the channel.

We'll leave our friends in the pool for now and follow Pigsy as he made his way into the town market, his silk shirt still streaming water. He was hungry, as usual, and viewed the produce stalls with a keen porcine eye. There were squash and turnips, parsley and cilantro but mostly dates — red dates, yellow dates, black dates, fresh dates, dried dates, dates in bags, Dates, dates, dates.

Pigsy still had a few odd coins tucked away in his ear for a rainy day. It didn't rain much here, but the silver was burning a hole in his ear, so he kept looking for the right kind of stall, and finally, he found it.

"Joseph's Fruit and Nuts: all you can eat, two silver coins."

Pigsy's Hebrew was poor, but he pointed at the sign, and with a few grunted words, and some tourist sign language, it was clear what he intended. He shook out two silver coins from his ear, handed them to Joseph, who inspected the foreign coins, decided they were acceptable, and waved his odd customer towards the tables, sacks, and baskets. It was a good day; it was rare for a tourist to fall for this. Two silver coins was an astronomical price to pay for...oh no!

Our dear Pigsy had already poured an entire basket of dates down his throat and was reaching for a second one. The storekeeper was making croaking noises as the second, and then the third basket disappeared. A few huge cakes of figs soon found their way down the porcine gullet, and the entire supply of almonds soon followed. By the time Joseph could react, there were only a few scattered dry dates on the table, and one satisfied Pigsy was on his way back to his friends.

Joseph grabbed a broom and chased after Pigsy.

"Hey you! Pig! Thief!"

One blow of Pigsy's rake would leave nine holes in that storekeeper's chest, but now that he had achieved merit, it would not do to kill people, so our Pigsy ran on, and jumped straight into the pool, making a huge wave and splashing half the water out of the pool.

Joseph was soaked but stood on the edge of the pool shouting, "all you can eat for two coins! Not the entire store!"

He didn't know that one of the foreign tourists, despite his shaved head and odd robes, was actually a former sage. Travel-for-Wisdom immediately understood the situation.

"I see you are upset. Did this Pig steal something from you?"

Joseph calmed down, thinking he'd found someone to support him.

"He didn't steal behind my back. He just ate all of my wares."

"Without paying?" Travel-for-Wisdom asked.

"He only paid with two silver coins. That doesn't even cover one hundredth of my stock."

Pigsy managed to grunt out the key question, "What did it say on your sign?"

"All you can eat, two silver coins! But that didn't mean the entire stall! That meant five or ten dates. What normal people eat."

Travel-for-Wisdom knew this was a disaster for the stall-keeper, but a disaster he brought upon himself.

"Yes. You intended it to apply to what normal people eat, but did it say that on the sign?"

"Not in so many words" admitted Joseph, the storekeeper.

"As you may have learned, legally speaking, what's in your heart stays in your heart, it has no legal standing. And if I may be so bold as to ask, when normal people take up that challenge, how much do they eat?"

Joseph looked sheepish, "about half a coin's worth."

"Perhaps you'd…"

"Yes, I guess I will…" And with that, Joseph wandered away.

Xuanzang was glad this had ended calmly. Pigsy had taken advantage of the merchant, but when it came down to it, Joseph was asking for trouble. And anybody who took one look at Pigsy should have realized that he had an appetite.

Noon was long past, so it was time to get moving. They all climbed out of the pool, and following local custom started on their way dripping wet. Even Donkey didn't mind having a wet Tang Monk on his back for a few cool minutes. They didn't have far to travel, and by late afternoon they'd reached the ford across the Jordan stream. The 'Jericho Ford'.

"Since we are headed back East, we need to cross to the other side. And there's somebody I'd like you to meet." Bear said.

Monkey trained his diamond eyes on the river but didn't see anything unusual; then he caught it. There was an auspicious radiance above the middle of the river. Below it was a young man with a black beard, wearing robes woven of camel hair and a leather belt. He was standing in the middle of the river, shouting at people who were crossing the ford.

"You brood of vipers! Repent! Who warned you to flee from the coming wrath? Repent! Confess your sins! The ax is already at the root of the trees, and every tree that does not produce good fruit will be cut down and thrown into the fire."

Xuanzang knew that Monkey could see what was real far better than the others could., "Disciple, what do you see? Is he a madman or a holy man?"

"Both, Master, both! He is holy, but also mad. Be glad that you never asked that question about yourself!"

Xuanzang knew that he was totally holy, having perfected himself through ten reincarnations. He also knew that only a madman would go on these long journeys into foreign lands.

"Bear, do you know of this man?"

"He must be John the Baptist. Called that because he dips

THE SECOND JOURNEY

people in the water to purify their bodies and souls. Some travel here to confess their sins and be cleansed by him. The others view him as a minor and noisy annoyance. Listen to him:

"Anyone who has two shirts should share with the one who has none, and anyone who has food should do the same."

This sounded familiar to Xuanzang.

"Those of us who have left the family no longer have two shirts. It sounds like he's telling everybody to become monks."

Their turn to cross the river soon came. They crossed on foot, letting Donkey ford the river without the burden of the Tang Monk on his back. As they passed, the prophet-madman went suddenly silent, closed his eyes, and raised his arms to heaven. Finally, he said, "God can raise up children for Abraham from the very stones."

They set up camp on the far side of the river, along with other groups of travelers.

"Bear, what did he mean by 'children for Abraham?'"

"Abraham, Our Father, was our ancestor, so 'children of Abraham' means us, the people of our nation. He was paying you a great compliment by saying 'God can raise up children for Abraham from the very stones.' You've become an honorary member of our people."

"It is a great honor, though I am not one to seek compliments or honors," said Xuanzang

"It's a tough climb up to the Red Rock City, so let's get some rest, and get an early start tomorrow morning."

Bear's advice was sound. There was a musician in one of the other groups, who took out a flute and started playing a mournful tune. Xuanzang wasn't much of a singer, but the stars, the river and the flute combined to make him homesick, he who had left all attachments behind. He sang quietly.

JOEL BIGMAN

Before my bed there's a pool of light
I wonder if it's frost on the ground
Looking up, I find the moon bright
Then bowing my head, I drown in homesickness.*

Xuanzang fell asleep and dreamed of Sage Abraham.

He was Sage Abraham, but as a child, of ten or eleven years. His father, Terach, owner of an idol store, had left him in charge while he went out to buy more raw materials for the manufacturing part of the business. A young man walked in and demanded to see a strong Hero idol. "I'm strong! I want a strong god!"

"Here, this one on the top step is the strongest."

The man paid, and was walking out when Abraham asked, "Sir, how old are you?"

"I am thirty years old."

"So why do you want to worship an idol that we made just yesterday?"

The man returned the idol and took his money back.

An elderly woman was the next customer. She wanted a poor weak god, like herself. So, he pointed to one on the bottom tier. She paid, and then, when she was on her way out...

"Venerable grandma, how old are you?

"I've lived foolishly for seventy years."

"So why do you want to worship an idol that we made just yesterday?"

She returned the idol and took her money back.

Xuanzang-Abraham was feeling a bit guilty about ruining the family business, but he knew what was real and what wasn't. He had an idea: he'd break off a few arms and legs of the smaller idols, a nose or two as well. He'd put a stick in the hands of the largest idol and claim that the idols fought among themselves!

Just then he heard an argument outside:

"I'm not going in there first! You're always cooking up some trick to get me in trouble!'

"You're such a lazy, idiot pig, you deserve to be fooled!"

The two potential customers crowded through the door, quarreling as they went, while a third followed them, trying to calm them down. Abraham didn't know who they were, though of course Xuanzang recognized his disciples.

The fat one had a pestle-like snout.

The hairy one had a thunder god's beak.

The dark one looked as mean as could be.

The dark one was Sha Monk, known as Sandy, who traveled with Xuanzang on his first Journey, but did not accompany him on this second Journey.

"Been idol smashing, young man?" Monkey asked.

"What if I have? They're just baked clay with gilt paint," Xuanzang-Abraham replied.

"We can help you. Do you have a Bureau of Five-Grain Transmigration here?' Monkey asked.

"A what?'

"A privy, a pit toilet!"

"Out in back," said Xuanzang-Abraham

"Which are your top three gods?"

"Those in the top row, of course! The Three Holy Ones."

"Sounds like Three pure Ones" said Monkey.

"Ready, Pigsy?"

"Yes! Yes! But first, a prayer!"

> *O Pure Ones Three, I'll confide in thee:*
> *From afar we came, Staunch foes of bogies.*

JOEL BIGMAN

You've sat too long; now join the privy.
Today you can't avoid facing something dirty
When you become Celestial Worthies Most Smelly!'

He grabbed all three statues off the top tier, loaded them on his broad shoulders, and took them out to the toilet pit.

Xuanzang-Abraham shuddered. This was fun, but there would be hell to pay.

———∽∽———

Xuanzang shuddered and woke up. He smiled at the recollection and went back to sleep.

We don't know what will happen to our friends on the way to the Red City; let's find out in the next chapter.

Judge

They woke before sunrise, as did all the other travelers, and headed up the ravine in near darkness, without even taking the time for breakfast. They were used to desert travel now, so they had prepared plenty of water for the climb.

The trail started out wide enough, but soon became narrow, and wound through a steep ravine. The only scenery were the colored stripes in the rock walls, and the narrow strip of sky above them. Soon they were ascending a steep slope, rocks blocking their way. Xuanzang had no choice but to get off of Donkey in order to make the climb easier for our talkative beast of burden.

They took a short break mid-morning to eat a quick breakfast in the shade of the rock wall, before continuing on their way. They were part of a long line of travelers slowly snaking their way up. Everybody was concentrating on the climb, there was little breath left to waste on idle chatter.

Occasionally you'd hear a "rough spot ahead" or "This rock is unstable" or a curse followed by "Are you okay?", but not much more.

They reached the top before noon. The ravine grew shallower, though narrower, and finally they were on top. The Red City, carved out of the living red sandstone, was spread out in front of them.

"It reminds me of the rock-carved temples of Yungang or Dunhuang. Magnificent! But a poor Tang monk like myself will not find a single statue of the Buddha here."

Their amazement at the Red City lasted for about ten minutes, until the heat of the sun, no longer hidden behind the walls of the ravine, hit them, and they decided to rest in the nearby Khan, and continue sightseeing later in the day. We will leave our friends resting and join a meeting in the Red City courthouse.

The Roman judge was sitting in the seat of honor, with an angry crowd of plaintiffs and defendants in front of him.

"You call yourself a judge?"

"You always find in favor of the Roman, no matter what!"

"Justice! Justice!"

"You've ruined me! I'll starve to death!"

The judge nodded at his pair of armed guards, who obediently knocked down a few of the more unruly ones, but this only served to incite the crowd further.

"Idiot judge!"

"Dishonest!"

"Justice! Justice!"

"A donkey could do better than you!"

"A donkey? A pig!"

"Yeah! We want a pig judge!"

This became a chant.

"Pig judge! Pig judge! Pig judge!"

Meanwhile, most of our friends had fallen sleep, and were napping as best as they could in the afternoon heat. Pigsy, however, had not had much to eat on the road, so he got up and decided to see what could be done about some food.

The red buildings cut into the rock were astounding, but he

THE SECOND JOURNEY

barely saw them. Where could he find a tavern or any place that sold food? He heard noise, doubtless some rowdy partying in a pub or restaurant of some sort. A party meant food, and even if he wasn't invited, he wasn't going to let good food go to waste. His stomach was really grumbling now, so he stomped into the building that the noise was coming from and heard the chant...

"Pig judge! Pig judge!"

Before he understood what was happening, the Roman judge had stepped down, and Pigsy found himself being shoved into his place. "Here! Take my place! Let's see how these lowlifes really like a pig judge."

Pigsy looked around and panicked at the sudden change in his position. His brain froze; what to do? He did what he always did when faced with a problem, he turned to food.

"I can't think straight when I'm hungry!"

"Bring him food! Pig Judge wants food!"

Soon piles of buns and vegetable were brought in, enough to get the edge off of Old Hog's appetite. He could delay no longer; it was time to judge. Pigsy let loose a great burp, to the amusement of the audience, and sat up straight in the judge's chair.

"Bring the first case!"

Two old men came into court, one carrying a cane walking stick. The one without a stick said:

"Your honor! I did this man a favor, and lent him twelve silver coins, on the condition that he return them when I asked for repayment. I knew that he needed the money, so I delayed my request for several months, but I was getting nervous that I might never get paid. So, I asked him to repay me, once, twice, three times, but he refuses!"

As you may recall, Pigsy had once played the role of one of the Daoist Three Pure Ones, after tossing the original into the pit toilet. So, he figured he could play the role of a Roman judge as well.

"And you, the venerable gentleman with the cane, what do you have to say about this matter?"

"It's true, he did lend me money, but I paid him back!"

"Liar!"

"Quiet!" Pigsy growled. "The court has no way to determine what is true here. What will satisfy you, lender? I cannot force him to pay you, without proof."

"If that liar is willing to swear that he paid me back, I'll leave the court quietly, but it has to be done properly, he needs to hold scriptures and swear by all that is holy."

"Sure, I'll swear," said the borrower.

Somebody ran off to bring the scriptures. The courtroom was murmuring quietly until he came back.

"Here."

"Okay, can you hold my cane while I hold the scriptures and swear?" asked the borrower. "I can't manage both at the same time."

"Sure, liar. I won't get in the way of your false testimony."

So, the cane was handed to the lender, and the borrower took the scriptures; he swore on God's holy name that he had borrowed the money and returned it. Every penny.

The lender shrugged as the holy scroll was handed back to its owner.

"If he's willing to risk his soul on such a false oath, I can't stop him. But I can give him a beating! Here, you can have your cane back!"

Before anybody could react, he gave the borrower a huge whack on the head! Fortunately, he was no Monkey, and this was no magic compliant rod, or Pigsy would have had a steaming meat patty on the floor of the courtroom, and on his first day as judge.

The borrower screamed in outrage, the attacker raised the cane again, but by now the guards had sprung into action. One grabbed the attacker, the other grabbed the weapon, but the cane had cracked from the first blow, and silver coins started leaking out of it.

Pigsy smiled, "and so, our first trial ends, with a thief who swore truthfully, but remained a thief and a liar."

At this point, the borrower was shaking in his sandals. Doubtless the usual punishment was a beating, exile, or worse.

"I see no point in punishing you further. Your reputation will follow you, and you will be miserable for the rest of your life. Go!"

The shamefaced borrower quickly left the room. The audience applauded.

"Good Judge!"

"Pig Judge better than Roman Judge!"

The Roman judge was not pleased by this at all. He nodded at the guards, who headed towards our favorite pig. Pigsy could easily have ventilated them, nine holes per guard, but he was a Reformed Pig now, one who 'keeps ants out of harm's way when they sweep the floor', so he stomped right past them, ignoring their feeble attempts to stab him with their spears, and ponderously rushed back to the khan.

"Master! Disaster! Disaster!"

"What sort of disaster?" a startled Xuanzang replied.

"A judge! They made me a judge! I was too successful, and now the real judge is after me with a couple of soldiers!"

"Younger brother, you could easily...No. You don't want to lose merit. I never thought Old Monkey would say this, but maybe it's best that we just quickly leave this place."

"Monkey, my eldest disciple! You have indeed gained wisdom. I never thought I would see the day that you would walk away from a fight!"

They quickly gathered their luggage and headed out of town. There were several roads leading away from the Red City, aside from the one they had climbed up earlier that day. Xuanzang chose the one headed east.

"It's time. We have learned much, and even if it isn't enough, Donkey and Travel-for-Wisdom can certainly help our friends in Kaifeng. Besides which, I am not young, and have traveled much. It's time to get back to my monastery and finish my life's work."

The sun was already low in the west behind them as they picked their way along the mountain trail.

We don't know if our friends will leave the Red City without suffering violence or losing their merit; let's find out in the next chapter.

Escape

We were telling you about our Tang Monk, Xuanzang, who was escaping the Red City with his disciples, Monkey and Eight-Rules Pigsy. Elisha Travel-for-Wisdom, once known as The Other, had joined them, along with Bear, their Foreign Guide, and the occasionally talkative Donkey.

They had not gone far when they heard the sound of marching feet behind them.

"Master, there are at least a hundred men coming after us. They delayed following us while they got the troops organized," Monkey said.

"Why do you worry, Elder Brother? You can turn them all into meat patties in a minute. Or I can do a little agricultural work on them with my rake." Pigsy pointed out.

"Idiot Pigsy, of course, we could destroy them all, but that would take away from our merit, and they'd only send more soldiers after us."

"Monkey," asked Xuanzang, "do you have a way to save us without killing anybody?"

"Master, you are forgetting how many tricks I have!"

Monkey bit off a handful of hairs, blew on them and whispered "change!" Marvelous Monkey! The hairs turned to exact copies of all the travelers. Now there were two monks, two Monkeys, two Pigs, two Bears, and even doubles of Travel-for-Wisdom

Elisha and Donkey.

"There went in two and two unto Noah into the ark…"

"What was that? Travel-for-Wisdom asked.

Bear laughed, "You also have much to learn. It is from the story of the flood; every child knows it. But we don't have much time. Brother Monkey, what now?"

"Let us step aside in this ravine, behind those rocks! The soldiers will take my hairs and return to their city."

They followed his advice, slipped up the ravine, and hid behind a rocky outcropping.

In the meantime, the specious travelers continued down the road. Sure enough, the soldiers arrived. The false travelers put on a show of being distressed and tried to run away before they were grabbed by the soldiers, dragged into town, and thrown into a prison cell for the night.

The next day they were dragged into court and beaten while the Roman judge questioned them, then threw them back back into the cell for another night. The following morning, however, the cell was empty. Monkey had called his hairs back; they had turned into flies, flown out the small window, and gone back to the hairy monkey they had come from.

In the meantime, our real travelers waited until the soldiers' footsteps had died away, then came out of the ravine. They hurried east as best as they could, to put some distance between themselves and the Red City. When night fell, they decided not to light a fire, as it was far too easy to see from a distance. So, they had cold food and went to sleep. When they woke up, Bear had disturbing news:

"We can't continue due east from here. It's all desert, no water. We must go north first, before we can head east again."

Xuanzang shook his head, but Monkey answered. "Once Master has gotten an idea into his head, it stays there. If he weren't so obstinate, he would never have reached the Western Heaven during his first Journey. If he decides to go east now, to head back home, that's what we'll do. We will overcome the hardships, as we always do. Besides which, you underestimate our powers."

> *So, they continued east. The trail faded till there was no sign of it. There was not a bird to be seen in the air above, nor an animal on the ground below. Though you look all round most earnestly to find where you can cross, you know not where to make your choice, the only mark and indication being the dry bones of the dead left upon the sand.*

Their water lasted for two days. On the afternoon of the third day, just when Xuanzang was getting seriously concerned, they saw sheep in the distance. When they got closer, they could see a shepherdess and a well. There was a large rock on top of the well.

"Disciples, I know you can be quite unruly. Let me approach the shepherdess and find out about this well." Xuanzang approached her, "Bodhisattva, we are travelers from a far foreign land. Can you tell us the nature of this well?"

"This well is shared by all the shepherds of this dry region. This large rock which covers the well is too heavy for one person to move by themselves. Every evening all the shepherds all gather together and roll the rock off the well, so we can water our sheep. Once they are all here, you can draw some water as well."

Xuanzang bowed and reported his findings back to the rest of our friends.

"This is a small matter, Master. Let Old Hog take care of it."

Dear Pigsy! He walked up to the well, and with one push of his snout, rolled the rock off the well. The shepherdess, who was at first aghast at Pigsy's appearance, was impressed by his strength. "You are a strange-looking person, but strong! You would be very useful to have around the tent!"

She gave him a look that Pigsy was quite familiar with. "Would you like to come back with me and visit my father? I think the two of you may have something to discuss together."

Pigsy bowed as best as he could.

"Thank you for your kind offer, dear lady. Once I would have immediately accepted, but now I am one who has left the family. In fact, due to my merit, I have been made Janitor of the Altars. I regretfully cannot join you."

He then turned and walked back to his friends, muttering all the while, "It's hard! It's hard!"

They all drank their fill, including Donkey, who wished he had been born a camel, filled up their water skins, and continued on their way.

Two days later, they were in a similar situation; their lips parched, their water skins empty. Xuanzang got off Donkey, to offer him a little relief, but then their going got even slower. The sun beat down mercilessly.

"If we weren't this far west, I would invite some of my water dragon friends to help us out with a little rain."

Bear had an idea, "Monkey, your compliant rod can help us here. See that rock up ahead? Go and give it a sharp blow."

"The rock will shatter into gravel, but how will that help us?"

"Hear now: are you to bring forth water out of this rock? Just do it, you'll be surprised."

Monkey pulled his Compliant Rod out of his ear, gave it a shake, and it was as thick as a rice bowl! He hit the rock twice and water poured out from the base of the rock!

There is a verse for this: "Water came forth abundantly, and the congregation drank, and their cattle."*

Though, in this case the congregation was rather small, and

THE SECOND JOURNEY

the closest they had to cattle was Donkey.

A few days later, they found themselves, yet again, running short of water. Monkey looked anxiously ahead with his diamond eyes. Yes! There was water, a spring-fed pool. He peered again, it wasn't a mirage, it was real.

"Master! Don't worry! Don't worry! There's water up ahead!"

A half hour later, they were at the spring. Date palms surrounded the pool, and birds sang their afternoon prayers. It was truly an ideal oasis.

Xuanzang dismounted from Donkey, who immediately went up to the pool to get a drink. Bear and Travel-for-Wisdom started unloading the empty water skins so they could be refilled. Pigsy rushed to the pool and knelt down to drink just as Donkey bent his head down, and...

"Yechh!"

"Bleeh!"

Now Xuanzang was worried!

"Pigsy, what is it?"

"The water is bitter! Tastes like poison!"

"Donkey?"

"Not fit for man or beast!"

Xuanzang panicked. "I knew this Second Journey was a mistake! Why did I let Guanyin pressure me into this? Bear? Travels-for-Wisdom?"

"I'm a guide and a strong man, not a miracle worker."

"I'm a rejected ex-sage."

"No, now you are one of us, Travel-for-Wisdom! Don't talk like that, I'm depressed enough as it is."

"Let me think," said Travel-for-Wisdom. "It is written:

> And when they came to Marah, they could not drink of the waters of Marah, for they were bitter. Therefore, the name

of it was called Marah. And the people murmured against Moses, saying: 'What shall we drink?'
And he cried unto the LORD; and the LORD showed him a tree, and he cast it into the waters, and the waters were made sweet. *

Now if only the Lord would show us that magic tree...."

Travel for Wisdom saw a rock but didn't notice the thorn bush right behind it. He sat dejectedly on the rock, then quickly jumped up. "Ow! Damn! It figures I'd set my rear end down on a thorn. My God has shown me a tree alright, a thorn in my butt!"

Xuanzang looked at Bear, then at Monkey. Bear looked at Monkey, then at the Tang monk. Their eyes shifted back and forth, who would break first?

Our impetuous Monkey couldn't play this waiting game very long. He ran to the thorn bush, pulled off a branch, and threw it into the pond. Everybody waited, expecting something to happen, but there was nothing. Monkey scooped up a handful of water, sipped it, and spat it out.

"Old Monkey doesn't understand! It should work! It should work!"

Travel-for-Wisdom finally understood. "And the LORD showed him a tree, and he cast it into the waters. I was shown the tree, I have to throw it in."

Travel-for-Wisdom gingerly pulled a few twigs off the bush and tossed them into the water. Nothing dramatic happened, except that the birds stopped singing.

Donkey bent his head down to the water again, sniffed it, and started drinking. Pigsy didn't wait any longer and threw himself on the edge of the pool and started noisily slurping water. Bear and Monkey scooped up water with their hands, Xuanzang with his begging bowl.

THE SECOND JOURNEY

They decided to rest at the oasis for a few days, before continuing on their way.

On the third day, Xuanzang decided it was time to continue. It was pleasant with water nearby, but they couldn't stay there forever, and their food was running out, even with the dates they could get from the trees.

They got an early start, Bear and Monkey leading, followed by Xuanzang on Donkey, accompanied by Travel-for-Wisdom, while Pigsy brought up the rear, carrying the excess luggage.

The day was especially hot. There was no sight of shade, no spec of green, or any sign of life besides a few snakes and scorpions that they carefully avoided. After all, one should keep ants out of harm's way when you sweep the floor, and the desert was the home of these creatures.

When the sun was high in the sky, they decided to take a break. Monkey found a small cave: "Let's go in here! It's the hottest part of the day, we'll have some shade in here!"

"Disciple, are there monsters in there?"

"No monsters! No monsters!"

Xuanzang remembered the caves on their first Journey that hid monsters.

"But something is written above the entrance in a yet another foreign language. I can't understand it. Maybe it says Black Wind Cave, or Lion-Camel Cave, or Golden Helmet Cave...we know what monsters there are in caves!"

"Let me look." Travel-for-Wisdom knew many of the local languages, "The Great Sage, Equal to Heaven, has made a tour of this place."

"What? No, I haven't! This isn't one of the Buddha's fingers!"

Travel-for-Wisdom laughed. "I've heard that you're quite a

trickster, Elder Brother Monkey. Tricksters sometimes get tricked themselves. But what's that bit about the Buddha's fingers?"

"Before I was enlightened, I caused havoc in Heaven. Only the Buddha could subdue me. I thought I could escape him using my magic cloud, but it turned out I was always in his hand. I thought I was pissing on a rock pillar, but it was his finger... What does the graffiti really say?"

"The Infantry Sucks."

"Ha! If they knew how to cloud-travel, they wouldn't have to walk so far."

They ate a few dates, drank a little, and waited for the day to cool down.

Xuanzang sighed.

"Master, what is it?"

"Monkey, you know how many adventures we've had..."

"Eighty-one on our first Journey!"

"Yes, we did not have so many on this Journey, yet it seems impossible to get back to Tang lands again."

"Don't speak like that, Master! Idiot Pigsy will decide to sell our belongings and buy you a coffin."

"Elder Brother, in the past I would have," said Pigsy, "but not today. We'll get through this desert somehow."

Xuanzang looked at their supply of water. It looked like a lot, but in a few days' time, it would be gone, and then what?

It's a mistake to take a break when traveling. It can be very hard to start again. Muscles are sore, feet ache; but they had no choice but to get up and go, unless they wanted to make 'The Infantry Sucks' cave their tomb.

They trudged silently along, keeping the sun to their backs, watching the ground, keeping an eye out for snakes and scorpions. The hours went by, until Bear suddenly stopped. They all stumbled to a stop as well and looked up: the horizon was a

THE SECOND JOURNEY

dark green. Bear knew where they were.

"It's the river. The Euphrates. These are civilized lands again."

They stepped more lightly with the river in sight and reached it before dark. They stayed in a khan overnight, then took a ferry across the river, and traveled to the Tigris, then north to Tigrit.

They left Tigrit, and went to Erbil.

They left Erbil and went to Qeydar.

They left Qeydar and went to Semnan.

They left Semnan and went to Bukhara.

We don't know yet what happened to our friends in Bukhara; let's find out in the next chapter.

Welcome

Bear had decided to stay in the West. Bukhara was the last city he would accompany them to. "I would be useless as a guide farther to the East, and that is a route that you know already."

They stayed one night in a small inn in Bukhara. Monkey, Pigsy and Travel-for-Wisdom, whom we had known as Elisha, The Other, went to sleep. Donkey rested in the stable, dreaming donkey dreams of endless hay and spirited conversations with the sages of the East.

Xuanzang and Bear sat on the roof, looking at the stars.

"Master Xuanzang. I have not shaved my head, or 'left the family'."

"I never expected you to. You have your own land, your own tradition, your own Way."

"Yes. I follow the Way of Sage Moses. Yet, I have learned much from you. In a way, I am your disciple, and I will remain such."

"What have you learned?"

"Compassion, of course. And wisdom."

"Are illusion and enlightenment not the same?"

"Master, you have managed to both confuse and enlighten me. I shall miss you. Grant me a gift before you leave."

"A gift? asked Xuanzang. "You know that I have nothing besides the clothes on my back and this begging bowl. Even old Donkey doesn't belong to me, he belongs to himself."

THE SECOND JOURNEY

"Give me a religious name."

"A name? You have a name."

"I am called Bear for my build and my strength. I need a name for humility and enlightenment."

"You don't need another name. But, so you will remember my teachings, we can call you 智承, Zhicheng."

"Which means?"

"Responsible Wisdom. That is your essence."

"Thank you."

The two sat on the roof quietly together for the rest of the night.

In the morning, Bear bade his companions goodbye. There wasn't much to say that hadn't already been said, so they lined up and bowed to him, and he bowed back, turned to leave, but then turned back and said:

> "*The LORD is thy keeper; The LORD is thy shade upon thy right hand.*
> *The sun shall not smite thee by day, Nor the moon by night.*
> *The LORD shall keep thee from all evil; He shall keep thy soul.*
> *The LORD shall guard thy going out and thy coming in, From this time forth and forever."*
> *Psalms 121*

Zhicheng Bear bowed one more time, turned, and left.

The rest of our company continued East, from Bukhara to Samarkand, where they stayed for few days to build up their strength. Pigsy noticeably gained in circumference, if not in wisdom.

Finally, they headed toward the Tianshan, the Heavenly Mountains. Though it was summer, it was cold high in the mountains. Day by day they trudged through the snow and ice. They walked up to the highest pass, only to climb down, and then back up again to the next pass. Donkey's endurance was useful now, as he carried Master Xuanzang up and down the mountain trails.

Finally, they reached lower and warmer altitudes, and saw the Jade Gate of Yumen Pass in the distance. They paused to take in the view. They had once again reached the edge of the Tang lands!

Breathing a collective sigh of relief, they started down the last slope towards the pass. As the trail went around a bend, they saw an elderly sage sitting under a tree.

"Monkey, who is that venerable sage?" asked Xuanzang.

Old Monkey peered with his diamond eyes and jumped excitedly, "It's Olam-Tzu! World-Master! The Western God!"

"He's come to bid us goodbye."

"Yes, yes!"

The World-Master rose as they approached, "I shall accompany you till the Jade Gate. That's as far as I can go."

Xuanzang understood. "You've been with us all along."

"Since you left Bukhara. Bear blessed you that 'The LORD shall guard thy going out and thy coming in,' so I thought I'd oblige."

Elisha, our Travel-for-Wisdom, was nonplussed.

"You're here."

"Yes."

"You watched over us during our travels?"

"Indeed."

"Even myself?" demanded Elisha.

"Of course."

THE SECOND JOURNEY

"What about 'Return, rebellious children. All apart from The Other?"

Olam-Tzu shrugged, "I was a bit overdramatic there."

Travel-for-Wisdom Elisha grew red in the face. "A bit overdramatic? I could throttle you!"

"Practically speaking, no, you couldn't.

> *Hast thou entered into the springs of the sea?*
> *Or hast thou walked in the recesses of the deep?*
> *Have the gates of death been revealed unto thee?*
> *Or hast thou seen the gates of the shadow of death?*
> *Hast thou surveyed unto the breadths of the earth?*
> *Declare, if thou knowest it all."**

"What is that supposed to mean?" Travel-for-Wisdom demanded.

"In short, there's more going on than you're aware of."

Elisha calmed down, "Okay, I can accept that. But what about that fellow who climbed a tree to follow your law and a snake bit him and killed him?"

"There's more going on than you're aware of," The World-Master repeated.

"You're saying just accept it, because you're God?"

"Yes. Return, rebellious children, even The Other."

"That helps a little," Travel-for-Wisdom admitted.

World-Master Olam-Tzu nodded and walked back toward the West. Soon, he flickered out of sight. None of our friends heard him mutter, "Then again, there's a lot going on that I'm not aware of either."

The Jade Gate was a green-roofed fortress, strategically placed directly on the Chinese end of the trade route. On one side, foreign lands. On the other side, Tang lands.

As they walked past the fortress, the soldiers lined the ramparts, waved, and bowed.

Xuanzang had gotten a hero's welcome when he had returned from his first Journey, so he was not completely surprised. But how did the garrison know who they were? He soon found out.

Monkey noticed first. "Master! There's a welcoming committee ahead. A hundred welcoming committees!"

Soon a flotilla of magic clouds arrived.

First was Guanyin, willow branch in hand.

Lord Guan the loyal was next.

Then were Lingji Bodhisattva and Pilanpo Bodhisattva.

Followed by the Eighteen Arhats, then

Ananda, Mahākāśyapa, Mahamayuri, and

Ratnadhvaja, Jingang, Niaoge Daolin!

The Four Heavenly Kings.

The Five Gates.

The Ten Yama Kings.

And then, horses!

Monkey clapped in delight! "My heavenly horses! I was only Heaven's Horse Officer for a short time, but I loved the horses!"

Then came the Heavenly host:

The Three Pure Ones.

The Queen Mother of the West.

Zhenwu, the Great Emperor, along with his Turtle and Snake generals.

Little Zhang Crown Prince, and the Five Sacred Dragons.

Five Elders of the Five Positions.

The Duke of Thunder, the other of Lightning, Marquis of Wind and Master of Rain.

Lords of the Five Elements: wood, Fire, Metal, Water, Earth.

The Barefoot Immortal.

The Nine Stars.

THE SECOND JOURNEY

The Twenty-Eight Mansions.
Three Stars of Luck, Prosperity and Longevity.
And countless more. Far too many to name here!
Oh, but let's not forget the Dragon Kings of the Four Seas:
Ao Guang, Ao Qin, Ao Shun, Ao Run.

All welcomed our travelers to the deafening sound of gongs and drums.

Guanyin explained, "Everyone is here, except for the Jade Emperor, since somebody needs to keep an eye on the world; and Lao Tzu, who's afraid some other ape will steal his elixir. He's become quite paranoid."

Travel-for-Wisdom had quite a headache, "We manage with one deity. Wouldn't two or three suffice for you?"

"We have the opposite view. We wonder how you manage with only one deity, and how you ignore all the spirits that surround you everywhere."

"We think you have vivid imaginations, and you think we are blind. Which goddess are you?"

"I'm the Bodhisattva Guanyin, not exactly a goddess. Your languages don't properly differentiate between heavenly beings." Guanyin explained. "You're the one who sent the monk to the West?" Travel-for-Wisdom asked.

"Yes."

"Why?"

"To help your people who live here. You will be their teacher." She saw that Travel-for-Wisdom was confused. "I'm compassion personified and deified. I help people. It's my calling, or job description, if you like."

"How many of my people live here?" Travel-for-Wisdom asked.

"Fifty families."

"A lot of effort to help fifty families, in a land of many

millions."

"You are indeed a sage. I am trying to bring fresh ideas into Tang lands. Xuanzang helped with Buddhist scriptures, but Buddhism has been in our lands for centuries. It is time to bring some fresh ideas into our lands."

"I can hardly teach fifty families, let alone millions."

"We shall see."

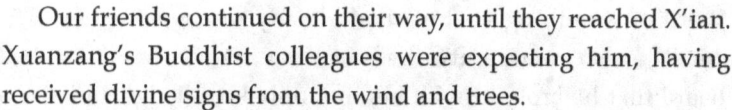

Our friends continued on their way, until they reached X'ian. Xuanzang's Buddhist colleagues were expecting him, having received divine signs from the wind and trees.

Their Master had returned, and was welcomed with boundless joy by the monks and scribes of the Temple of Great Blessing.

After spending one night back home, Xuanzang went to pay his respects to Emperor Taizong. Following a vegetarian banquet, he went back to the Temple of Great Blessing. The following morning our friends sent out for Kaifeng.

We don't know what kind of welcome awaits them in Kaifeng; let's find out in the next chapter.

Return to Kaifeng

Word of Xuanzang's return had already reached Kaifeng. The small Jewish community, the Sect Who Extract the Sinew, had heard that he brought with him not only knowledge, but also a teacher! There were also rumors of a magic donkey, though of what use it may be was yet unknown.

They came to the western gate of Kaifeng to greet the returned travelers. Their neighbors, excited at the return of the famous monk, all joined them at the gate as well. Some brought images of the gods from their temples, along with gongs and drums.

They lined the two sides of the main road, and cheered as Xuanzang entered, leading the donkey. He was followed by the teacher, Travel-for-Wisdom Zhixing, then by the famous Eight-Rules Pigsy, and finally a prancing, dancing Old Monkey!

The Buddhists chanted:

> *I submit to Dīpaṁkara, the Buddha of Antiquity.*
> *I submit to Bhaiṣajya-vaiḍūrya-prabhāṣa, the Physician and*
> *Buddha of Crystal Lights.*
> *I submit to the Buddha Śākyamuni.*
> *I submit to the Buddha of the Past, Present, and Future.*
> *I submit to the Buddha of Pure Joy.**

The Jews chanted:

Give thanks unto God, for He is good, for His mercy endureth forever.
Give thanks unto the God of gods, for His mercy endureth forever.
Give thanks unto the Lord of lords, for His mercy endureth forever.

Who giveth food to all flesh, for His mercy endureth forever.
O give thanks unto the G-d of heaven, for His mercy endureth forever.*

Here Ends the Second Journey
Finished and Complete. Praise to God, Creator of the World

Sources:

Most of the poems are from *The Journey to the West*. Anthony C. Yu translation, University of Chicago Press.

Biblical verses are from the *JPS translation of 1917*.

The comment about Moths flying into the flame is from *Archy and Mehitabel*, Don Marquis.

Xuanzang's comment about writing is from *The Great Tang Records on the Western Regions*

Poem about the Bellows from *Tao Teh King*, Legge translation.

The Jewish mystical statements are from the *Zohar*.

Comment about alphabet from *The Great Tang Records on the Western Regions*.

Patience chapter, quote about teachers from *Ethical Teachings of the Ancient Jewish Sages*.

Before my bed there's a pool of light – poem by Li Bai.

So, they continued east... *Record of Buddhistic Kingdoms*, Xuanzang

Afterward

The Second Journey was a Journey for myself as well. My native culture is Jewish, and over the years I've developed a great interest in Chinese culture. I was reading The Journey to the West a second time and studying a daily page of the Talmud as I wrote the novel. My hope is that it will be a bridge between cultures, and a bridge to both cultures for many Western readers.

This started out as "I wonder if you could write a book combining Jewish and Chinese stories?" At first I thought of a Biblical Romance of the Three Kingdoms, but after reading the Romance, I realized that it wouldn't go. When I picked up The Journey to the West, I knew I had the right story.

The historical Xuanzang was a real monk, who lived in the 7th century, during the early Tang Dynasty, and did in fact travel to India to bring Buddhist Scriptures back to China. He did not take a superhero Monkey or a talking pig with him- that legend grew over time, into the Ming Dynasty fantasy The Journey to the West.

I took some chronological license in having the Monk meet the Rabbis, as the Talmudic period ended over a century before the time of Xuanzang. I hope that the gentle reader who enjoyed this fantasy will excuse this minor inaccuracy.

The Talmud is a compilation of ancient Jewish legal discussions, spiced with a scattering of folklore and legends.

THE SECOND JOURNEY

The Rabbis had extensive arguments about legal details, and the same discussions and arguments continue to this day in Talmudic study houses.

Most of the characters existed long before I was born. Xuanzang, Monkey, and Pigsy are wonderful characters, and they graciously agreed to join the story, even without Guanyin's encouragement. The Talmudic characters were waiting for centuries on my bookshelf, and were glad to join the adventure.

Bear is my own invention. I needed someone to serve as a guide, to explain things to the Chinese heroes, and incidentally to the reader as well.

The adventures are based on stories from the Talmud, with one exception, when Honi travels magically to China for a rainmaking contest in the Slow Cart Kingdom.

The style of the novel is loosely based on that of the Chinese Classic. It is episodic, with each adventure standing on its own. I've incorporated a few poems and quotations in the text as well, in the Ming tradition. The "let's find out in the next chapter" teaser is also common in the Chinese Classics.

I read Anthony C. Yu's full translation of The Journey to the West, which I highly recommend, though it is a bit long. Arthur Waley's Monkey is a shorter version that is more easily digested.

The legends from the Talmud are scattered through the Talmud and related literature. The classic compilation is The Book of Legends, compiled and translated (into Hebrew, many of the originals were in Aramaic) by Bialik and Ravnitsky. The book is available in English translation.

Podcast enthusiasts who want to learn about Chinese history and culture would do well to listen to Laszlo Montgomery's China History Podcast.

The Talmud itself is available online, with English translation, at the Sefaria site.

Though my knowledge is limited, I find that I am a local "expert" in Chinese culture, because most people in the West are completely ignorant of the other half of the world. Every schoolchild in China, Taiwan, Korea and Japan knows of the Monkey King, but few in the West ever heard of him.

The widespread ignorance of Chinese history in the West is disturbing. Everyone has to deal with China, and it is always best to understand who you are dealing with.

Some thanks are in order: To my 'critical cheerleader' editor Sana Abuleil. And my love and thanks to my wife, who has managed to put up with me for many years, has put up with my Chinese craziness, and who is my Talmud study partner to boot.

And what better way to end than with the famous line of Rabbi Judah Halevi:

我的心在东方，但我在遥远的西方
ליבי במזרח ואנוכי בסוף מערב
My heart is in the East, but I am far in the West.

About The Author

Joel Bigman is the author of *The Second Journey*, the world's first Chinese-Jewish historical fantasy. He works in the semiconductor industry, and has travelled widely in Asia. He's a proud father and grandfather. Joel lives in Israel with his patient wife and wild imagination.